Mom never m
Sunday's *Richmon*
an article or two at the kitchen table and after was pacing
the section into the recycling bin while Sam worked
through the rest of the paper from the comfort of the
living room. This Sunday's routine was cut short.

When Sam went to the kitchen to refill her coffee
cup, the paper lay open on the table, but her mom was
gone. On the Celebrations page, opposite an article titled,
"Preparing Your Soil for Next Year's Bounty," was a
photo of a smiling Al nestled up next to a woman. The
short announcement bore the caption, "Albert Hobson and
Elena Fairchild to Wed."

He'd sprinkled salt in the wound. The date was set
for Valentine's Day, the day Mom married Dad. When
Sam lifted the page to read more, the top half of the photo
fell back.

Mom had cleanly cut off their heads.

To my neighbor Judy –
May you enjoy & perhaps
gain new perspectives.

Judy Whitehill Witt

Spectrum
of
Secrets

by

Judy Whitehill Witt

Spectrum of Secrets

Cover Art by *Jennifer Greeff*

The Wild Rose Press, Inc.
PO Box 708
Adams Basin, NY 14410-0708
Visit us at www.thewildrosepress.com

Publishing History
First Edition, 2022
Trade Paperback ISBN 978-1-5092-4242-9
Digital ISBN 978-1-5092-4243-6

Published in the United States of America

Dedication

To all those on the autism spectrum who struggle
to overcome negative perceptions: may you find
appreciation for your unique strengths.

Chapter 1
Sunday, October 26, 2008

"It'll be ruined," Clair Hobson shouted as she jumped from her daughter's idling car and ran down the flagstone walk, her open parka flapping like an injured bird's wings.

Her front door, barely visible through billowing sheets of rain, gaped open. She stepped cautiously into the mess.

Puddles in the foyer had splotched and swelled the hardwood flooring. A drift of red and yellow maple leaves looked almost picturesque piled in the niche where the hall table used to stand. A musty odor, most likely from the wet floor, assaulted her. But there was another element in that odor. Two medium-sized cartons were stacked beside the door. Yes, the smell of damp corrugated cardboard.

Clair stood rigid, rocking side-to-side. She scanned the barren living room, then focused on the scuffed wall above the fireplace where her favorite print, Van Gogh's *Starry Night*, had hung. Moving from her home of so many years was hard.

Renting out the house was her last-ditch way to raise enough money to cover both the small mortgage and the huge home equity loan which had gone dangerously delinquent. If the lousy real estate market turned around in a few years, maybe the house would be worth enough

1

to sell and pay off both loans.

Water dripping from her drenched jeans, Samara McNeer dumped a shrink-wrapped stack of flattened cartons and two bags of packing materials in the living room. She closed the door, taking extra care to ensure the finicky catch clicked shut.

"I bet this mess is Al's fault," Clair said, still rocking and staring. "He probably came by. Those two brown moving boxes weren't here when we were packing last Sunday. He never did get the hang of closing that door."

"It's okay, Mom. Your homeowner's insurance will cover the water damage. And your renters will get a freshly refinished floor in the bargain. Here, I've got your list. We've already done number one: take packing materials to the house. Let's keep going. Number two: pack everything from kitchen cabinets into cartons."

Samara picked up the flattened cartons. Clair brushed back the silver-white ringlets plastered to her forehead and grabbed the two bags.

In the kitchen, Samara flipped the light switch. No light. The clock display on the microwave was black.

"No power, Mom."

"They weren't supposed to cut off the power. They should have just transferred the service to the Jamisons. Now the pipes will freeze when the temperature drops tonight. The forecast is for a low in the twenties—might even break the record for October 26th, set in 1952. That's fifty-six years ago, the year I was born—"

"I know—"

"—and it dropped to twenty-six degrees. We're right on time this year. The first killing frost in Virginia's piedmont is usually this month between the nineteenth and the twenty-ninth. These poor pipes… Preston always told me to keep the pipes under the sink warm by opening the cabinet doors. How can I protect the pipes if there's no heat? Samara, what should I do?"

Samara shrugged. Clair walked to Preston's antique oak telephone box mounted on the wall by the back door, gently lifted the earpiece from its hook, and turned the crank, jangling the two bells.

"I wish I could ask Preston. He always had the answers when I needed them."

As she replaced the earpiece, a low growl sounded. Both women spun around to locate the source. With Clair behind her, Samara edged toward the open basement door. At the bottom of the staircase hunched a black shape, its eyes and shiny collar reflecting the half-light of the stormy day. It growled again and advanced slowly, toenails ticking on each step. When Samara slammed the door, the stray let out a fury of barks.

Samara scowled. "When will folks stop abandoning their unwanted pets out here? He must have run in after the unlatched door blew open. At least in here he'll be safe from the weather. I'll call Animal Control when they open tomorrow. Meanwhile, you gave me a great idea, Mom."

"What's that?"

"You picked up the earpiece of Dad's old phone. Remember when I was little, how I'd phone you from the matching one in the playhouse?"

"You only did that a few times—when it rained—to ask me to bring you an umbrella. What does that have to do with anything?"

"Dad not only linked up the two phones but put a heater out there for wintertime. Isn't it still there?"

Clair nodded.

"If I can find the kerosene, we can warm up this kitchen."

The rain and wind had diminished, though thunder rumbled nearby. Samara crossed the screened porch and descended the steps to the sloping lawn. She sloshed downhill through fallen leaves, past the vegetable garden. Clair's staked plants were withering, but no weeds blemished the symmetry of the rows. Cabbages were almost ready for picking. Thankfully, the Jamisons were fine with Clair finishing her fall gardening after they moved in, but what would she do next spring with nothing to tend?

She understood plants. If she planted them properly, nourished them consistently, and protected them from pests, they flourished, rewarding her with their beauty and bounty. That relationship had always worked well for her. Not so much the kind with people. Especially in Al's case. Even to some extent, in the relationship with her own daughter.

At the edge of the woods sat the big playhouse Preston had built decades ago repurposed as a shed. As Samara disappeared inside, Clair quickly set up the first carton. From under the sink, she grabbed her lidded blue plastic box labeled "Cleaning Cloths," placed it in the carton, and wedged it tight with a bottle of window spray so it wouldn't shift. She'd taught Samara to always use paper towels for cleaning tasks; Samara had never opened this box. That was as it must be. Clair had promised Preston that their daughter would never see the contents.

When Samara returned with the heater, Clair sat cross-legged on the floor, pulling dish detergent and gallon cans from the cabinet under the sink.

"Pack the detergent, Mom, but leave those leftovers

4

from refinishing the cabinets. We have no use for them, but the Jamisons might want them for touchups. Stuff often gets scratched up during a move."

"But the list said to pack *everything*."

"Well, the list should have said 'everything you can use.' Hand 'em to me. I'll put them on the countertop where they'll be seen."

"Should I leave this dog chow here, too? It must be a year since Mookie died, but those Jamisons have a dog."

"You're a wellspring of great ideas today. Have you packed the mixing bowls yet?"

Clair cast a what-planet-are-you-from look at her daughter. "Why don't you ever make sense? And the answer is no. What are you doing?"

"Setting up a buffet and the finest water on tap for our ill-tempered outcast in the basement."

"How're you going to do it without him eating you first?"

"I'll work out something."

Clair chafed her hands together. "Before you do that, get the heater running."

Samara centered the heater in the kitchen, brushed some gritty rust from her hands, filled it with kerosene, and turned it on. A welcome warmth began radiating around the room.

By the time the last of the cartons were packed and loaded into Samara's SUV, the sky had darkened. Another squall brewing. The living room still held a two-sweater chill, but the kitchen was almost toasty. Clair hoped it would retain enough heat overnight to prevent frozen pipes. Preston had done a thorough job insulating this place.

After Samara turned off the kerosene heater, Clair

drew the thermal drapes at the sliding door to the porch.

Samara said, "Once you're in the car, I'm going to open the basement door, then sprint out."

"Be careful, Samara. And close the front door securely."

"I wish you'd call me Sam, like everyone else."

"But that's not the name I gave you."

In the car, Clair stared anxiously at the front door. She relaxed only when Samara emerged and pulled the door until it gave a solid click.

Sliding behind the wheel, Samara said, "Hey, it's only 1:30. We can still salvage a few hours of this rainy Sunday."

"Actually, it's 1:36. I never could teach you to be precise. And we have all those cartons in the back to deal with. That's sure to take a while."

Samara responded with a heavy sigh.

Halfway out the narrow drive, oncoming headlights forced them to a halt. The other vehicle stopped a couple of yards away and cut off its lights.

"Son of a bitch." Samara spat out the words.

Then Clair recognized the driver. Turning her head and gazing into the woods' undergrowth, she started her rocking. "Son-of-a-bitch is too nice a term for him. Dogs don't ruin their own families. Son-of-a-viper. Yes, son-of-a-viper fits that snake better."

"Stay put, Mom. I'll handle this." Samara stepped into the quickening rain, as Al Hobson did the same.

Clair kept her head turned but cracked the window and looked askance toward Al.

If he'd been in his dapper banker's getup, his sexy salt-and-pepper hair would have reminded her of Richard Gere. But in those saggy sweatpants and a battered corduroy jacket straining at the buttons? Closer to a vagrant. The eyes? Nothing like Gere's. Clair had learned the hard way that Al's were you-better-watch-your-back eyes.

Al grinned and broke the silence. "Got everything taken care of at the house?"

"You mean the house you stole from my mom?"

"Come now; nothing's stolen. The house is still a hundred percent Clair's. And her equity earns a much better return, parked in a terrific investment."

"You mean fifty percent of that equity."

He'd snookered her out of the other half in the divorce. Clair wished she'd heeded her daughter's warning before she'd agreed to marry the man.

"I paid more than my share of the taxes, the mortgage, the utilities. You know as well as I do, Clair is no picnic to live with."

Clair wondered if Samara really felt that way. Preston certainly never thought so.

"I earned a share of that property." Al propped one balled fist on a hip.

"You call that sharing? Living with her for two years, refinancing her house—oh, pardon me, the house you shared—then dumping her. She's saddled with a loan she can't pay. Why are you here, anyway?"

"I only have a couple of things to pick up. Look, this is going nowhere. I'll back up to the road and let you out."

"How thoughtful of you. I'll show you what *thoughtful* truly means. When you go in the house…" Samara paused and cocked her head.

"What?"

"Never mind."

She returned to her car, soaked and shivering.
But grinning.

Chapter 2

After a ten-minute drive, Samara and Clair came to the railroad crossing in Ashland, Virginia, and encountered the inevitable—the gates were down. A freight train lumbered along Center Street's steel median strip, the CSX railroad tracks. No "wrong side of the tracks" here, aside from times like this.

Living in The Center of the Universe, as Ashland residents proclaimed their town to be, meant being able to walk a mile or so in most directions and see more farmers' fields than neat houses with kids playing on tree-shaded lawns. But the whole "Center of the Universe" thing had stopped making any sense to Clair in second grade when she'd learned what a minuscule speck the entire earth was in its solar system, let alone in the real universe.

Whenever an AMTRAK train glided through on July fourth, passengers might be treated to the imprecise precision of the lawn chair brigade parading down Center Street or to three-legged races and watermelon-seed-spitting contests on the lawn of the Hanover Arts & Activities Center. Clair thought Ashland could inspire a Norman Rockwell painting if he were still around. On the flip side, however, townsfolk were never far from the inconvenience of trains at all hours or the racket of volunteer fire and rescue squads racing to the latest emergency, sirens shrieking.

When Samara parked beside the small vinyl-sided rancher she rented, those sirens were at it again. Samara paid no attention, but Clair covered her ears. The noise pierced her sensitive eardrums like an ice pick.

"That makes three today," said Clair, her hands still cupping her ears.

"Three what?"

"Sirens. I don't see why they can't make them quieter. Did you know our fire department responds to two thousand calls every year? Thank goodness the sound is fading away now."

No sooner had Samara opened her front door than her cell rang. She answered it while Clair set down a carton and went back for another. Clair returned with a carton labeled "Cleaning Supplies," and near the door, she met Samara with keys in her hand.

"Who was that on the phone?"

"A wrong number. We'll figure out what to do with these cartons when I get back. I need to pick up something for dinner. Have a couple of errands, actually. I'll be back in a while."

Before Clair could respond, Samara was out the door. The same old annoyance niggled Clair. Her daughter spoke in such nebulous terms. What would they have for dinner? What errands? How long did "in a while" mean?

She picked up the heavy "Cleaning Supplies" carton and headed to Samara's attic. This one wouldn't get unpacked here.

****

The phone call had been more than a wrong number; it was a disastrous number. As Sam sped back toward her mom's house, she replayed the call in her mind. It had sounded like Al was in a bar blasting some god-awful rock with heavy bass.

"Leave me alone. You'll only dig yourself deeper, Al."

His voice grew even louder. "You need to get over here."

"When hell freezes over."

"Clair's house is on fire. I called it in, and the first engine is already here."

"What? How can it—I'll be right there."

This would have done her mom in, hence a cover story.

The rain stopped. Where's a good downpour when you need one? The drive seemed interminable, giving Sam plenty of time to curse. *Did I create a disaster with that damn heater? Or was it Al? It must have been Al. What a bastard!*

No train appeared, and few cars were about on a gray Sunday afternoon, but traffic lights didn't cooperate. Her hands shook so badly it was hard to steer. When she finally parked on the shoulder behind a police car, she fumbled to open the door.

"Ma'am, you need to stay back and let us do our jobs," said the burly policeman, blocking her from walking even five feet down the long driveway.

She could see three fire trucks, their flashing lights turned off and sirens silenced, but the deep rumble of their engines and the hiss from water hitting flames forced her to shout to be heard. "That's my mother's house. The house where I grew up. I—"

The whine of something like a chainsaw pierced the sodden woods, followed by the clatter of shattering glass, then three shotgun-like blasts.

"What's happening?" she yelled.

"They're ventilating the fire by cutting a hole in the roof and breaking some windows. It lets the smoke and heat escape instead of spreading to the rest of the house. Makes a mess, but it helps contain the damage. They should have it under control shortly. Mr. Hobson told us the house is vacant. Is that right?"

"No! There's a dog in the basement." She bolted toward the house, but the policeman snagged the hood of her coat and pulled her up short.

"I said you can't go down there. I'll relay the info about the dog. Why don't you have a seat over here? We may have some questions for you." He gripped her elbow, led her to his patrol car, and motioned to a spot on the front bumper—right beside Al, a cigarette dangling from his lips.

"No, thanks." She couldn't stand either the man or his stinking cloud. Her mom wouldn't have married him if he hadn't lied about how much he smoked.

"Suit yourself," the officer called over his shoulder as he returned to his post.

She tried to look through the half-bare trees, but all she could see beyond the engines was a growing bloom of black smoke against a flat pewter sky. A rosy glow wavered from behind the roof's peak as if the sun couldn't decide whether to rise or set.

She turned to Al, who was watching her watch the fire. "What did you do? Use the kerosene from the heater so you could watch a piece of Mom's life go up in smoke?"

"What heater?"

"The one I set up to keep the pipes from freezing. The power was off."

"I never even made it into the house. After I let you

12

out, I drove up and parked. That's when I saw the smoke. I ran around back and saw the kitchen drapes flaming, so I called 9-1-1 and moved my car out of the way. Then I phoned you."

She studied his face and posture for any hint of a lie, but it was futile. Duane Chanesky, who lost to Al at poker every Friday night, said he'd never seen someone who could hide his tells so well. If he were a shark, you'd never know he had teeth until they sank into your leg.

Sam kicked at the leaves collecting on the berm and crossed her arms against her chest, both to warm herself and to try for some measure of control. It was a good thing she hadn't brought her mom. Aside from the trauma of watching what was left from Mom's marriage to Dad destroyed, she would have freaked at the sounds. Firefighting was noisy business.

"Perhaps the damage won't be too extensive," Sam said. "Maybe they can limit it like the policeman said."

"These woods sure do isolate the house from the neighbors. Lucky I was here; otherwise, it would have been entirely too late." Al puffed his chest as if presenting it for a medal.

"Tell me again—why were you here? I thought you'd finished clearing out all the junk you'd left in the attic over a month ago."

"Yeah, I'd mostly gotten it, but I was picking up the last bit. While we're on the subject, why were you in the house? Hadn't movers taken it all?" He tilted his poker face toward hers.

"We'd left packing kitchen stuff for last and ran out of time. It's not like we needed it. My cabinets are already full." All her mom's remaining furniture and belongings that hadn't been sold or shoehorned into Sam's house had gone into a storage unit, pending finding a new place for her. Another thing to figure out soon.

She would never admit it to Al or let her mom see it, but he was right about one thing—Mom was a challenge to live with, twenty-four/seven.

A Fire Medic unit pulled away from the house and came up the drive. When its lights and siren turned on as it neared the road, both of them flinched.

Do they use ambulances for dogs?

The policeman backed toward Sam and motioned the vehicle in the direction of I-95. She rushed to him.

"Will he be okay?"

"How should I know?" He resumed his post on the driveway.

"I told you to tell them about the dog. If you'd done it right away, maybe this wouldn't have happened," she yelled, scowling at the policeman.

"What difference would that make? He was blown off the roof by those small explosions you heard."

"How in the world did he get on the roof?"

"How do you think? By a ladder." He walked a few paces away.

"Wait. Dogs don't climb ladders."

The policeman came back, shaking his head.

"Right. But firefighters do. Like I said, he was blown off the roof after he cut the hole to vent the fire. Must have been knocked out or broken some bones when he hit the ground."

How could this get any worse? First, her mother forced to rent out the house Sam had grown up in, then the fire, now a firefighter badly injured. She prayed that at least the dog escaped unharmed.

As the policeman returned to his spot at the end of

the drive, Sam looked toward the house. The red glow was gone, but black smoke still billowed toward the sky.

A firefighter carrying a balled-up blanket approached Al and Sam. "Which of you reported the dog in the house?" he said, offering the blanket to Al, who hadn't budged from his seat on the patrol car's bumper.

Al shrank back and pointed at Sam.

"That would be me." Sam hesitantly reached for the proffered bundle.

"Careful, now. When we went in the backyard door to the lower level to search for your dog, this little guy was the only one we found. He was whimpering in a corner, on the side farthest from the fire. Maybe the dog already took the rest of the puppies somewhere safe, but if she was in the kitchen, well…we won't know more until everything's under control. Sorry." He eased the bundle into her arms, then lifted the folds until a black head appeared, eyes tightly shut.

Sam stroked the pup's short fuzz, feeling the trembling body shrink away from her cold hand.

The firefighter added, "You'd better get him warmed up; I recommend a hot water bottle. You'll need to bottle-feed him, too, unless his mama comes back."

"It wasn't my dog. It was a stray that somehow got in. She must have used the basement as a safe place to have her puppies."

"Well, this one is yours now, unless you want me to take it to the animal shelter. What do you say?"

The blanket was no heavier than the wool one Sam had recently put on her bed, but the burden of caring for an orphaned puppy, one like the black lab her fiancé had had…not sure she could take it. Too close a tie to the worst day of her life. However, the shelter might not have enough staff to nurture a newborn night and day.

"I'll take care of him for now, but…I guess I'll work something out."

"One more thing. The fire investigator will need to question everyone who's been in the house recently. Are you the homeowner?"

"No, this is my mom's house. She and I packed up the last of her things earlier today. Also, her ex-husband, Al Hobson, came this afternoon." Sam tipped her head in Al's direction. "He reported the fire."

"Well, the three of you can meet the investigator here tomorrow morning at ten and walk him through what happened." His brows drew together at Sam's frown. "Is that a problem?"

"Maybe, but I'll see what I can do. My mom is going through a rough time right now."

"It could get rougher if she doesn't cooperate. Get her here tomorrow. Ten o'clock."

Sam started to her car, but remembered the ambulance and went back. "How's the fellow who was injured?"

The firefighter turned grim. "Don't know. He was still unconscious when they took him away."

"How awful! Who is it?"

"Ryan Bennett. He's—"

"Ryan? Oh, my God! I took AP classes with Ryan in high school." Memories flooded her mind—philosophical arguments over just about everything in English Lit, heated arguments about how to best solve problems in Trigonometry, puzzlement over why he'd asked her to the senior prom until she realized that nobody else had asked and it was the only way *either* of them would attend. "I need to go. I'm so sorry."

The firefighter strode back down the drive. As Sam opened her car door, Al rose and called out half-heartedly, "Anything I can do?"

"Yeah, leave me alone."

She nested the pup's bundle onto the floorboard in front of the passenger seat, started the car, and turned the heater to "high."

Hitting the gas, she wheeled from the shoulder onto the road, shooting gravel at the man who'd torpedoed her mom's tenuous hold on life. She watched him in the rearview mirror as he sank back onto the patrol car's bumper.

****

By four o'clock, Sam had picked up a hot water bottle, a wind-up alarm clock, a puppy feeding kit, and puppy formula, plus three takeout dinners. When she'd phoned Mariah, she'd told her only that she needed a huge favor. Her best friend, as well as her bookshop's assistant manager, Mariah Gabrielli, never let her down.

As always, Mariah replied, "Anything but asking me to murder Al."

When Mariah's parents had died in a plane crash, she'd inherited their small Cape Cod house on Maple Glen Lane. From the day the two girls met in first grade, Sam had considered it her home, too. Mrs. Gabrielli had supplied her with all the hugs and warmth her own mom didn't seem to have.

Mariah and Sam became closer than many sisters. Even though they were polar opposites in the looks department—Mariah ended up with all the voluptuous curves Sam lacked and was almost a head shorter—Sam spent so much time at the Gabrielli place, some folks mistook her for a member of the household. She carried a key, but the house was seldom locked.

"Oh, for Petey's sake, come in. I'm in the kitchen," said a muffled voice from the back.

"I can't. I need help with the door."

"Give me a minute to finish washing my hands. I sure hope you brought dinner, or I might be forced to open a can of spaghetti."

No way. Mariah didn't believe in recipes involving fewer than twelve ingredients, several of them unpronounceable. As part-owner of Gabrielli's Classic Catering, the business started by her parents and now run by her brother, she created scrumptious new recipes that kept customers coming back for more. Sam's job as chief taster, though unpaid, had resulted in significant gains to her bottom line.

When Mariah opened the door and saw the bag from the barbecue place on England Street, she said, "Only kidding about dinner. I was getting ready to start a batch of lasagna and a spinach salad. Join me?"

"You're not going to have time to make lasagna, so I brought this." Sam handed her the barbecue bag, then nodded toward the bundle in her arms. "Here's the favor I told you about." As Sam peeled back the edge of the blanket, the puppy yawned, punctuated by a high-pitched yip. "This orphan needs a foster home for a while."

"He's so tiny. What happened to your mama, little guy?" Mariah rubbed the velvet under his chin with one finger.

All through the retelling of the day's disasters, Sam kept her emotions in check, but when she came to the part about the ambulance, the first tear leaked out, followed by the dike giving way. Mariah dumped magazines out of a large basket and set the puppy in it, blanket and all. She then held Sam until the sobs subsided.

When Sam pulled back, she said, "I don't even know what to tackle first. How do I tell Mom? I sure can't take a newborn puppy home without getting hit with a load of questions I'm not ready to answer. I could have sworn I cut off the heater. Was it still hot enough to relight itself if the dog knocked it over? Or did Al do it then lie like a rug?" She hiccupped a breath. "Is the damage fixable? Will it fall on Mom to pay for it? No way the Jamisons can move in now. And Ryan… what if he dies?"

"Small stuff first. Tell me how you want me to care for the puppy, and I'll do it. I'll open Paperbacks tomorrow and take him with me so I can feed him every few hours. We must stock a book on puppy care—all I have to do is read it."

On cue, the puppy whimpered. She reached into the basket and stroked him until he quieted, then she heaved a sigh.

"Now about your mom…"

"You know how any change sends her off the rails. Regardless of when I tell her about the fire, she'll hole up in her bedroom for a week, like she did when Dad died. A funeral can be delayed, but she's got to meet with the investigator tomorrow." Sam flopped back on the sofa and searched the ceiling for an answer.

"Maybe you shouldn't give her the option of hiding. Don't tell her. *Show* her by taking her to the house in the morning. That way, at least it will look to the investigator like she's cooperating by being there."

"How will it be cooperating when she shuts down?"

"You'll just have to explain about your mom. You can answer all his questions. He'll understand."

"Maybe." Sam shrugged. "But you're right. That's

probably the only way."

After they stumbled through the intricacies of giving a days-old pup his first bottle-feeding and then settled him back in the basket with the warm water bottle and the ticking clock for comfort, Sam couldn't delay going home any longer. Her mom would be suspicious enough; her "couple of errands" had taken almost three hours, and all she had to show for them were two cold takeout dinners.

She slipped on her coat. "Wish me luck tomorrow. I'm going to need it."

Mariah gave her one last hug. "Luck wouldn't hurt, as long as it's good luck. But you're a survivor. Put those brass ovaries to work."

Chapter 3

By morning, frost sparkled on the lawns, and a crust of ice coated low spots on the roads. Sunlight had thawed a deceptive sheen on top of the ice as if the roads were merely wet.

When Samara turned the car toward Clair's house instead of the bookshop, Clair thought her daughter wasn't paying attention to the road.

"You're going the wrong way."

"Mariah offered to open up this morning. I thought you'd want to check on your garden, maybe pick those cabbages." Samara made no move to change course.

"Today is not her day to open. Turn around." Clair stared straight ahead.

"Mom, we have to go to the house. There's something you need to see."

Clair sat rigid, hands clasped in her lap. "I don't care what you want me to see. Today is our day to open the shop. Turn around now."

"Sorry, Mom. Not now."

The two passed the rest of the trip in cold silence.

She wished for the early days when her daughter always did as she was told and enjoyed the beautiful name she'd given her. Her favorite tree, the maple, produced samaras—winged seeds that helicoptered on the wind. Each spring of Clair's childhood, she'd fill a pail with samaras, fling them into the air, watch the aerobatics, then do it all over again and again. When she was pregnant, she thought of the baby as a samara, gracefully spinning away on a breeze, taking root in a fertile spot, and, with careful nurturing, growing strong and independent. Clair succeeded too well. Samara grew up to be annoyingly headstrong. A child should never disobey a parent, regardless of age.

When Samara turned down the driveway, Clair spotted a truck parked near the house.

"Is this truck what you wanted me to see?"

"There was a fire at the house yesterday. Al called it in and then notified me. I spent the afternoon here watching the firefighters."

"You lied to me about your errands. I thought I taught you to always tell the truth."

Then the onerous weight of Samara's message sank in. Clair wrapped her arms around herself and cast her gaze on the dashboard. What was she supposed to feel under these circumstances? She didn't know. Numbness set in.

"I didn't want you getting all upset until we could assess the damage. I'm here for you, Mom. I'll help you. We'll deal with this together."

At least her daughter knew enough to refrain from reaching for her. Clair didn't want to be touched at times like this. They both got out.

Clair studied her house. Charred rafters were all that remained of the back corner of the roof over the kitchen. Shards of glass glistened on the sooty ground. The brick façade stood nearly perfect, but sunlight poured out the kitchen window instead of into it. Now the Jamisons wouldn't be able to move in, and the bank could take the house.

Clair's stomach clenched in a painful knot. As she was about to tell Samara to take her anywhere but here, a man carrying a small shovel and three pails emerged from the back yard, picking his way over long, deep ruts in the grass.

"What are you doing at my house?"

He peeled off a thick glove and offered his hand but awkwardly pulled it back when Clair didn't shake it. "I'm Don Truitt of the Fire Marshal's office, investigating the cause of your fire. You must be Mrs. Hobson. I have a few questions for you."

Samara stepped between them, not touching Clair in any way. "I'm Samara McNeer, her daughter. Most folks call me Sam. Pleased to meet you." She reached for his hand and shook it firmly. "We were here yesterday packing up the last of our things in the house. You see, the house is being rented out shortly and—"

"Pardon me, but I'd rather speak with the owner of the house. Mrs. Hobson, what time did you arrive here yesterday?" He sidestepped around Samara, closer to Clair.

Clair backed up two steps and looked toward her house. "At 10:28 a.m."

Mr. Truitt opened a small notebook, flipped to a fresh page, and wrote. "Tell me what you did while you were here."

"I packed kitchen stuff."

He circled his hand in the air. "And?"

Silence. She continued staring at the house.

"Ma'am, please answer the question."

Clair focused on his scuffed black boots. " 'And' is not a question."

"And what else did you do?"

23

"Left. At 1:36 p.m." She spoke loudly so he'd be sure to get it straight.

"I'm trying to figure out what happened to your house, and you don't seem overly concerned about all the damage. If it were any other woman's home, she'd be extremely upset. Your eyes aren't red, are they?"

"No, they're brown."

Mr. Truitt huffed and turned to Samara. Most people did eventually. At a time like this, that was fine with Clair.

"Why don't you help me fill in a few of the holes, Ms. McNeer?"

"Gladly. Call me Sam."

Glancing at the small spade in Truitt's hand, Clair said with a slight smile, "You'll need the bigger shovel from my tool shed." Samara let out a tiny chuckle.

Clair strode toward her garden, giving long, muddy ruts a wide berth. Those ruts must have come from fire engines running over the soggy ground. As if getting fire damage fixed wasn't enough, she'd have to patch and reseed the lawn next spring, too, if the house was still hers.

"Is she always like this? I mean—help me out here— is she mentally...you know...challenged?" Truitt quietly asked.

Clair winced. Why did people often talk as if she couldn't hear? She was a mere two dozen feet away. She wasn't deaf. Anything but.

"There's nothing wrong with her intellect. In fact, she might be brighter than you and me put together. But she doesn't handle anything outside of her normal routines very well."

"Why isn't she upset by all this?"

"Believe me, she's upset. See her there? Gardening is her thing; it calms her."

"Sorry, but her behavior looks out-and-out uncooperative to me."

While Samara related the events leading up to the fire, including admitting she'd set up the heater but cut it off, Clair steadily worked in the garden—pulling up withered plants, harvesting the last cabbages, and straightening fence posts to a perfect vertical. She didn't once look back toward the house but sneaked sideways glances at the investigator. Despite the distance, she didn't miss a word.

"Are you finished with your questions, Mr. Truitt?" Samara asked.

"For the moment, yes."

"I have some questions for you if you don't mind. Could you tell what started the fire?"

"I've got a pretty good idea, but there's nothing I can share with you at this time," he said, tucking the notebook and pen into his coat's breast pocket.

"And how is the firefighter who was injured—Ryan Bennett?" Samara crossed her fingers.

Hoping for a good answer? That was the young man who'd taken Samara to the prom. What kind of injuries?

"You'd have to check with the hospital on that one."

"How much of the house was damaged?"

"The kitchen and back porch are a total loss. Beyond that, only smoke and water damage. Your insurance adjuster will let you know."

Now, who was being uncooperative? At least she'd given him definitive answers.

"By the way, don't set foot anywhere near the house until I tell you it's okay. Both for safety's sake and, until

25

we can rule out arson, it's considered a crime scene."

Clair lost her hold on an armload of cabbages, and they tumbled to the ground.

Samara asked, "Have you seen a black Lab wandering around here this morning?"

"No, but in the kitchen, I bagged the charred remains of what could be a medium-sized dog…"

Samara gasped.

"And three tiny ones under her, apparently her pups. Sorry. Are you the one who took the pup found in the basement?"

"Yes."

What pup? Samara hadn't brought a pup home. What else had Samara not told her?

Just then, Al's gleaming black car rolled to a stop, and he stepped out. He'd upgraded from yesterday's grunge to a coat and tie, plus a dark gray overcoat. He looked the part he often bragged about—being the well-connected son of a Connecticut appellate court judge. If that was for real, no one in Ashland had seen proof or cared enough to check it out. Neither the elder Mr. Hobson nor any of his influential associates had ever shown their faces here—not even for her wedding to Al.

Al sauntered over as if the world should wait for him, then greeted the investigator, shaking hands with the right while passing his business card with the left.

"Sorry I'm late, but I was hung up on an overseas conference call. I'm Al Hobson, Clair's former husband. I was told you'd have questions for me since I discovered the fire."

"I appreciate you coming, sir," said Truitt. He tucked the card in his pocket and retrieved his notebook.

"I arrived here yesterday about one-thirty, as Sam

and Clair were leaving. After talking briefly with Sam, I backed up to let them out the drive, then drove down close to the front door. I'd come to look for something I thought I'd left in the attic."

"What did you see when you entered the house?"

"I never got that far. When I saw an odd light flickering from the front window, I ran around to the backyard and saw the kitchen drapes burning, smoke everywhere. I called 911, and you know the rest."

Samara broke in. "You told me you first saw smoke, not a flickering light. Which is it?"

Al waved her away dismissively, turned to Truitt, and said, "Of course, where there's smoke, there's fire. I saw both."

Next, Samara asked, "So you never picked up your boxes?"

"What boxes?" Al's voice rose.

"The ones you left by the front door."

"I didn't put anything there. I haven't even set foot inside since early September." Al turned back to Truitt and crossed his arms. "Who's supposed to be doing the questioning here?"

"Enough with the arguing. Ma'am, there weren't any boxes by the front door. Besides what I found in the kitchen, I saw absolutely no contents in the house—not in rooms, not in closets, not in the basement, not in the attic."

"Well, that settles it," Al said. "If you have any more questions for me, Truitt, you know where to find me. I'd better get back to the bank." After his handshake declared the meeting over, he shambled back to his car, followed by Mr. Truitt.

As Clair watched them both leave, something elusive

nagged at her—Al was different somehow.

****

Sam went to help her mom carry the produce she'd gathered. As soon as she moved downwind from the kitchen, the breeze hit her with the noxious smell of burnt roof shingles. Looking back at the house, the irony of it all struck her. Her mom's house was now like her marriage to Al had been—both looked fine from the front but had been gutted in the core.

On the drive to the bookshop, Sam's mom said, "You know, some things they said don't make sense. Boxes don't just disappear. And Al would have noticed the shrieking smoke alarms first."

Sam wasn't surprised that her mom had overheard the conversation. Most kids have mothers with eyes in the back of their heads. Hers had the ears of a barn owl that could hear the slightest rustling of a mouse in the grass. It used to embarrass Sam to no end when her mom would ask about something a boyfriend had whispered to her the night before. This time, with the wind carrying the words straight to the garden, Sam was sure she hadn't missed a single syllable. Plus, her mom had picked up on the obvious—smoke alarms. She had overlooked that.

Sam thought for a moment. "If the fire started when Al was leaving the house with the two boxes, instead of when he arrived, why wouldn't he just admit it? Do you think he's afraid he'd be accused of starting the fire if they knew he'd been inside?"

In spite of the lack of response, she knew gears were turning, processing the details and trying to put them into some semblance of a picture.

After a full two minutes, Mom answered, "No, they'd never accuse him of starting it. People don't start fires, then call 9-1-1 right away, unless it's accidental. If it had been an accident, he might have been burned, and then he'd have to tell them the truth." She paused to tug at her seatbelt.

"I didn't see any sign of burns, either yesterday or today. But..." Sam thought back to the way Al had walked to his car after speaking with Truitt. "Al's gait today wasn't his normal, smooth stride. He seemed slow, moving gingerly as if he was in pain, but trying to mask it."

After a quiet minute, Mom said, "That must be what seemed odd to me. How did he walk yesterday? Did his pants have any holes or tears?"

"He had his normal swagger before the fire when I spoke with him in the driveway after we'd packed kitchen stuff. As for later yesterday, I couldn't say. The whole time I was at the fire, he sat on a police car's bumper. He stood for a moment as I drove away, but he never took a step. And he had on that ragged pair of black sweatpants. Holes—if there were any—wouldn't look out of place. You're thinking the dog bit him, right?"

"Yes. And another thing, the timing's not right. It was fifteen minutes from when we left Al to when I heard the sirens. What did he do in those fifteen minutes? I don't understand why people lie."

To Clair, lies were illogical and wrong. She took everything at face value, as she saw it. And she noticed a lot.

"And Samara, where's the puppy? Why didn't you tell me about the puppy?" Clair folded her arms. "While you're at it, also tell me how that firefighter—Ryan Bennett—got injured."

Although thoughts of Ryan in the hospital and the

dead mama dog and her puppies in the kitchen brought tears to Sam's eyes, she started from ground zero and brought her mom up to speed.

That evening, Sam phoned Memorial Regional Medical Center. All she could learn was that Ryan was listed in serious condition. No phone calls or visitors allowed except family. Did he have a wife and kids? With a town as small as Ashland, you'd think she'd know, but their social circles had never overlapped, except during high school. And that was more of a collision than an overlap.

She remembered him having a much older brother in the Army. Ryan had followed his example at some point after college, but Sam had no idea if his parents were still in the picture. Did he have anyone to visit him, to look after him?

****

Over the next few days, every time a phone rang at home or work, Sam dreaded answering. At each jangle of the bells on the bookshop's front door, she checked to see if a uniformed officer entered. With the house heading for foreclosure, an unexplained fire could arouse suspicions. Would she and her mom be questioned again, be arrested for arson? Or if Ryan died, for something far worse?

If the spotlight of blame hit them, maybe they could point to Al—see if the dog really did sink teeth into him. Could a crime lab match bite marks to the poor dead dog's teeth? Al would probably weasel out of it somehow, but one ace up her sleeve was better than nothing.

On Wednesday afternoon, Sam placed her tenth call to the hospital in three days. "Hi. I hate to bother you. I'm—"

"Ah, you again, Ms. McNeer. Well, this time I have good news. Mr. Bennett's condition has been upgraded to stable, so you're free to visit him if you like. He's in Room 245. Would you like me to put you through?"

"Oh, I wouldn't want to wake him if he's sleeping, but thanks so much." As she put her phone back in her pocket, she mouthed a big "Yes!"

Over her mom's protests, she closed the shop at five instead of six. Sam spent only enough time at home to scarf a bowl of cereal for dinner, freshen up, and call Mariah to make sure the puppy was doing okay. She flew out the door, leaving Clair in mid-rant over breaking every precious bit of their daily routine.

As Sam drove to the hospital, she mulled over her speech. *Wow, you haven't changed a bit since graduation; that would be...fifteen years ago.* Wrong approach if he's bruised or bandaged. *Thanks for almost dying to save my mom's house, though it might not be hers much longer.* Perhaps, *Boy, you avoided landmines overseas only to get blown up in Ashland.* The third one is not always the charm.

She decided to wing it.

She stopped in the gift shop and bought a "GET WELL SOON" balloon—a dark blue one with neon yellow and purple stars. When she peeked through the half-open door to Room 245, he appeared to be dozing, propped by pillows and the raised head of the bed.

Ceiling lights were off, but a fixture on the wall behind the bed cast a puddle of light, enough for her to survey the scene. No bandages on his face, no scary traction apparatus. An IV line stretched up to a bag of clear fluid hung on a monitor stand, and his right hand loosely held a control button on a long cord. When she'd had an appendectomy, she found that little button blissful. One press and—*voila*—the attached PCA pump (patient-controlled analgesia) delivered a shot of painkiller straight into the IV.

When did he become a hottie? Although Ryan probably hadn't shaved since Sunday's fire, his blond hair made it not so noticeable. What had been an unruly mass of long hair in high school was now rumpled but trim. His clunky glasses weren't on his face or bedside stand. Maybe he wouldn't be able to see her without them, especially in the dim light.

She might pass for a hospital volunteer coming to cheer him up. Sam tiptoed in, heading for the visitor's chair to wait for him to wake up, but the door handle snagged her purse strap and yanked it off her shoulder. The overloaded bag landed on the floor buckle first, with a loud metallic clink. Ryan flinched, groaned, and opened his eyes. He slowly turned his face in her direction. A moment passed.

"I should have known. Whirly-girl. You were a headache then. You're an even worse headache now." He spoke haltingly, hushed as if the effort pained him. He groaned again and hit the happy button.

"I still go by Sam, by the way." Thanks to him. When he discovered what a samara was in high school, he saddled her with the nickname. Others who wanted to get under her skin latched onto it. "How do you even know it's me? You can't see squat without your glasses."

"The miracle of lasers."

"Oh." She tied the balloon's ribbon to the bed's footboard, adding it to the flock of similar ones floating there. "If you're not up for visitors, I can come back another time."

"Long as you're here, sit, stay."

Did he think she was a dog? She slid a chair nearer to the foot of the bed and sat down. That's when she noticed a squarish contraption about the size of a pizza box standing on its narrow edge below the side rail. Three tall see-through cylinders were inset into it, each with graduated markings. Two of the cylinders held a murky red liquid. A tube ran from the device toward Ryan's chest. Thank heavens the tube disappeared under the sheet.

"What's this device on the floor?"

"It collects fluid from a place where it doesn't belong, namely my right lung." He pulled the sheet back and then pointed to where the tube plunged into his chest. When Sam recoiled, he covered it again and changed the subject. "Thanks for the balloon. I'm getting quite a collection."

Before Uncle Sam sent him overseas, Ryan had been engaged to someone he'd met in college, but Sam had never caught mention of a wedding. Or any further word about him, for that matter. Better play it safe.

"Your wife must be worried sick. I'm so glad you've graduated from ICU."

"No wife. Never been married." He studied Sam as if he'd never met her. "Does your husband know you're here?"

His grapevine must be as weak as hers. Guess he was away in the service when her fiancé Kyle was killed. "No husband. I'm living with my mom now. No, reverse that. She's living with me."

"Why was her house vacant? She sell it?"

"Not in this market. She'd planned to rent it out, a long story for another time. What about you? What's the damage report?"

"Concussion, two fractured ribs, one collapsed lung."

"Ouch. I'm so sorry this happened. At my mom's house, of all places."

"Comes with the job. Not your fault."

How Sam wished she could believe that without a doubt. She felt an overwhelming urge to leave. "Guess I'd better not let you stress your lungs with more talking."

"Opposite. They say it's good for me; keeps my lungs inflated. They torture me with deep breathing exercises…every two hours…" As slowly as an automatic garage door closing, his eyelids drifted shut. "And talking's not as hard as holding my eyes open. Drugs…"

Quietly Sam picked up her purse and put the chair back. On the way out the door, she heard, "Later, gator."

****

After opening Mariah's front door, Sam called, "ISC Convention time."

Amid struggling with the angst of middle school, Sam and Mariah had banded together, forming the Introverts Social Club—where one is a quorum, and two's a convention. Conventions had occurred at least twice a week ever since.

Sam inhaled a mélange of tempting aromas. "Something sure smells good in there. I detect marinara sauce, garlic bread, and an open bottle of white zinfandel. Anything left? I've not eaten anything resembling a dinner."

"Dufus, you can't smell wine from the foyer. Come on back. There's plenty."

"I said 'detect,' not 'smell.' It's Wednesday; hence the featured vino of the day."

In less than a minute, Mariah had dished up a plate of

spaghetti, ladled her homemade sauce on top, poured a glass of white zin, and served it to Sam. After topping up her own glass and taking a slice of garlic bread from the basket, Mariah said, "You're a whole lot more upbeat today. What gives?"

"It doesn't look like I'll be arrested for negligent homicide." Sam ate a huge forkful of spaghetti. "Ryan is out of Intensive Care, and I just had a chat with him. From what I could tell, he's doing pretty well. The fall rattled his skull, broke a couple of ribs, and collapsed a lung, but knowing him, he'll be back on his feet in no time. He's morphed into a pretty good-looking guy, but one thing hasn't changed; he still annoys the heck out of me."

When Sam glanced up from her plate, Mariah's eyes were smiling, but she didn't say anything. Sam scanned the kitchen.

"Hey, how's our littlest survivor doing?"

"See for yourself. I'm getting ready to feed him. And, like it or not, I'm calling him Phoenix. You know, out of the ashes. Come here, Phoenix, you hungry little dickens."

Mariah slid an open cardboard carton out of the corner and scooped up the puppy. She nestled him on a fluffy towel in her lap. He opened his eyes a crack, squirmed around, and found the long nipple on the puppy bottle she held. It had been just three days, yet Sam could have sworn he'd grown, at least in the tummy.

"Why do you think this one was in the basement while the others were in the kitchen?"

"After I left the house on Sunday, I guess his mama found the food I'd put out in the kitchen and carried the puppies up, one at a time, for the warmth from the heater.

The fire must have started before she had a chance to move this last one. She died rather than leaving those three. No wonder she'd growled at me—she had pups to protect. And I'd assumed *she* was a *he* with an attitude."

Mariah tilted the bottle higher; the formula was more than half gone. "Do you still suspect that Al used the kerosene to set the house on fire?"

"Yeah, if they could prove the dog attacked him, he'd have to admit he'd been in the house before the fire started. But I thought of one way he could claim it was accidental. If he and the dog got into a scuffle, he could say one of them knocked the heater over, and some kerosene leaked out. Add a little glowing ash from Al's ever-present cigarette, and—poof—fire."

"If it happened that way, why didn't Al at least get singed in the flare-up?"

"He'd figure out some way to explain it. The key to dealing with that snake is to anticipate where he'll slither next." With a hopeful smile, Sam asked, "Any ideas on what he'd say, oh wise one?"

"Not really. Hey, you'll work it out. You always do. I'm still with you, betting that cold, calculating Al set it deliberately."

"And left no telling evidence behind. No other help to offer?" Sam pleaded.

"You mean, aside from taking care of Phoenix for you?"

"Point taken."

Aside from being a personal, all-purpose support system, too. She wasn't an ungrateful ass for expecting so much from Mariah. It had always been a two-way street. They'd taken turns relying on one another to make it through tough times—the deaths of Mariah's parents, the murders of Sam's dad and her fiancé. The thinnest thread of that thought rushed the horror back in high-def. Sam put down her fork.

How much longer would it be until the dreadful scene seven years ago would start to fade?

Her dad and Kyle hadn't returned from a short run to Kyle's house for a spare propane tank, and guests were nearly due for a cookout. When Kyle didn't answer his cell, Sam figured they must have broken down in a spot with no reception. She'd grabbed her keys.

Roads on the outskirts of Ashland changed in a heartbeat to a hundred percent rural. Almost no traffic. Fields planted in corn and soybeans lined the left of the shoulderless road, and scraggly woods leaned in from the right. As she neared Kyle's ten rolling acres, an ambulance with siren blasting sped in the opposite direction.

When she rounded the last bend before Kyle's driveway, she came to a knot of fire and rescue vehicles. She stopped and sat frozen to her seat. Only when Officer Giles Joyner, a friend from high school, walked up did she summon the courage to open the door.

As Sam tried to peer past a fire engine off the side of the road, she could only make out a clearing at the edge of the pine forest, a clearing that hadn't been there before. She looked at Giles and tried to force the question out, but it wouldn't come. No matter. Giles understood. With eyes brimming, he shook his head.

The two most cherished men in Sam's life—her dad and her fiancé—gone. Police had an easy time with the how—someone had rammed Dad's car off the road—but not with the why or by whom. The case had quickly gone cold, but the pain burned relentlessly.

Even now.

"Earth to Sam," Mariah said. "Hey, where'd you go?"

"No place that's happy." Sam pushed the memory into a dark corner. *Enough already. Suck it up, girl.*

Sam ran her hand over the puppy's silky fuzz. A small smile warmed her face.

Mariah settled the contented puppy back in his carton. "You know I'll gladly put in more sleepless nights feeding him every two hours, but…"

"Not to worry. I'll take over nursemaid duty next week as soon as I cover the bases with the insurance adjuster. On second thought, could you manage if we made that week after next?"

"I suppose so, but it'll be your fault if I suffer irreparable damage from so little beauty sleep."

"Like you need it."

Despite hanging with the wallflowers, Mariah had always been the first one to be asked out by the guys. Like many of Italian descent, she carried a few extra pounds in the most enticing places on her softly rounded, five-four frame. Even when she stumbled through an awkward conversation with a prospective boyfriend, her big dark eyes sparkled with the promise of fun.

In Sam's case, though lean and lithe, she scared the shorter fellows off with her height of five-eleven. That height was a waste when it came to basketball or any ball for that matter. She had no aim, even at miniature golf or ping-pong. But her dad had made sure that given a drill, a hammer, some screwdrivers, and a project, she excelled. Prospective boyfriends didn't like being one-upped in that department.

"Would you like to take your mom a plate of

leftovers?"

"Thanks, but you know the drill. If it's not listed on Mom's menu planner for the week, she won't eat it. She'll never know what she's missing."

****

At home, Sam found a note on the kitchen table:

Proper dinner in fridge
Listen to message on machine
Goodnight

Judging by the light seeping from under her mom's closed bedroom door, she would be reading well into the night, the same as she had every night since the fire. Reading, for both her and her mom, was the drug of choice when coping with stress. Sam loved getting lost in a gripping mystery novel, but Clair stuck to nonfiction. How studying the classification of trees or the lifecycle of a peculiar moss could capture her interest, Sam couldn't begin to understand. Those books would bore her into oblivion.

She pressed the play button on the answering machine.

"This is the Fire Marshal's office calling for Clair Hobson and Samara McNeer. Please be at our office tomorrow morning, Thursday, October thirtieth, at ten a.m. If you are unable to keep this appointment, call 555-0183 as soon as possible. Thank you."

If they were filing charges of some kind, the police would have come to arrest them. So the Fire Department must have more questions—not a fun prospect where her mom was concerned. Damn. At least it was Mariah's regular day to open the shop; disruptions to routine would be minimal.

Was Sam's budding headache a case of sympathy

pains for Ryan's concussion? She picked up the latest Victoria Thompson mystery, *Murder on Bank Street*, and headed to her room.

It was going to be a long night.

Chapter 4

Sam shifted in the hard chair but couldn't get comfortable. Her mom sat beside her, ramrod straight, hands folded in her lap, rocking slightly side-to-side ever since they'd arrived. Footsteps broke the silence. Sam put a firm hand on her mom's leg—the quit-rocking signal that often saved them both from embarrassment.

Truitt opened his door and ushered them in. With papers, books, and cartons stacked everywhere in the investigator's windowless office, the place looked like a firetrap. Ironic.

"Have a seat." Truitt waved them toward two wooden chairs opposite his cluttered desk. Before they were even seated, he handed Sam a sheaf of papers from his open folder. "My investigation of your fire is now complete. Follow along on your copy if you'd like. Sorry to tell you this, but the bottom line is that you, Ms. McNeer, set the stage by lighting that kerosene heater."

"But we'd used that heater hundreds of times with no problem," Sam said, her voice quavering. "I placed it in the center of the room with nothing near it, and before we left, I turned it off. Did the dog knock it over?"

Or did Al kick it over?

"No, the heater was warped but still upright. Those 'hundreds of times' were the problem. That type of heater uses gravity and a partial vacuum to slowly feed kerosene from a vertically oriented tank to a shallow reservoir with

41

a wick. But in your case," he said, his stare boring a hole into Sam, "over time, rust had eaten away at the tank. It just takes a pinhole leak to break the vacuum and overfill the reservoir. At the first sign of rust, that heater should have been tossed."

He glanced down at his report. "Based on the burn pattern, the fire traveled over the vinyl flooring to the open cabinets by the sink and worked its way to all the cabinetry, countertops, wallpaper, drapes, and ceiling."

The horrifying scene replayed in her head, complete with the dog cowering in the corner, nuzzling her puppies closer. "But I turned it off."

"All the way to off? Or just to low?"

"Off. I'm sure." Was it supposed to click when switched off? She hadn't heard a click. "What caused those explosions that knocked the firefighter off the roof?"

"I found shards of paint cans. When the fire's temperature hit the flashpoint, they blew. Were you repainting anything?"

"It must have been those cans we left behind for touchups," Clair said.

It stunned Sam to hear her speak. She'd almost forgotten her mom was beside her.

"They were leftovers of stain, polyurethane, and such." Clair turned to Sam. "If we'd stuck to my list and packed up everything, there would have been nothing to explode."

Truitt closed his folder and filed it in the cabinet behind his desk. "And you could have avoided the whole disaster simply by waiting for the power to be restored. Dominion Virginia Power crews fixed all the lines downed in the storms by approximately 6 p.m. that evening."

Sam shuffled through the copies he'd given her and gave the summary sheet a close look. Truitt's report listed the cause as accidental. His form didn't have checkboxes for negligence or stupidity.

****

The meeting initiated a bizarre reversal of moods. Mom spent the rest of the day cleaning and reorganizing Sam's kitchen and alphabetizing all the spices. Now that she could chart the precise sequence of events and define the reasons for every failure, her world was back in order.

Sam retreated to her room, shut the door, and didn't come out, not even for her mom's classic meatloaf. She pulled a "Mom stunt"—curling up with her pillow and drawing the comforter over her head.

She had set up the dominos and started the whole cascade. *She* suggested the kerosene heater. *She* ignored the rust on her hands. *She* lured the dog and all but one pup to their deaths. And *she* had planted the can-bombs on the counter. So much for hoping to dump the blame on Al. He'd been in the house all right, probably removing those two boxes and getting bitten in the process. But even if he or his damn cigarette played a part in lighting the leaked kerosene, the investigation was closed.

That horse was dead, dead, dead. No sense beating it.

****

A power tool whined and whirred. Sam's eyes popped open, and she sprang from the bed. The shadow of a birdfeeder—complete with birds—danced across her comforter. The book she'd been reading well past 1 a.m. was on the floor. The bedside clock showed 8:15 a.m. and the date. It was Halloween.

She followed the intermittent racket to the kitchen

and found her mother drilling holes in the wall by the back door. Given her mom's penchant for inflicting damage on herself, property, or unwary bystanders when using tools of any kind, Sam unplugged the drill.

"What are you doing to my wall?"

"Drilling pilot holes for screws," Mom answered, stepping back to admire her handiwork.

"Why?"

"To make it easier to screw in the screws, of course."

Of all the days to test her tolerance. "I meant, what are you hanging on the wall?"

"If you meant that, why didn't you ask that in the first place? I'm hanging the antique phone where it belongs, right by the kitchen door. I'm so glad we got it before the fire. You should have told the movers to take it on moving day."

"It had been hanging there so long, it'd become another fixture to me, like the woodwork or the kitchen sink."

"That's your biggest problem. You take too much for granted. You stop seeing things that are right in front of your face. I don't. I see everything. Every time." Clair strode from the kitchen.

Though tempted to retort, Sam didn't bother. It would serve no purpose. In the concrete sense, her mom was correct. Nearly every time they walked together, Clair would spot coins in a crack on the sidewalk, occasionally dollar bills in the bushes. Tax-free income. Her dad used to say she could pick fly shit out of the pepper. But in the arena of seeing Sam's emotional needs growing up, she'd been blind.

No hugs before or after school, no "I love you" when tucking her in bed. Not even when her dad and Kyle died could Sam share the burden of grief. One thing she never had the luxury of taking for granted was that her mom loved her.

Oh, there had been benefits to having a mom so different from everyone else's. As long as Sam told her mom well in advance, she let Sam spend the night at Mariah's house anytime she asked. She let Sam decorate her room any way she wanted—with mesh bags tacked in the corners holding a menagerie of stuffed animals and a galaxy of glow-in-the-dark stars stuck all over the ceiling. All Sam had to do was keep it neat.

As soon as Sam surpassed her mom in height, Mom figured she was big enough to take care of herself, even to the point of allowing Sam's friends to sleep over when she and her dad attended a booksellers' conference out of town.

Her friends were jealous of that, but they didn't envy Sam when they saw her mom act weird—doing her rocking thing, going silent at times, or rattling on *ad nauseam* about bizarre plants. They rarely came by the house if her mom was home. Mariah had been the exception.

Two patched holes and an indeterminate number of choice words later, the heavy phone box became a new fixture on her wall. Despite Sam's irritation over her mom putting up Dad's phone without consulting her, she admitted—to herself—that it belonged right there.

****

Going through the familiar motions of opening the door to McNeer's Paperbacks by the Tracks, setting out the till, and stocking the latest arrivals, Sam could understand the comfort her mom derived from sticking to routines.

While Mom busied herself in the office—ordering books, paying invoices, and handling all the minutiae Sam hated—a stream of Randolph-Macon students trickled through the shop, sometimes buying the latest paperback. A guy wearing devil's horns kept leering at two classmates dressed as Playboy bunnies, but most of the students were more interested in the huge bowl of candy corn she'd set by the register. True to long-standing custom, they used the scattering of overstuffed chairs as off-campus housing, taking up residence for hours at a time—studying, snacking, texting, surfing with the free Wi-Fi, and napping. Rarely was there an empty seat. She should have charged rent.

There were days when most of her profits came from the coffee and decadent pastries Mariah's brother supplied via Gabrielli's Classic Catering. Thankfully, the refinanced loan on the bookshop's building wasn't too onerous. If it weren't for the rental income from the building's other three stores and offices on the second floor, Paperbacks would have folded years ago, even before Sam had inherited it.

She'd relished the quiet and calm atmosphere ever since her own days in those chairs, from age four when she learned to read to age twenty when she graduated from Randolph-Macon with a major in English Lit. Sam had never questioned what she'd do after college. The bookshop, peopled with friends and family, was more her home than any structure that housed her bed had ever been.

During a lull in business, instead of reading in her own comfy chair behind the register, Sam pulled out scratch paper and started several lists. Sometimes things didn't look so bleak once they were in black and white.

On the first one, labeled "Must Do," she wrote:

Meet w/ insurance adjuster Mon. 11:00
Mardigan @ bank – Mon. 3:00
Study foreclosure process—ways to avoid?
Take shed stuff to storage
Pick up Phoenix by Fri. 11/14, latest

The next she titled "Should Do:"

New chairs for shop
Find apartment for Mom
Help her move to said place
Keep tabs on Ryan

The last one—"Want to Do"—brought a smile to her face.

~~*Learn to crochet*~~ *Learn scuba diving*
Fly to Bahamas—30 books—no phone—no Mom
Eat 1 qt. double dark choc. ice cream
Hire masseur for back & neck massage every afternoon

After tucking the first two lists into her purse, Sam opened *Murder on Bank Street*, dropped its bookmark on the counter, and replaced it with the third list. How many other folks could say they go to work to escape days off?

****

When Sam arrived at Mariah's that evening with a grocery bag and a DVD of *Dead Poets' Society* for their Friday night flicks, Mariah announced, "The movie will have to wait. There's a new book I need to show you."

"You mean there's one I haven't seen?" Sam chuckled, tossing her coat on the back of a chair and handing Mariah the bag. "Put this in your freezer first."

"Hey, I'm serious," Mariah said, setting the bag on the floor. She plopped on the sofa and patted the cushion beside her. "Here, this won't take long."

"You haven't been reading up on the perils of foreclosure, have you?" Sam slumped back. Much as she loved reading, she'd been counting on an evening in Robin Williams' classroom.

"This has to do with your mom. My Uncle Edmund, bless his difficult soul, is like her in lots of ways. He's super bright. He can spot an obscure bug in thousands of lines of computer code. But conversations with him are awkward. He either gives you curt answers to questions, or he talks your ear off about steam engines—always steam engines—even if the topic under discussion is politics."

"That doesn't sound much like Mom, except for the 'awkward conversations' part, and she is bright, but steam engines? Debugging?" Mariah had lost her. This must be what it was like for her mom when Sam went off on a tangent.

"Hear me out. What about her obsession with plants? When she gets going about gardening, you can't slide a word in edgewise. Yet you often have to speak for her when she has to deal with strangers. Others don't know how to work around her quirks."

"Tell me something I don't know." Sam fidgeted with a curl that kept falling across her forehead. "Where does a book come in?"

"Patience." Mariah shot her an inscrutable look. "Uncle Edmund called me last week, spent forty-five minutes telling me about his discovery. He's been diagnosed with Asperger's Syndrome, you know, high-functioning autism. He was so excited to learn *why* he's always been different from most people."

"And the book?"

"I hoped we'd have something about Asperger's in

the shop. There was only one; the paperback just came out. You absolutely must read it." Mariah handed her *The Complete Guide to Asperger's Syndrome* by Tony Attwood. "I've read the whole thing. It fits your mom to a T."

Sam was struck by the book's cover. Three nautilus shells were pictured in cross-section, their many chambers spiraling outward.

"Wait. How could your uncle or my mom be autistic, yet no one ever recognized it?"

"That's the 'high-functioning' part at work. They're bright enough to get by or even excel, but their social problems win them labels like difficult, quirky, misfit, or anti-social. And when psychologists first started diagnosing Asperger's in the early 1990s, they were looking at kids, mostly boys having trouble in school. Girls and women with Asperger's are better at camouflaging their difficulties, slipping under the radar. They're much better than boys at mimicking other children's normal behavior. Your mom was nearly forty in 1990, in a stable marriage. If she were managing passably, why would anyone think of looking for a diagnosis?"

"I'm not convinced, but if you're so sure it's worth it, I'll take a look. Even if Asperger's fits her, what's to be gained by hanging a diagnosis around her neck? It's not like there's a cure."

"No cure, but at least you might understand why she's the way she is." Mariah peeked in the grocery bag Sam had brought, and her brows shot up. "Sweet! I'm gonna skip the freezer and get us some bowls. BIG bowls. We'd better kill off this *Death By Chocolate* before it finishes melting."

Mariah rattled dishes in the kitchen while Sam focused on the book cover. Like the nautilus, her mom's shell had walls within walls. Could any book ever show her what was locked inside the inner chambers?

****

They arrived at work early on Saturday. Sam drove past the shop front before parking in the back. As they'd anticipated, Halloween tricksters had left one of their occasional calling cards, but this time the two of them had come prepared with a stock of window cleaners, scrapers, and squeegees.

While Mom tended to her back-office duties, Sam got to work removing the spray-painted *ZOMBIES ROCK* on the shop's picture window.

Removing the black paint cost twenty minutes and ten frozen fingers.

****

On Monday morning, the insurance adjuster showed up at Clair's burned house a half-hour late, giving Clair and her daughter time to survey the damage undisturbed.

Outside, a faint odor of smoke hung in the still air. The front door was locked. As Clair turned the key, she took a deep breath and let it out. The acrid smell hit as soon as she stepped into the foyer. The walls in the living room looked like they'd been painted dingy gray. Except for the blistered living room ceiling, major damage seemed limited to the kitchen. What remained was nearly unrecognizable. Blackened chunks of debris littered the floor. A twisted black snake of something, maybe the faucet, poked up like a cobra ready to strike. What must have been parts of cabinets, countertops, and rafters lay askew.

"That would be where the dog and puppies were,"

said Clair, pointing to the breakfast nook.

"How can you tell? Everything is black on black, truly fly poop in pepper."

"No, we packed the pepper." The corners of Clair's mouth twitched up; she was proud of her little joke.

Samara huffed and leaned back against the charred doorframe. "How can you make light of this disaster?"

"Don't blame me. You brought up the old pepper thing. Anyway, we're here to learn what happened. Just look. See that boot print in the ash and the parallel scrape marks in the corner? The investigator must have removed the mama and then used his shovel to pick up the pups. And when we first saw him, he was carrying three little pails."

"I've seen enough. Let's wait outside. I'm feeling nauseous."

Clair followed Samara toward the front door, then halted. "Wait. Look around. What do you see?"

Samara did a three-sixty around the living room and foyer. "Gray. Everything is gray."

"Right. What's wrong with that?"

Samara took a second look, then shrugged her shoulders.

"What did you see before the fire?"

"Ah, now I get it. The boxes! Those two boxes stacked by the door."

"I'll teach you yet. And that means…"

"If the boxes had been removed *after* the fire by someone—a firefighter or anyone else—that spot under the boxes wouldn't be gray. The floor would have a clean spot."

"So…"

"So now we have proof Al lied. He must have been

51

in the house. He removed the boxes before the fire started. Good job, Mom."

"It doesn't change much. Still our word against his that there were any boxes in the first place."

The crunch of gravel announced the arrival of the adjuster. He got out of his car with a clipboard, a bulky tape measure, and a camera and hustled to the front stoop. Without so much as an introduction, he barged in.

"Sorry for running late. Thanks for unlocking the door. I'll take over from here. I don't recommend that you follow along; you might not recognize some hazardous areas. I'll lock up when I'm done, not that it'll do much good from the look of things." He gave Clair a business card. "I'll be in touch, probably in about a week. Have a good day." He held the door until they left, then shut it.

As her daughter drove away, Clair slipped the man's card into Samara's purse. "How dare he kick me out of my own house! I could have helped." She started rocking.

****

Clair and Samara arrived at Ashland Community Bank a few minutes early for their afternoon appointment, but Mr. Mardigan didn't make them wait.

"Come in, come in. Make yourselves comfortable."

They sat down in front of his imposing mahogany desk. Its finish gleamed, not even a smudge. The surface held only a phone, a leather blotter with gilt trim, a full business card holder, and his engraved brass nameplate: Squire T. Mardigan, President. Clair recalled he was in his mid-forties. His light brown hair, with only a hint of a receding hairline, was impeccably groomed.

"Hello, Mr. Mardigan—" Samara began.

"Please, call me Squire. We're all on a first-name basis here. Al told me about your fire, Clair. I'm so sorry.

I wanted to meet with you personally to extend my sincere sympathy. You must be distraught, but hopefully, your insurance will cover it adequately. You've met with the adjuster, I trust?" He looked straight at Clair, but she peered behind him, reading the framed diploma on the wall: Wharton School, University of Pennsylvania, Squire Thomas Mardigan. "Right, Clair?"

"Right. This morning."

"When you get the estimate, please forward a copy for our records. I need to project how long repairs will take. We'll postpone any actions toward foreclosure until they're complete. In the meantime, maybe you could bring your loan current, and we won't have to suffer the indignities of foreclosing, will we, Clair?"

Clair now focused on a collection of golf trophies on his credenza, many from charity tournaments.

Samara fidgeted in her chair. "And what indignity would you be suffering with us, Squire? Having to sign the paperwork? You might suffer a paper cut."

He raised one hand. "I'm sorry, Samara. Poor choice of words. I can understand how difficult this must be for you, watching your mother risk losing her house and all. Let's see what we're dealing with. I have the payment records right here." He pulled a thin file out of a desk drawer. After shuffling through a few sheets, he stopped to suck on a paper cut on his index finger. Not lifting his focus from the page, he continued, "Clair, your small first mortgage is current, but payments on the home equity loan are significantly in arrears. Then there are the penalties and accrued interest…" He looked up, a kindly smile on his face. "But in all, not so bad, considering how many payments you've missed."

Not bad? Clair saw the situation as impossible and

getting worse by the day. She'd always kept her promises. What was a loan if not a promise—in writing no less—to repay the money? If Samara hadn't insisted she had to attend this meeting, she'd be back at the bookshop, dealing with the doable, instead of sitting here, her chest cramped with shame.

"She's doing all she can do," Samara said.

She and Clair cleared a pittance from running the business. Clair's savings had barely covered Preston's final expenses and then, years later, the lawyer for her divorce from Al.

Mardigan leaned toward Samara. "Did she spend all the loan proceeds on the home addition and remodeling, as stated in the application?"

He'd given up addressing Clair. People often did. Clair continued her mental survey of the room. She noted what wasn't anywhere in sight—a picture of Mardigan's wife.

"What addition?" Samara said. "There's no addition. I never saw those papers. I wasn't in close touch with Mom at the time."

Al had made sure of that. After he'd married Clair, he'd insisted Samara move out. She was beyond old enough to live on her own, he'd said. Clair had agreed, mostly to spare herself from all the loud arguments between Al and Samara. After Samara left, Al talked Clair into the home equity loan. Once all the paperwork went through, Al seemed to change. Not for the better.

"Well, where did the money go?" Mardigan narrowed his eyes.

"Al locked up Mom's proceeds in some investment that's paying a good return, but since he claimed half of the investment in the divorce settlement, the income doesn't amount to much."

"Can't you help her out?"

"I'm stretched thin already, paying student loans, a car loan, and rent for my house."

"Hey, I want to help you here. Maybe I can arrange a loan using your business real estate as collateral."

"I don't know how I'd pay it back, but I'll think about it. Thank you for your time, Mr. Mardigan." Samara stood, and Clair followed suit.

Clair looked at his tie—shades of gray with thin navy and maroon diagonal stripes—and said, "Thank you, Mr. Mardigan."

Without rising from his chair, Mardigan gave a slight nod in acknowledgment. His thin lips twisted up at the corners. "That's *Squire*. You can call me Squire. Good day."

They left quietly.

Before starting the car, Samara said, "If I'd uttered his first name, I would have gagged. Mark Twain was right. He said, 'A banker is a fellow who lends you his umbrella when the sun is shining but wants it back the minute it begins to rain.' So much for getting any help from Mardigan. Don't worry, Mom. After the repairs are done, we'll find another tenant."

Clair tugged at the tight shoulder belt and began rocking. "Those repairs will take months. By that time, the loan will be farther behind. What then?"

"We'll come up with something."

"No, it's a hopeless mess."

Chapter 5

At dinnertime, when Sam dialed the direct line to Memorial Hospital's Room 245, thinking she might offer to bring Ryan a double cheeseburger or some hot wings to spice up his bland diet, the phone was answered by a gravelly-voiced old lady begging her to tell the nurse she needed more meds. After instructing the woman how to hit the call button, Sam phoned the hospital's operator.

"Could you please tell me the new room number for Ryan Bennett? I believe he's been moved."

"Sorry, we have no Ryan Bennett registered here. He must have been discharged. Have a nice day." *Click.*

It didn't seem possible. When she'd called Saturday morning, Ryan said the doctors considered him "stable," but he felt awful, and the tube draining fluid from his lung was driving him nuts. He apparently went straight to "Go" without passing "Good." Then again, these days, hospitals kicked you out as soon as you could make it on your own to the bathroom and back without passing out.

No matter where Sam searched, she couldn't find his home number in a directory or online. The firehouse surely had it, but Stacie Evans, Ashland's biggest gossip, did clerical work there. If Stacie caught the slightest whisper of "Sam" and "Ryan" in the same sentence, the whole town would soon be under the impression they were nearly engaged. No way could she let that happen. This situation warranted obfuscation, i.e. lying, though

56

her mom was forever telling her lies brought trouble. Her dad, on the other hand, had said, "If you gotta go, go big."

Sam called the non-emergency number for the firehouse and was relieved when a man answered, but she still needed to be careful.

"I'm Sarah Reinhart calling from Memorial Regional Medical Center." She spoke quickly, doing her best imitation of a beleaguered nurse. "It seems Mr. Bennett left his watch in the drawer of the bedside stand. It's one of those fancy Ironman watches with all those dials and such. I have no way to reach him. They've already filed his chart, and I don't have his number. I'm sure he'd want to know we have it. His number, please?"

"Hold on a minute." By the sound of several muted voices, Sam could tell the guy had covered the mouthpiece with his hand while discussing the situation. "Yeah, okay. You can call him on his cell. I'm sure he'll be glad to hear from you." He gave the number.

"Thanks. Bye." Next time, Sam thought she should come up with a better alias. *Sarah* sounded too close to *Samara*.

Call number four. Ryan picked up on the third ring.

"Hello?" His voice was still weak like his breathing was constrained.

"Hi, Ryan. It's Sam. Glad you're finally home. I thought you might not have anything stocked for dinner, and I was just going out to get a burger. Can I bring you anything?"

"Thanks for the offer. I sure could use a cheeseburger with everything, large fries, and a chocolate shake. They didn't feed me anything decent in there." Some shuffling and rustling sounded in the background.

"Is anyone there with you? I mean, I could bring

them something, too."

"No, just me. Do you know where my place is?"

"Actually, no."

"It's in the Camelot Townhomes, 849 Broadmoor Court."

"How about a half-hour?"

"No hurry. I'm not going anywhere." Was that a chuckle she heard right before he hung up the phone?

****

Thirty minutes later, fast food in hand, she rang the bell.

"Come on in. It's unlocked," Ryan called weakly. "I'm upstairs."

Across from the front door was a narrow staircase. Funny. They'd never had a date except for the prom, and here she was, heading straight to his bedroom.

"Turn right at the top," he said.

In fact, there was no other choice.

The scene was quite a contrast to the hospital. Propped up in a four-poster, double size, he looked like a model for the cover of a romance novel. Minus his Clark Kent glasses, he resembled the alter ego—with that strong, square jaw—but why was she reminded of Red Riding Hood's wolf? Maybe it was the way the quilt was pulled up to mid-chest, a navy and green plaid flannel shirt revealed above. He'd set a folding chair near the bed and had placed the nightstand between, like a table for two.

"It's not the Ritz, but thanks for the room service." He sat up a bit straighter, then winced, putting a hand to his chest.

"You look a far sight better than the last time I saw you. Am I famished! I'll dish up. We can talk later." She spread out napkins into a makeshift tablecloth, divvied up the burgers and fries, and handed him the milkshake.

The silence didn't last long.

"You don't know how I've been craving this," he said, taking a long drag on the straw, then starting on the burger. "The only thing we ever agreed on was chocolate—the more, the better."

After a few fries, Sam asked, "When did they release you?"

A mouthful of burger muffled his answer. "Sat'day aft'noon."

"No more danger from the collapsed lung?"

"You wouldn't know it from how much it hurts to breathe, but no, not as long as I stay pretty quiet. At least the fluid stopped draining, and they could pull out that damned tube."

Recalling the sight of the chest tube and bloody fluid collecting in the device on the floor made Sam give up on her half-eaten burger. "How long do they say you'll be out of the action?"

He was already crumpling the empty wrapper and digging into the fries. "Well, the concussion headache is getting better, but it may be another week or so before I can cut out the pain meds. Once I'm not under the influence, I'll be able to get behind the wheel, but the ribs will keep me from firefighting for at least eight weeks. You know, with the heavy lifting and all."

"You'd better slow down on that shake. I don't imagine brain freeze would help the headache any."

"Good point. Hey, this has been great. And we've been in the same room for ten minutes, not a single argument. This belongs in the record books."

When he set down the empty cup, Sam noticed his

watch. She'd guessed right—precisely like 'Sarah' had described it. "Nice watch."

"Yeah. One of the guys lent me this beauty. My cheap digital watch didn't survive the fall. That one you found must have been someone else's." A grin played at the corners of his lips.

"The one I found?" An unwelcome warmth blossomed in her cheeks.

He couldn't hold it in, even though laughing obviously pained him. "I was at the firehouse catching up with the guys when you called. Thanks for allowing enough time for me to borrow a watch like you described and to have Don bring me home and set the stage." He threw off the quilt. He was still wearing his jeans.

She'd been right about the wolf. Her cheeks grew hotter. Without a word, she stuffed the trash into his wastebasket, picked up her purse, and, with all the dignity she could muster, headed to the door.

"Aw, come on. Don't leave. The guys and I were just having a little fun—"

"Yeah, at my expense, like in high school. Haven't you outgrown that in the last fifteen years?"

"You walked right into it with that crazy tale about the watch. It was too perfect to resist."

When would she learn not to lie? Her mom's dictum—lies cause trouble—was spot-on.

Ryan's smile peaked, then faded. "It's not like I don't appreciate you coming; I do. Still friends?"

"Were we ever?"

The crestfallen look on his face immediately made Sam feel like a jerk. Their relationship had always generated sparks—sparks of the wrong kind. Even the right kind scared her. Sparks can lead to flames, getting burned.

The wounds from losing Kyle seven years ago hadn't healed.

****

Although Sam finished the book about Asperger's Monday night, it took her till Thursday to skim through the few books on autism she'd found on her shop's shelves. Her mom certainly wasn't on the low-functioning end of autism's spectrum. However, the high end was a different story. An Asperger's diagnosis fit her like a custom-made glove. But Sam was on the fence about where to go from here. She scheduled an ISC Convention at Mariah's that evening.

Mariah met her at her door. "Saw you drive up. Why are all the conventions at my house these days? I'm going to raise my facility fee."

"Would you prefer to share a facility with my mom? Besides, the food at this place is top-rated."

The aroma of something yeasty wafted in.

"Since you put it that way, maybe I could give you a frequent booking discount."

Sam poked her head into the kitchen, just enough to see a soup pot on the stove, rolls cooling on a baking sheet, and Phoenix napping in his box. "I need a sounding board. You were right about Mom."

"Of course. Aren't I always?"

They both kicked off shoes and sat cross-legged on Mariah's cushiony sofa. "No comment. I'm in a quandary. If I bring this up with Mom, the first thing she'll tell me is that there's nothing wrong with her. She'll say any communication problems are my fault, or everyone else's fault since we don't express ourselves clearly. I doubt she'd even go for an evaluation; you know how she hates dealing with strangers. Anyway, how could a psychologist diagnose her if I'm the one doing all the talking?"

"If you can get her to go for an appointment—granted, half the battle—I think she'll be okay. They'll probably take her to a quiet place and have her fill out an assessment form, like a multiple-choice test. She can read and write perfectly well."

"But what about the bigger issue, what's to be gained? It's not like she'll attend a remedial class in communication skills. Try picturing a fifty-six-year-old woman on a pint-sized chair in a room full of grade school kids."

That image made them both crack up.

"Maybe we're going about this wrong. Here's a radical idea. Tell her about it and see what *she* wants to do."

"That would certainly get me off the hook. Do you have any idea how exasperating it is, trying to anticipate her moods, her reactions, intervening in all the situations she can't handle? I don't know how Dad did it all those years. And he loved her deeply, to boot. Ever since he died, I've felt like the captain of a rudderless sailboat, unable to navigate Mom away from rocky shoals. Oh, well. In spite of her behavior, she *is* an adult. If she doesn't want to have anything to do with getting a diagnosis, I'll simply drop the subject."

"Regardless, maybe you could read up and see how they help kids overcome the communication issues. You might learn some new techniques to help you cope with her."

"We'll see."

Over a dinner of pea soup with ham and lots of warm

yeast rolls, Sam said, "We met with Mardigan at the bank on Monday. What an ass! He acted like he was sympathetic about the fire, but all he really wanted to do was to make sure Mom's insurance would cover the house repairs. The good news is that it buys us a little time because he doesn't want to proceed with foreclosure until it's in saleable condition." She sank her teeth into a roll—thin crust on the outside, light but chewy on the inside. "God, these are so good… The bad news is that Mardigan merely postponed the inevitable. He offered to float a loan against my shop's building so that I could make good on Mom's equity loan. That's about as helpful as putting pontoons on a camel. I couldn't repay it, and Mom couldn't keep up with future loan payments, anyway."

"I know you've looked at it before, but isn't there some way she could sell the house?"

"Not in this market. The sum of the mortgage and the home equity loan puts her deep underwater. Even with a good sales contract, an agent told me the house would bring $60,000 less than the balances owed, *not* counting the late fees. A loan servicer at the bank told her months ago that they'd never agree to that much of a short sale. She'd have to make up the difference. I was sure I'd done the right thing—talking her into moving out, generating some rental income, and moving on with her life—but now she can't rent the place until the damage is fixed. You know the most aggravating part?"

"Not a clue."

"Mardigan tried to insist that we call him 'Squire.' Pompous ass, but he comes by it naturally. Al told me Mardigan's parents really did give him that as a first name. Way over the top for Irish farmers from West

Virginia. Maybe they thought it would give him a shortcut to respect. Didn't work on me."

"Parents mean well. Look at your name. I've always loved the story behind it. Clair selected something she loved—a winged maple seed—something full of the promise of new life, creative energy freely making its way in the world." Mariah cleared her place, then in the center of the kitchen, she threw her head back, stretched her arms out, and whirled in a circle. When she stopped, her long, dark-brown hair swirled gracefully over her shoulders. "She gave you something beautiful to aspire to."

Sam put her empty soup bowl in the sink. "But she needs me planted right beside her. Where's the freedom in that?"

****

Clair was pacing in her bedroom when she heard the front door open and close. Samara was finally home.

"Samara, come in here. I've been waiting to talk to you," she called.

Samara appeared and braced herself against the doorframe but didn't step into the room. "What about, Mom?"

"Why was this book buried under your bras?" She waved Tony Attwood's book on Asperger's over her head. "I found it when I was putting away your clean laundry. The last time you hid a book, you were thirteen, and I'd discovered a sizzling romance novel under your mattress. Why did you hide something like this?"

"I didn't mean to hide it. I, uh, must have stashed it in there when I was doing a quick cleanup." Samara still didn't set foot into the room.

"Whose book is it?" Clair scrunched her brows

64

together.

"Mariah bought it at Paperbacks and gave it to me to read."

"Thank goodness. I couldn't help myself. I marked all over the pages and crimped lots of corners. You'll never believe it, but this book is about me!"

Samara nearly stumbled coming into the room. "I need to sit down."

"Suit yourself." Clair paid little attention to her daughter and barreled ahead with the same intensity she usually reserved for the taxonomy of plants. "I know this book almost entirely talks about children, but it's how I was when I was little, and it mostly fits today. Painfully shy. Misunderstood. Takes everything literally. Trouble understanding humor and figures of speech. Hates change. Loves routine and rules. No close friends. Well, Preston was the exception there... Strong interest in specific areas. The list goes on and on." She flipped through the dog-eared pages. "Over-sensitivity to sound and touch. Doesn't like hugs or shaking hands. Uncomfortable with eye contact. Inability to read body language. Rocking to soothe agitation." She wasn't rocking now. She shook with energy, barely pausing to breathe.

"I never told you what it was like for me in grade school," Clair continued. "Whenever I became overwhelmed in class, of course, I rocked. The teacher would say, 'If you have to go that badly, get up and go to the lavatory, for Pete's sake.' I never knew why it mattered to Pete Burkhardt or why I couldn't go to the library—my favorite place—instead of the lavatory, but I didn't question it. It worked for me. I escaped from that class. And, oh, the bullying because I was different.

Starting all the way back in kindergarten…"

She rolled onward for over an hour. She vented about the hurt and frustration that still churned inside like it was yesterday. The anger that built until it blew up into tantrums and meltdowns. The rejection by other children, teachers, strangers…

In looking for solutions to cure Clair of her unusual behaviors, her mother had tested out all the "fixes" she could find. Though she was sure her mother acted out of love, the only message Clair received was that she was hopelessly broken. The bombardment of negative messages from all directions drove away any possibility for self-respect. Drowning in a sea of self-loathing, the one thing she had clung to like a life preserver was her sister Patrice's support and guidance.

"…and now I finally know, after all these years I finally know *why*! I'm me because I have Asperger's Syndrome. I'm wired differently from other people. I'm not defective like everyone tells me. I'm different. Just *different*."

****

Mom's reaction to learning about Asperger's stunned Sam. She thought her mother would fight to avoid a label of any kind, stubbornly deny that she displayed any of the symptoms, or at least be sad and withdraw farther into her impenetrable shell. Instead, she embraced the probable diagnosis as the long-awaited answer to a prayer, much like the way Mariah's Uncle Edmund had reacted.

Before Sam climbed into bed, even though the clock read 11:45 p.m., she had to phone Mariah. "I know it's beyond your bedtime, but you're never going to believe this…" Now it was Sam's turn to cut on the verbal faucet full blast.

The next morning, Sam dragged herself out of bed and into the bathroom. She shouldn't have glanced in the mirror. Her frizzy hair looked like she'd tangled with a blender…and lost. At breakfast, Mom still had a full head of steam. She nattered on with more stories of the indignities she'd suffered throughout her life. Sam, however, was running on empty.

"Mom, have you seen my giant yellow coffee mug? It's not with the rest of my mugs. I need a triple dose."

"I put it on the shelf with the soup bowls. It looked like a soup bowl to me."

When Sam opened the cabinet door, she found not only her mug and soup bowls but her soup pot and ladles, too. "What's all this stuff doing here?"

"I fixed your kitchen, so the things that go together are stored in the same place."

Sam had been in this house for almost three years and had everything just where she wanted it. Her mom had been here for a month, and the house was turned upside down. Sam snatched her mug and closed the cabinet door a bit hard, rattling the dishes. Anyone who came between Sam and her morning caffeine was in a dangerous spot. That went double when she was short on sleep.

"I wish you hadn't done all this."

"I was trying to help. Your home is so disorganized."

"Not to me. My home is exactly the way I like it. I want mugs with mugs." And her mom was just being Mom…again. If this were an object lesson demonstrating the Asperger's mind, it could be titled: *Extreme focus on own point of view and no consideration for anyone else's feelings.* It took the last shred of Sam's low reserve of tolerance to keep from lighting into her mom. Yes, Mom's attitude had changed, but would her behavior ever become less frustrating? Maybe she could turn this into a teachable moment.

"Next time you want to do something like this, *please* ask me first."

"I don't see why, but if that's your rule, okay. This is a classic example," said Clair, smiling and putting her hand over her heart like she was pledging allegiance. "I see things differently, that's all. I like being different. I'm not ashamed of who I am, not anymore."

It finally dawned on Sam. An Asperger's diagnosis could be a one-way ticket to a place her mom had only dreamed of visiting, a place where she could live with self-respect. But could she continue to live with her mom?

Then and there, she resolved to make finding Mom a place of her own a top priority.

Did I free the genie from the bottle or open Pandora's box?

She was leaning toward the box.

Chapter 6

The deadline for picking up Phoenix arrived too quickly. Sam was already losing sleep over sharing her house with her displaced mom. Maybe she should put out a sign: Homeless Shelter. Before going to work on Friday, Sam stopped by Mariah's and, while Clair waited in the SUV, she loaded the puppy and his paraphernalia into the back. As she drove away, she peered in the rearview mirror. The long look on Mariah's face told her she'd become attached, as Sam knew she would be, too, in short order.

Her mom asked, "Where are we going to put that big cage? Why isn't he in the box Mariah's been using to bring him into the shop? I don't think that thing will fit behind the register like the box did. And it will be more of a pain to carry home every day."

"Mariah said he'd started teething on the carton, so she borrowed a friend's crate. They call it a crate, not a cage. We'll just have to make it fit. She gave me good news, though. He's down to four feedings a day—at seven, noon, five, and eleven—then he sleeps until morning."

"That's better than when you were a baby. I couldn't handle your crying at night. Preston took over nighttime feedings when you were two weeks old. I went to bed with headphones on for five months until you slept through the night."

Sam's dad had told her about this. She'd always taken it as a sign of Mom pushing her away, not caring enough about her welfare. In light of learning about Asperger's traits, however, the real issue must have been Mom's extreme sensitivity to sound.

****

Though the risk of more humiliation loomed, Sam thought she should do more to ease Ryan's recovery. Bottom line, she was ashamed of her cutting remark when she'd left his place in a snit. A care package—something she could deliver and then make a hasty exit—seemed the best choice. Over the next week, she gathered anything she guessed he might like and loaded the items into a shipping carton she'd received books in. Reusing— always the best recycling. When the carton was nearly full, she picked up the phone.

"Hi, Ryan. It's Sam. I have a little something I'd like to drop off on my way to the grocery and was wondering if it'd be convenient for me to come by now. I won't stay long. Ten minutes."

"It's not my watch, is it?"

Sam cringed. "Very funny."

He never let anything go.

"Just kidding. Really. Yeah, that'd be fine. See you shortly."

This time when she rang the bell, Ryan met her at the door. Since the day the fire reintroduced them, this was the first time she'd seen him standing, instead of lying in a bed, covers pulled up. He seemed a bit taller than she remembered—had to be at least six-two. He still possessed "the bod of a V-man," as she and Mariah used to call it. Broad in the shoulders, tapering to narrow in the hips, no extra padding in between. Impressive, considering he was a decade past his college years.

"Come on in," he said, eyeing the carton. "Good grief, Charlie Brown. I thought you said a *little* something."

"Actually, it's a lot of little somethings I thought you could use. You must be going bonkers cooped up here." She put the carton on his coffee table and started unloading. "A few books…"

The stack grew one by one, up to about a foot high. Out of the corner of her eye, she spotted floor-to-ceiling built-in bookshelves on both sides of the fireplace—every shelf full. Her heart sank.

"You have so many paperbacks over there. Where do you buy your books?"

"Online at used book sites and a few from used book stores and library sales. My money stretches a lot farther when I buy them that way."

That explained why she'd not seen him in Paperbacks.

"Well, if there are any in this stack you don't want or already have, bring them to Paperbacks by the Tracks. I'll exchange them for you."

"That's your dad's store, isn't it? Do you still work for him?"

"It's my store now." She took a deep breath and huffed it out. "Dad died seven years ago."

"Sorry, Sam. I had no idea. That was when I was stationed in Germany. What happened? Couldn't have been old age."

"We're pretty short on answers. Two guys in a pickup tailed Dad from our house and rammed his bumper several times. While Dad hit the gas and tried to outrun them, Kyle—he was my fiancé, and they were going to his house—he immediately called 9-1-1. Kyle only had a minute to describe the truck and the guys before the pickup knocked them off the road into the trees. They were both killed, and the bastards were never found. But that's more than you ever wanted to know."

Ryan, the man with a ready comeback for everything, was speechless. Sam choked back tears and rummaged through the half-empty carton.

"Let's see what else we have here."

By the time the carton was empty, the coffee table looked like a setup for a yard sale. The assortment included two used jigsaw puzzles, a deck of cards, a Richmond Braves water bottle, Sam's old three-by-three color block cube (scrambled), and a pair of new corduroy bedroom slippers (men's XL).

She pasted on a grin. Surely at least one thing would appeal to him.

"What do you think?"

He twisted the cube's colors so fast she couldn't follow. In less than a minute, he set it down. Each side—a single, unscrambled color. Well, that didn't last. She hoped the rest would give him a little longer stretch of entertainment.

"Hey, this is all great stuff, and I do appreciate you bringing it over. Really." He picked up the Braves water bottle and matched her grin, then turned serious. "This isn't the best time to bring this up, but the fellas told me what caused your fire. You were always so good about knowing how things worked. You really never knew how dangerous it could be to use such a rusty old heater?"

"Maybe this is the perfect time to ask; why do you always ask the worst questions?" Sam was painfully aware of the truth in his words and needed no reminding.

"I'm not blaming you. It's just that, with your smarts and all…"

Sam couldn't read the enigmatic look on his face.

Before she could come out with something stupid, like she did on her last visit, she flattened the empty carton. On the way out the door, she tossed, "See you around" over her shoulder.

When Sam arrived at her driveway, she didn't pull in. Instead, she circled the block several times, waiting to cool down. This was the way it had always been with Ryan. One minute they'd be having a normal conversation, and the next, a zap would hit her dead center. She'd gone most of her adult life without encountering him. She could just as well go the rest of it that way, too.

On the third pass along the street behind hers, Sam noticed a small "Private Apartment for Rent" sign hanging on a handrail by a front door. The modest two-story colonial didn't look big enough to have anything of the kind. She pulled up next to the mailbox to get the phone number for her mom.

Before she could fish a pen out of her purse, a stoop-shouldered, gray-haired lady in gardening boots clomped from around back, dragging a trash bag to the curb. Sam was almost sure it was Mrs. Moody, who'd won Ashland's Fourth of July pie-baking contests quite a few years in a row.

"Are you lost, young lady?"

"No, I just saw your For Rent sign and was curious. What kind of apartment do you have?"

"Well, I might as well show you. Easier than telling." Instead of going toward the front door, she led Sam around back. "I'm Zena Moody, by the way. And you look familiar. Let's see, where have I seen you before? Do you work at Ukrop's? No, that's not it. Don't tell me and take all my fun away. Not at my church, not at Megan's Mega Deal—you don't look like the Deal type…"

"McNeer's Paperbacks by the Tracks. I'm Sam McNeer."

"Ah, you've spoiled it." The wrinkles on her cheeks sagged even lower. "Oh well, I haven't won that game for years. Here we are." Zena opened a side door on her oversized detached garage and walked in, but Sam turned to look at the back of the house. "Aren't you coming, Pam?"

Zena must have been short on either hearing or memory. Sam let the error go.

Could she suggest to her mom that she live in a garage? No harm in looking. When Zena switched on the overhead lights, Sam gaped. Instead of oil-stained concrete, there was a beige vinyl floor. Walls painted pale yellow wrapped three sides of the open room, and the fourth—where she'd seen garage doors outside—was lined by kitchen cabinets, counters, and appliances, plus a dinette in one corner and a pantry closet in the other. At the opposite end of the room, another closet, probably for coats, was tucked in the corner, and an open-riser spiral staircase rose to a loft.

"Is that the bedroom up there?"

"Yup. Go see for yourself. Your knees are better than mine." Zena walked to the dinette and sat on its upholstered, wraparound bench to wait.

As Sam wound her way to the loft, she tried to envision wrangling a bed and chest of drawers up the twisting stairs, but when she reached the top, she saw there was no need to worry. The room was complete with a platform double bed, large drawers underneath, a bookcase headboard, and built-in nightstands on each side. On the wall opposite the bed was a closet that would be adequate for Mom's meager wardrobe; she wasn't much into collecting fashion. The lower portions of the sloping walls were lined with shelving and cabinets.

No nook went to waste. Two dormer windows on one side of the room and two skylights above the other flooded the room with light. When Sam checked the view from a window, she couldn't believe what she saw. Through a tree line separating the back-to-back lots, she spied her furled red patio umbrella only two lots away. She had known this house would be close to hers but didn't expect it to be that close. Was this a good thing or a bad thing?

Downstairs again, she asked, "But where's a bathroom?"

"You're staring at it. That's it in the corner." When Sam opened the door she'd thought was to a coat closet, she found a mini-bathroom—sink, toilet, and shower in a space not much bigger than a nook for a stacked washer and dryer.

"This is just like on a cruise ship."

"Because that's what it is, without the ship. The whole room—walls, plumbing, and all—came as a single unit, perfect for here. Well, you've had the nickel tour. Is this the kind of place you're looking for?"

"It's not for me; it's for my mother. She'll have to take a look. What's the rent?"

"I'm asking $625, including water and electric. Bring her by any day but Tuesday. That's when I play bridge. And not before nine o'clock or after five-thirty. Out you go, now. I've got a pot of soup on the stove."

After Sam closed her car door, she glanced back at the house. Zena and Mom might make quite a pair. Maybe Zena stored her soup bowls with the pot and ladles, too.

That evening over dinner, Sam broached the subject. "Mom, I think I've found a place that would be great for you, a place where you can set things up any way you want."

"I don't want to move again. I just moved here," She stirred some sour cream into her chili. "Don't you like having me help you with the cooking and cleaning?"

"It's not that at all, Mom." She had to bite her tongue. "You've been really helpful. This apartment is just around the block. You could still come by for dinner, or I could join you at your new home."

Sam took her bowl and glass to the sink and rinsed them. She didn't dare tell Mom the apartment was a refurbished garage. That would nix the whole deal, sight unseen.

Her phone rang. After glancing at the caller ID, she rolled her eyes. It was Ryan.

"Sam?"

"What do you want? I'm finishing dinner." She'd just lost any appetite for dessert.

"It won't take long. I called to apologize. It was a low blow, but I'm so sick of this freakin' headache and the rotten ribs and going stir crazy." When she didn't respond, he continued, "I do like a couple of the books you brought. And I started the puzzle of the lighthouse. I've always liked lighthouses."

"I remembered your term paper on the history of lifesaving stations along the Atlantic coast. And the one you wrote about Ocracoke Island and Blackbeard, Arthur Teach."

"Edward Teach, yeah."

"I never could get it right. I always confused him with Arthur Treacher, the British actor who lent his name to a fish and chips chain."

"Well, don't let your dinner get cold. See ya."

"Bye." She sighed. An apology from Ryan—that was a first.

As her mom washed the dinner dishes, Sam dried, putting the pot and bowls back where they used to be.

"Those don't go there," her mom announced matter-of-factly.

"My place, my system. Remember? When you have your own, you can store things any way you want."

"I told you, I don't want to move." She stole another glance at Sam's "disorganized" cabinet and scowled. "But I'll take a look."

There was a light at the end of the tunnel, and maybe it wasn't an oncoming train.

****

Taking advantage of their day off on Thursday, Clair and her daughter walked around the block to see the apartment. Samara led the way single-file along the two-foot-wide sidewalk, where there was one, and by the edge of the narrow street when there wasn't. The oddity of sidewalk placement was so typically Ashland. The homes they passed were a random mix of ranchers, bungalows, and plain two stories. The only one that looked like it could accommodate a separate apartment was a lone Victorian on the corner, but Samara kept walking toward the middle of the block.

Clair paused to pick up a tarnished penny peeking out

from under the dried leaves. It was almost the same color as the leaves, but more "old teapot" than "wrinkled, brown pants."

"Here it is, Mom," Samara said.

Clair looked up and saw the rental sign; she examined the house. The boxy little colonial seemed lost on its wide lot. A two-car garage sat behind the house, at the end of a gravel driveway.

"How can this be an apartment? It's a house. I can't afford to rent a house. Why did you bring me here?"

"You wouldn't be renting the whole property, just one part of it."

"Which part? I don't want to share a kitchen and living room with another renter, a complete stranger."

"Do you always have to be so negative? Don't worry; you wouldn't be sharing any living space. Give it a chance. Let's ring the bell and have the woman show you the place."

Zena Moody answered the door in a below-the-knee paisley dress, a crocheted shawl, and chunky shoes with two-inch heels. "Hello, Pam. See, I remembered your name. And I remember you, Mrs. McNeer."

"Her name is Samara. I'm Clair Hobson now."

Clair didn't offer to shake hands. Neither did Zena.

Hands on hips, Zena stared at Samara. "Why did you tell me your name was Pam?"

Samara blushed. "I must have mumbled. Sorry. Would it be convenient for you to show my mom the apartment now?"

"I was getting ready to go shopping, but it can wait. It's not like I have an appointment for a fitting at Megan's Mega Deal."

Zena and Samara laughed. Clair didn't.

As Zena led them through her living room, dining room, and kitchen, Clair studied the jumble of knickknacks that coated tables and shelves. If she were to rent the apartment, Zena surely could use some help getting her place more orderly.

When they exited the back door, Clair asked, "Wait. Where is this apartment?"

"Out here," Zena said. "Come on. Watch your step. Tree roots are making the paving stones all humpy-jawed."

Clair made note of every overgrown shrub, weed-choked flowerbed, and fallen limb. As she was about to comment, she felt Samara's firm hand on her shoulder. She shrugged it off but didn't voice a word.

Zena unlocked the side door to the garage. *Whatever could Samara have been thinking? A garage?* They stepped inside. Clair didn't break her silence until she'd explored every cranny.

"How much?"

"As I told your daughter, $625 a month, including utilities. It's worth every bit of that, probably more. That's what my dear Vernon told me was right. He's the one who designed and built this, so I could have a little gravy with my serving of Social Security after he was gone, bless his soul. It's been nine years, and the income has been a godsend."

Clair fell back into silent mode. The smile that had lit Zena's face faded. Clair went over to a window and cast a long look at the backyard. Move? She hated the word. Her heart hammered so hard she could hear it. Could the others hear it, too?

"How about $550? I can help you get this yard into shape. You see, I'm an expert gardener. You'll get at least

$75 worth of yard work every month. I can change that flowerbed along the side fence into a vegetable garden, and we can split the produce."

Now it was Zena's turn to pause. She tapped her foot in an odd rhythm as if she were performing some kind of difficult mental tally. "If you plant lots of peas and butter beans next spring, it's a deal."

This time when Zena extended her hand, Clair shook it.

The walk home proceeded in comfortable silence. As they rounded the corner onto their street, Samara suddenly started laughing so hard she had to stop walking.

When Samara regained control of herself, she asked, "The old story is really true, isn't it, Mom? I just witnessed the sequel with my own eyes. That's exactly how—"

"There you go again, talking nonsense." Clair placed one hand on a cocked hip.

"Let me finish, and you'll understand. You used exactly the same technique to get Dad to hire you as a bookkeeper. You offered plant care to parlay your way into what you wanted. Out of more than a dozen applicants, your unique offer to rescue the wilting plants in front of Dad's shop tipped the balance in your favor. You even wrangled an extra ten bucks a week out of him. You've done it again. Way to go!"

"My sister taught me the way to succeed at anything was to focus on my strengths. My strongest expertise has always been in plants. What's funny about that?"

"I'd always thought that whole deal about the wilting plants was more of a fairy tale about how you two got together. It's just funny to watch a nearly identical scene play out decades later." Samara laughed again, but Clair still didn't see the humor in it.

"Mom, what do you like best about the apartment? Why did you take it so quickly?"

"It's simple. Because it's different from any apartment I've ever seen. Just like me. I'm different from all the others, too. And I can have a garden again."

****

At home, Sam's mom pulled out a notebook. "Samara, we need to make a moving list. It's what Preston would have done."

She was right, although Sam's dad hadn't been the one to come up with that coping strategy. He once told Sam about another list, a three-page one he'd received from Aunt Patrice as a sort of wedding present. It was titled "Helping Clair." The note penned at the top said, "There are no guarantees that come with a marriage license, but I thought that in my sister's case, a User's Manual could come in handy."

If Sam hadn't found the list when she'd sorted through her dad's papers to administer his estate, the last seven years would have been impossible. At first, she'd resisted using some techniques for dealing with Mom's quirks. She felt a deep resentment for being stuck with manipulating her. But the techniques Patrice had developed worked. Like putting a hand on her mom's shoulder to signal her not to make offhand comments. It worked during the tour of the apartment. Sam knew for certain that when her mom saw the disastrous state of Zena's landscaping, some less than polite unfiltered thought was about to pop from her lips.

But the most crucial item on the list was number one: Make and follow lists. For her mom, list-making diminished the anxiety brought on by her life-long nemesis: change. Broken down into small steps, each task became attainable, and changes came at a pace she could handle.

By Saturday, two days after seeing the apartment for the first time, they'd taken three-quarters of the contents of her mom's clothes closet and dresser drawers to the new bedroom and put them away. When it came time to unpack the kitchen stuff, Sam's mom ordered her daughter to go home and start dinner. That was fine with Sam. She'd never organize things the same way her mom would.

Needing a big favor to complete the sixth item, Sam decided to give Ryan a chance to redeem himself. Could his buddies provide pickups and muscles to move furniture from her mom's storage unit to the new living room? He promised they'd show up Sunday afternoon, as long as there were no emergency calls.

****

After Samara left, Clair stood in the middle of her empty "new living room" and shuddered. The momentum she'd gained from the revelation of why she had never fit in—Asperger's—had fizzled away. Yes, this place was different, like her, but…

For the first time in decades, she'd be alone in an unfamiliar place. Even with Preston gone, his comforting presence had permeated every corner of her house in the woods. At Samara's home, she could relax, knowing her daughter was only a room or two away. Now less than a block separated the two of them, but…

What would Preston have her do? Her gaze swept the room. Stacked by the kitchen cabinets was a pyramid of five cartons full of dishes, pots and pans, utensils, spices, canned goods, and more. Yes. Everything for a reason. Before Samara could call her away for dinner, she'd empty the most important one.

She removed the top tier of two cartons and put them aside. Slitting the tape of the box in the middle of the bottom three marked "Cleaning Supplies," she was pleased to see that, just as she'd packed it weeks ago, her window spray wedge had held the blue plastic cleaning cloths box secure. No need to check inside. By its heft, she knew all was well. She slid the box into its proper place at the back right corner of the under-sink cabinet.

****

Mom never missed reading the gardening page in Sunday's *Richmond Times-Dispatch*, often clipping out an article or two at the kitchen table and afterward putting the section into the recycling bin while Sam worked through the rest of the paper from the comfort of the living room. This Sunday's routine was cut short.

When Sam went to the kitchen to refill her coffee cup, the paper lay open on the table, but her mom was gone. On the Celebrations page, opposite an article titled, "Preparing Your Soil for Next Year's Bounty," was a photo of a smiling Al nestled up next to a woman. The short announcement bore the caption, "Albert Hobson and Elena Fairchild to Wed."

He'd sprinkled salt in the wound. The date was set for Valentine's Day, the day Mom married Dad. When Sam lifted the page to read more, the top half of the photo fell back.

Mom had cleanly cut off their heads.

Chapter 7

Ryan and his friends showed up at Sam's house just past lunchtime to help with the move. Mom couldn't be coaxed out of her room, so Sam left her alone to mope. The guys made short work of loading the last of the cartons Sam had stored for her mom in her tiny attic.

Ryan still wasn't allowed to lift anything…anything but the puppy, that is. He said the puppy was too little to count. Even though Phoenix would have been perfectly safe in his crate, he insisted on holding him "to keep him out of harm's way." Phoenix returned the favor by chewing a hole in his shirtsleeve. When the crew left to pick up furniture from her mother's storage unit, Ryan let Phoenix give him a puppy kiss on his nose, then put him back in his crate.

Mom had made the process easy. She'd listed every item to dig out of her storage unit. Then, for furniture placement at the apartment, she'd cut a tiny slip of paper to scale for each piece of furniture and taped it onto a room diagram precisely where it belonged. Ryan watched the action from the sidelines, occasionally poking fun at the guys if they dropped something.

And occasionally watching Sam.

Inside of two hours, the job was done. Sam issued paychecks in the form of hot pizzas and cold sodas or beer for the men not on call. Fate decided to save her an awkward goodbye. As the last slice of pizza disappeared, the guys got a report of an accident on Route 1. Even those not on call used this as the cue to clear out. Before she could dispose of her paper plate, they were gone.

She surveyed the room. Scattered plates, napkins, and cans gave Mom's new place a lived-in look and smell, but not one she would appreciate. She collected the debris in a bag and carried it home.

As she walked in the door, Sam found her mom reading in the living room. Sam cheerily announced, "Well, your apartment's all ready for you. You can spend tonight in your very own place."

"No, I can't. Most of my gardening books are still in the shed behind my house. I have to have my books nearby, or it just won't feel like *my* place." Mom went back to reading.

"Okay, let's go get them now."

Without looking up, Mom said, "No, that won't work. When we pick up my books, we need to get the rest of the contents of the shed, too. One trip is so much more efficient than two."

Sam let out a long sigh. "Then we'll get everything. Let's go before it gets dark."

"Too late. It's clouding up, and the barometer is dropping. Rain's coming. Before I move my tools, I need to use them to clean up the vegetable garden. I can't do that in the rain."

Her heels were dug in deeper than a bomb shelter. Sam surrendered. At least she managed to talk Mom into a backup plan. They'd leave Mariah in charge of Paperbacks the next afternoon—supposed to be sunny— while they took care of the books, tools, gardening, and all. Then Sam might—just might—get her house back.

After dinner, Mom retreated to her room for the

evening.

Phoenix trotted over to Sam and yipped. A signal to be taken outside? She certainly hoped so. Maybe if she rushed him out, he'd learn to associate the actions. She scooped him up, went out the back door, and set him on the grass. He sniffed around for a moment and then did his business. Sam picked him up, cuddled him close, and gave him his favorite rub behind the ears.

"You're such a good little pup. Whoever adopts you will get a winner. If you're not careful, I might have to keep you."

Any chance Ryan could be a keeper, too? Sam gathered her courage and called him.

"I didn't get much of a chance to thank you this afternoon."

"I didn't do anything aside from leading the cavalry, but I have to ask."

Here we go again.

"Did I pass the test?" he asked.

"What test?"

"Keeping my mouth shut."

Sam could swear she heard him grin. "You aced it." Amazing—the man was making a bona fide effort to be nicer. "Now it's my turn to ask. Would you like to join us for Thanksgiving dinner at the Iron Horse? Low-key. It'll just be me, Mom, my Aunt Patrice, and Mariah. We're not much into big to-dos."

"I usually feast with the firehouse families, but yeah, that sounds good and a lot quieter. Do you have any idea how loud it gets when fifteen kids—toddlers to teens, high on cupcakes and pie—chase around that cavernous firehouse? What time?"

"Our reservation is for two o'clock. Meet you there,

86

okay?"

"Yeah, thanks."

"Oh, one more thing. Don't take it personally when my mom doesn't look at you or engage in much conversation. That's just the way she is with everybody. No worries; Mariah and Aunt Patrice will have no trouble taking up the slack."

After Sam put down the phone, she chuckled. Nothing like asking a man in his thirties for a date and subjecting him to the scrutiny of three chaperones.

****

When Sam and her mom arrived at the old house, they had to steer clear of a flock of workmen hustling to get the new roof in place before the worst of the winter weather arrived. Sam emptied everything from the old playhouse while Mom tidied up the vegetable garden. Zena made room to store the tools, fertilizers, etc., in a nearly falling-down shed behind the garage apartment. Mom's gardening books found a new home on shelves in her loft.

By that night, Mom admitted the apartment was ready for her first night sleeping there. Sam was glad. Even when her mom had been holed up in her bedroom, it felt like a ghostly presence trailed cold drafts throughout the house. Despite that, Sam felt reassured that her mom would be so close by. Why is it you can't stand to live day to day with someone you love, but you'd never want to live without them?

Sam couldn't wait to have her house to herself, all except for Phoenix, of course. He was much less trouble now that he'd progressed to drinking his formula from a bowl and had figured out what to do with mushy puppy chow. The day was fast approaching when the animal shelter could care for him, too. They'd find him a permanent home. Could she let him go? The cute little guy, with his big, dark eyes and clumsy antics, had already wiggled his way into her heart, but was this the best time for her to raise a puppy? Probably not.

In the evening, after Sam's mom had left, Mariah came over to help undo her mom's "helpful" kitchen rearranging. When Sam told her of the change in Thanksgiving plans, she instantly regretted inviting Ryan.

"What's this? Has Ryan swept you off your feet? I suppose it's only fair since your inadvertent bombs knocked him off his feet."

"Good one." Sam laughed. "Watch out, or your teasing might start to annoy me worse than Ryan's does. Where'd my serving platters go?"

"I saw them under the dinner plates in your china cabinet. You know you love me anyway. Who's Holmes without Mrs. Hudson to look after him? I feed you. I shelter you when you need it. Who's Thelma without Louise?"

"If you'll remember, that duo didn't end so well."

"Touché. How's your mom handling all the change?"

"So long as she sticks to her lists, not too bad. And it doesn't hurt that we're busy getting the shop ready for Black Friday. Routines help. But she's driving me nuts with her 'I'm different' thing. Now she wants to see a psychologist and get the diagnosis confirmed. Hand me those pots, will you?"

"I think you ought to arrange an appointment."

"I looked into it; it's not that simple. A full evaluation involves a whole battery of tests and appointments costing hundreds of dollars, possibly thousands. It's not covered by our insurance. She's already scraping the bottom of her barrel to pay the rent."

"But I think it's important. Tell you what, I'll front the money. If one of you can pay me back someday, fine. If not, it's a gift."

Sam knew Mariah could spare the money, considering her inheritance from her folks and her part ownership in the successful catering business. But it simply wasn't right.

"No way can I let you do that. I don't pay you enough as it is. How can I *take* money from you?"

"Just think about it. Where do you keep these packs of birthday candles? I assume you don't want them in your cake pans."

****

Clair opened the door to her new apartment and turned on all the lights. She drew ten slow, deep breaths and surveyed the place. Yes, two moves within a month were almost more than she could bear, but living in her daughter's house, with so few of her own familiar things, was never going to work. Even though it was her daughter's place, she'd felt like an outsider, a feeling that had plagued her throughout life. She sat down in her favorite chair, the one upholstered in a botanical print. It felt good to be surrounded by some of her furniture, which she'd carefully arranged in the same order that it had been in her old living room. Even the lamps were placed precisely on the same spots on the end tables.

The first item installed on her apartment wall was the second antique phone, placed beside the dinette. Samara had insisted on doing the work by herself. The phone, a lifeline to her memories of Preston, made the place feel like home. But there was still the matter of deciding what to do with all the stuff in Clair's storage unit, two-thirds full even after the removal of living room furnishings. Maybe in the spring, they could have a big yard sale.

Clair knew she'd never return to the house in the woods. In only two years, Al had soured every precious memory of that house that she'd accumulated in the previous twenty-four.

****

On Thanksgiving Day, Sam, her mom, Mariah, and Aunt Patrice arrived at the Iron Horse Restaurant half an hour early, allowing time for a round of drinks. The carved mahogany bar trimmed with burnished brass accents set an old-world atmosphere, turning back the clock to a slower-paced age. The whole place hummed with the chatter of families and friends sharing holiday festivities. A long freight train started rumbling by on the Center Street median, only a couple of dozen feet from the restaurant's front door.

Right at two o'clock, they were shown to their favorite table in the quieter back corner, where Mom could sit facing the wall, her back to the other patrons. Ten minutes later, the hostess ushered Ryan through the packed restaurant.

"Sorry I'm a little late, folks. Freight train tie-up," he said, motioning toward the front window. He didn't need to say more.

Sam made the introductions. "Ryan, this is my mom, Clair Hobson, her sister, Patrice Givens, and I'm sure you remember Mariah Gabrielli from biology class."

"Happy Thanksgiving, everyone. Thanks for letting me join you." He smiled and sat on the open seat beside Sam. He'd dressed up for the occasion—dark gray suit, white shirt, and striped tie in muted fall colors. "It's a pleasure to be surrounded by such lovely women." Ryan had always been a quick study.

Patrice, who'd driven an hour from her home in Charlottesville, looked sharp, even at age sixty. She was relentless about exercising to keep in shape, not allowing a "meno-pot" to grow around her middle. Unlike Mom, she maintained the illusion—with an assist from her hairdresser—that she was still a brunette. The laugh lines around her mouth and at the corners of her eyes warmed her face and radiated her typical good humor.

Mom's face was as pristine as a woman twenty years her junior—one of the benefits of her customary lack of expression—and her classic figure still drew every male's eye when she entered a room. As for her curls, which had turned to silver in her early forties, she'd never considered dyeing them. She'd say, "That's the color my hair is now. I am who I am."

Then there was Mariah. Even ignoring her knock-out curves—if that were possible, given that clingy red sweater—her smile alone could earn her a gig in a toothpaste commercial. Sam couldn't understand why she hadn't been snapped up by some smart bachelor.

As for Sam, an added dash of eyeliner and shadow was as good as it got. She'd upgraded from her standard jeans to tailored gray slacks and a softly draping ivory sweater, but her appearance couldn't hold a candle to the others. She was way too tall, too broad in the beam, and her curly, chin-length hair could be as untamable as a hyperactive kid. She didn't see herself as unattractive, but she was far from model-perfect.

In the midst of the waiter taking their orders, another train roared by, this time an AMTRAK passenger train. As if a remote's pause button had been hit, they all stopped mid-sentence and then resumed speaking when the last car disappeared from the window.

While they waited for the main course, Patrice started questioning Ryan as if checking the credentials of a daughter's suitor. With no children of her own, Sam was often the target of her mothering instincts.

"I hear you're a firefighter, Ryan. What made you choose that profession?"

"As far as a profession goes, I'm an accountant. I volunteer as a firefighter. Our department here in Ashland is a hundred percent volunteer. Since I have a private accounting practice and work from home, it's not hard to schedule a shift each week."

Sam put down her buttered roll. "You never told me you're an accountant."

"You didn't ask. When you've driven by the firehouse, haven't you noticed the sign that says, Ashland *Volunteer* Fire Company? I have to do something to pay the bills." The table went quiet for a moment.

"Of course," Sam mumbled, "but I never stopped to consider the implications."

At this, Mom glared in her direction and gave a slight shake of her head. Sam's faults, her oversights—both Ryan and Mom had an uncanny knack for casting a spotlight on them. She was relieved when their entrees arrived. The conversation stuck to small talk during the meal, but Sam avoided looking Ryan's way.

As the waiter cleared the dishes, Ryan leaned toward Sam and whispered, "I've done it again. Sorry. Really. Is your mom mad at me, too? She hasn't once looked my way."

She whispered back, "I told you, that's the way she is with everybody. Don't let it bother you." She glanced across the table at her mother, certain she'd taken in every word.

Just then, the shattering of a plate halted all conversations in the room. Heads turned to the source of the noise. From the front of the restaurant, a red-faced waiter beat a retreat toward the kitchen, gripping his overloaded tray with two hands. Mom gasped, then stood up and made a beeline for the door. Sam dashed after her, intercepting her before she could go outside.

"What's wrong, Mom?"

"Didn't you see? Al is sitting at a table by the window…with *her*."

Sam turned and saw Al with Elena Fairchild at a table for two in the front corner. Elena looked even more eye-catching than in their engagement photo in the newspaper. As the couple laughed at some intimate joke, Elena tossed her wavy blonde locks over the shoulder of her backless black dress. Overdressed for the occasion, especially for Ashland.

"Wait here while I get our bill," Sam said. "I'm too full for pie anyway. We'll leave."

Again Mom reached for the door, but Sam held it closed.

"Stay here by the bar. It's too cold out there today. I won't be long."

Mom retreated to the far end of the bar and stood near the restrooms, rocking, half-hidden by a potted plant.

When Sam explained to the others what had happened, Patrice said, "While you get the bill, I'll have a few words with them."

Sam grabbed her arm. "Don't make a scene. Let's just go."

Patrice firmly removed the hand restraining her. "This isn't only for Clair's sake. It's for Elena's, too."

Once Patrice started on a warpath, all protest was futile. Sam could only watch from the sidelines while she paid the bill.

Even a train going by wouldn't have prevented patrons from getting an earful.

Patrice took her stand beside their table and curtly introduced herself to Elena, then turned to Al. "Let's see. This will make three, won't it, Al? Up to your underhanded tricks again?"

Elena fumed. "Excuse me? What gives you the right to speak to my fiancé that way? You're spoiling our holiday dinner."

On the table sat a half-eaten appetizer of raw oysters.

Patrice turned her attention back to Elena.

"You, my dear, are in line to become the third Mrs. Hobson, the third one who, unless I miss my guess, will be fleeced by this serial scammer. I can vouch for the first two."

Had Sam heard her aunt right? He had a wife before her mom? News to her.

Patrice raised a brow. "Did you tell her about them both, Al?"

With a sneer, Elena said, "Oh, I see, you must be a friend of that strange one he just divorced. Seems to me she's the one who snared him with her looks, with no personality to back it up. If anyone was scammed, it was him."

"Thanks, Elena. You just saved me from feeling sorry for you. Maybe you deserve what you'll get after you say, 'I do.' As for you, Al, the third time will *not* be the charm."

Al went on the offensive. "Since you seem so put out by our engagement, I should tell the police to add your name to the list of suspects. Maybe you're the one who ransacked my house last week. You could use an anger management course, though I doubt it would do any good. You're as unhinged as your sister."

If Patrice's eyes had pulsed with heat rays, he would have fried in his chair. "I'll make damn sure you never marry again." She spoke in an ominously low voice, but everyone in the now silent room distinctly heard her. She marched to the door.

It was one of those moments that defined "so quiet you could hear a pin drop." Sam gained a new appreciation for the intensity of her aunt's bond with Mom. And Ryan got a crash course in her family's dysfunctional dynamics. He said polite goodbyes and made a quick exit.

Patrice took charge of getting her sister calmed down, just as she'd done hundreds of times when they were young. On the way to Mom's place, she spoke in soothing tones, talking about plans for celebrating Christmas. When they entered the garage apartment, Patrice complimented her on the new abode. Mom listened but didn't utter a word, then went up the spiral staircase to her loft bedroom. Patrice and Sam called out their goodbyes and left.

At Sam's request, Aunt Patrice stayed an hour at her house before returning to Charlottesville. She had questions. Lots of questions.

"That was some performance. When I phoned you about the engagement, I didn't realize it upset you so much."

"It didn't at first. I was more curious than upset at the time, so I did some digging. The more I learned, the angrier I became."

A bolt of comprehension hit Sam. "So you found out about a third time? He'd been married to someone before Mom?"

"Exactly. We all knew he moved here from Connecticut in 2002, but we didn't know why. Now I do. He'd gone through a nasty divorce from a woman named Gail. I found the court's ruling online. To learn the juicy details, I tracked down Gail's phone number, and we had a chat. The bastard tried to pull the same stunt he did with Clair, but Gail and the court wouldn't let him get away with it."

"What do you mean by 'stunt'?"

"He talked her into refinancing the house she'd owned before the marriage, saddled her with a much bigger mortgage, and invested the freed-up equity. When he sued Gail for divorce, claiming half of the investment as joint property, she fought back and walked away with it all. It was rightfully hers, and the court agreed."

"Good for her, but I wish Mom had been savvy enough to take Al to court."

"Nothing we could have done about that, but there's one more satisfying bit to Al's history. When word of his underhanded dealings leaked to management at the bank where he'd worked, they fired his ass. Hence, the move to a new town far away."

"I guess the only difference in Mom's case is that she didn't understand what she was signing away in the divorce agreement."

Patrice stared at her lap and smoothed out a small wrinkle in her skirt. "I'll never forgive myself for allowing Clair to push me away when she married him."

"Me, too. Al sabotaged my every attempt to talk sense into her. Within a month after they'd married, Al convinced her he knew what was best, and I was just a meddling kid who ran a bookshop, an overgrown kid who shouldn't be mooching off them. She'd trusted Dad so completely, and all was well. I guess she assumed any man who'd put his name next to hers on a marriage license could be trusted. Al told her to ask me to move out of the house, and she did. I complied." Sam's pain went deeper than that, down to guilt that still rankled. She teared up.

Patrice cradled Sam's head on her shoulder. "There now, sweetie. Like I said, nothing either of us could have done."

"That's not it. The worst part is that I caved in too easily. Honestly, I was relieved to get away, let someone else wrangle with Mom's behavior. It felt like I'd drawn a get-out-of-jail-free card. I should have been stronger. There must have been something I could have done to protect her."

The unrelenting burden of memories weighed on Sam. She felt she'd let Dad down.

You'd think by age thirty-two I would have found some way to help her, but no, Mom would never see deceit in a smooth-talker like Al unless it was tattooed all over him.

"Did you know the terms of the home equity loan?"

"I didn't even know she was getting it until it was a done deal. She still won't show me the divorce papers. She told me about the settlement in general, but very few specifics. Same thing with her bank accounts and investments. She tells me bottom-line balances, but I don't even know the name of Al's hot-shot fund where the proceeds from the loan are invested.

"I'm sure Al had lots to do with her hiding things

from me, but Mom's never been big on sharing her business. I think she still sees me as a child." Sam laid her head back on the sofa and closed her eyes. "I'm so tired of rescuing Mom from herself when she doesn't want my help."

"Keep at it, honey. She needs you, even though she'll never tell you that. She doesn't make it easy, but you're doing the best job anyone could do. I'm too far away to keep close tabs on her. By the way, her new place will be perfect—private, quiet, totally under her control, yet she's nearly next door, so you can get there at a moment's notice. With the way she fights change, how did you ever get her to move there?"

After Sam told her the story, Patrice asked, "What's with this 'I'm different' thing? That's a new one. From the time I arrived, she kept throwing that into the conversation. And she seemed happy about it."

Sam explained about Asperger's Syndrome.

"So much of what you say certainly matches up with Clair, but she's no savant. Everything I've seen about autism shows people like Dustin Hoffman in *Rain Man*, someone who can memorize all the names and numbers in a phone book. She's smart and knows a lot about plants, but not to that extreme."

"The character Hoffman played was more autistic, not performing well enough in daily life to warrant a 'high functioning' diagnosis. Most people with the syndrome have super-strong interests and skills in specific areas, but they're not savants. Maybe if Mom gets a diagnosis, we'll find out for sure." She noticed Patrice poking her sleeve up an inch and stealing a glimpse at her watch. "I've held you up long enough."

"If you have anything else you want to discuss, my

cell is always on. I should be getting on the road. I-64 can be a bitch around the holidays. Love you, honey." After a motherly hug, Patrice left.

Curling up on her sofa with Phoenix by her side, Sam snuggled under the afghan, trying to replicate the warmth of that parting hug. It wasn't enough.

It was never enough.

Chapter 8

With the specials the bookshop offered to Black Friday shoppers, there was a nice uptick in business, but nothing compared to what the big box retailers could do. Considering most of Sam's regular customers—the students—went home for Thanksgiving, she was pleased with the tally. The holiday season's extended hours— open from 1 p.m. to 6 p.m. on Sundays—would also help. And quite a few customers had been coming by just to play with Phoenix. Perhaps she should rent him out by the hour.

Over the next two weeks, Sam used her Sunday mornings to prepare an early Christmas present for Mom. Starting at the edge of her backyard, she cleared a path along the property line, through the woods, brambles, and underbrush to Zena Moody's place two lots down. This would be worth it, in spite of all the scratches she collected in the process.

With the assistance of Ryan and an electrician—a volunteer EMT—they figured out how to reconnect the two antique phones, the same as they had been between the old house and the playhouse. She installed fresh dry cell batteries inside the hinged front of each wooden case. Then they strung a phone line from Sam's house to a tree, down the trunk, along the ground at the edge of the path, up another trunk, and—*voila*—to the eaves of the garage apartment. Not pretty, but it would work unless the phone company objected to what she'd done. She'd cleared the project with all the homeowners but not with them. It wasn't like her little private network would steal their business.

The day of the phone's grand unveiling stayed crisp and clear from dawn to dusk and beyond. So much for calling Mom to request umbrella delivery, like she did as a child. After closing the shop, Sam and her mom rode home together as usual.

When Sam parked in her driveway, her mom said, "I thought you were having dinner at my place tonight. I'm fixing a vegetable pizza."

"I wouldn't miss it. Let's walk over. Then I'll walk home after dinner. I need the exercise." Sam grabbed a flashlight from under her seat. Shining the light at the tree line, she said, "Follow me. I know a shortcut."

Mom looked none too pleased by the alteration of her routine but didn't object. As they started down the path, she said, "You did this, didn't you? The path was a good idea, but did you notice any poison ivy back here? *Toxicodendron radicans* is most prevalent in thinly shaded areas like this narrow strip of trees, and it's hard to recognize in the winter when it's leafless like—"

"We're here," Sam announced as they emerged by the garage.

"That *was* quick. I'll start the pizza."

"Will there be enough if I ask Mariah to join us?" *She'd better say yes.*

"Well, we won't have leftovers, but call her if you want to." Mom opened the freezer and took out bags of vegetables from last summer's garden.

Sam walked to the old phone, lifted the earpiece from its hook, and turned the crank. The jangling bells startled

Mom. Pucks of frozen zucchini skated across the counter.

"Hello. She said you could come over for dinner. See you shortly." Sam hung up the phone.

"Why did you do that? Even if the phone worked, it could only connect to another old one, not a modern one like Mariah's."

"Give it a minute."

After unlocking the door, Sam turned on the outside light. Right on cue, a breathless Mariah breezed in, hit a button on her watch, and set down a flashlight.

"I raced like the wind and made it in fifty-eight seconds. They don't call me Mariah for nothing. Thanks for inviting me, Mrs. Hobson. I love your pizza."

Mom's brow knit into a *v*. "How did you do that?" She glared at the two young women.

"I connected our two phones, like before. Mariah was waiting at my house for the call. From now on, no matter if it rains or snows, I'm just a jingle away. I promised Dad I'd always look after you. Using his old phones to keep in touch with you seems so right."

Sam gleamed with pride at her flawless plan, at least until Mom said, "You shouldn't have bothered. This is 2008; my cell phone is perfectly fine. And I'm still your parent; I can take care of myself. I'm different, not disabled." She turned her back and finished preparing the pizza.

Sam's stomach knotted into a fist. Spurned again. She wanted to lash back, but she let the issue slide. The heavy yoke of her duty demanded it.

****

Days earlier, Sam had asked Mom to dinner Thursday night. Following the rebuff, she thought, why sweat it with a time-consuming recipe; Mom wouldn't appreciate it. Sam opted for a "Dinner for Two" bag from Ukrop's. The night's special included pork chops with gravy, rosemary roasted potatoes, butter beans and corn, and their signature rolls—all ready to heat and eat. With Christmas a mere two weeks away, she also pre-ordered a complete Christmas dinner-to-go. It wasn't worth the effort to cook everything from scratch when she could buy a better feast from her favorite grocery.

After warming their dinners in the microwave, Sam turned on the small TV on the counter to watch the evening news. It would preclude the need for conversation.

"And now for the top story: Bernard Madoff, a former chairman of NASDAQ, was arrested today for securities fraud. He's confessed to running the biggest Ponzi scheme in history. By his own admission, his firm, Bernard L. Madoff Investment Securities LLC, has defrauded thousands of investors to the tune of fifty billion dollars. Yes, you heard that right—fifty billion with a 'B' as in 'Bernard.' Regulators say…"

While the newscast rambled on, Sam swallowed a bite of her roll and murmured, "Un-fricking-believable."

Her mom watched the headlines scroll across the bottom of the screen. "You've asked me the name. Well, that's it. What's securities fraud?"

"What do you mean? The name of what?"

"The name of the fund where Al invested all my money. I repeat, what's securities fraud?"

****

When dawn broke on Friday, Sam was still wearing the previous day's clothes. Her hands shook when she picked up her coffee mug—shook with a combination of rage, fear, and lack of sleep. Even pouring the story out to

Mariah in the middle of the night hadn't helped much. Could the hole get any deeper? That investment was supposed to be Mom's retirement savings. She was fifty-six. How could she start deep in debt and be able to retire in only ten years? Sam had run countless scenarios through her mind. Hire a lawyer and try to be first in line to recover money from Madoff... Sue Al and make him reimburse Mom for her losses... Sell the bookshop, the building, and then both of them get a fresh start somewhere else... The possibilities ranged from difficult to dreadful to disastrously stupid.

Sam grabbed her keys and loaded Phoenix and his crate into the car. It was nine o'clock. There was one thing she could do right now. It wouldn't lead to recovering a single dollar, but she'd feel somewhat better. She drove to Ashland Community Bank.

The lobby, as typical for early morning, held a scattering of customers—one at a teller station, another filling out a deposit slip, and one meeting with an account manager in a glass-fronted office. Al's office was empty. Sam made her way directly to Mardigan's office, ignoring a male voice ordering her not to go back there. A solid wood door muffled angry voices. When she opened it, she saw Al standing in front of Mardigan's desk, his arms rigid, hands clenching the edge.

"But I don't have them, I tell you! They're all gone. Burned. You saw for yourself, didn't you?" When the opening door smacked against the doorstop, Al's head whipped around. He glared at Sam, then continued his rant even louder. "How many times do I have to tell you... I lost everything. There's no way I'll ever get a penny back from Madoff. The big institutional investors and their fancy lawyers will jump to the head of the line.

He burned all of us."

Mardigan, seated behind his desk, stood and growled at Sam, "This is a private conversation. Get the hell out of here, Samara."

"Not before I have my say." She stood her ground. "This bastard, your trusted vice president, has ruined my mom. She has absolutely nothing left, thanks to his conniving. Remember that fund where I told you he'd invested the cash from the home equity loan? It was Bernard Madoff's. For all I know, Al wangled a cut or collected some kind of kickback."

"Hold on. He just told me he's in the same boat. He put his money there, too."

Sam was taken aback, but only for a few seconds. "Frankly, I don't care what he lost. He's the one who should have known better. His job is to keep money safe. He failed miserably, and my mom is paying for it. If you don't fire this idiot right now, I'll call the TV stations. How many customers will entrust their savings to this bank when they hear my story?"

"You'll do no such thing unless you want to get hit with a slander suit," Al shot back.

"Oh, but it gets even better. There's another scandalous tidbit the viewers will love." Sam smiled at Al, then faced Mardigan. "He's done this marry-and-refi scam before. In Connecticut. And it cost him his job there, too."

Mardigan's mouth fell open.

Just then, Duane Chanesky stormed into the room and slammed his fist into Al's face. Blood sprayed the desk, speckling a neat stack of papers, polka-dotting Mardigan's white shirt, and ornamenting his green tie. Just in time for Christmas.

"You broke my nose, you son of a bitch!" Al pulled out a white handkerchief and tried to stanch the streaming blood.

Sam looked at Duane and grinned. "I wish I'd done that." Mild-mannered Duane—who would have guessed? She'd never seen this side of Kyle's cousin before.

"How many other people have you screwed?" Duane spat out while massaging his knuckles.

When Duane lunged at Al, Mardigan rounded his desk and separated the two. "What's your beef, Duane?"

"This bastard convinced me to do a cash-out refi, then pulled strings to get my money into an investment he swore had been beating the market for decades. It did... until yesterday when Madoff was arrested." Duane charged toward Al again, but Mardigan blocked him.

"You can stop right there. If you don't leave peaceably, I'll call the police."

Duane shook free of Mardigan's grip and stepped back. "This isn't the end of it, Al. You'll see. And you'd better come get all the crap you have stored in my attic, or I'll pile it in my yard and burn it." He left, slamming the door shut behind him.

Mardigan returned to his seat. Al flopped onto a chair.

"Don't make yourself too comfortable. I've just buzzed Security to escort you from the building. You're fired."

Al leaped to his feet and, dripping blood, leaned over the desk. For a moment, Sam thought he would take a swipe at Mardigan.

"But Squire, you can't do this. You have no grounds."

"So sue me. You've just moved from the asset

column to the liability."

When a uniformed guard entered, Mardigan told him, "Take him straight out and don't ever let him back in here. I'll clean out his office myself."

The guard nodded. Al's scowl said more than any words could. He used those watch-your-back eyes.

"And close the door," Mardigan added.

"Have a seat." He waved toward the same chair where Al had sat.

Sam shook her head and sat in the other visitor chair. "That one's got blood on it."

"Happy now?" Mardigan took out a tissue and dabbed at the spots on his tie.

"I must admit, I do feel better, but 'happy' is not the word I'd use." She rested her forearms on the arms of the chair and waited.

"What would it take to make you happy?" He leaned back in his chair.

"Don't worry. I'm not going to go to the media. You don't have to buy me off."

He let out a long sigh. "I had no such intention. I'm only trying to help you overcome your current difficulties. I had no idea what Hobson was up to."

Interesting. "Mr. We're-all-on-a-first-name-basis-here" called him *Hobson*, not *Al*. After a brief pause, Sam said, "Well, I could use some help getting my mom's life put back together, but I don't know where to begin."

"Let me give the matter some consideration. For starters, I'll see what the bank's options might be for Clair's mortgage situation. No promises, but I'll look into it."

He rose and extended his hand, the bloody tissue still in it. He pulled it back. "Sorry, you've gotten caught up in this unseemly business."

"Actually, the last half hour has been a pleasure."
She just might have misjudged Mardigan.

Chapter 9

Ten minutes late. Eleven minutes late. No sooner had Clair opened her car door than Samara pulled up behind her at Zena's curb. Clair slammed the door.

Climbing into her daughter's car, she ranted, "I'd given up on you. You're eleven minutes late. Now we won't be able to open on time. Will we have to go back to driving separately? I can't afford the gas." She buckled her seatbelt. "I called your home phone *and* your cell, but they both went to voicemail. Don't tell me you forgot to turn it on again. I even tried the antique phone."

"Sorry, but I had an errand I had to take care of. I turned my cell phone's ringer off, so I wouldn't be interrupted. By the way, you'll be glad to know I took your advice. Tomorrow my home phone is scheduled to be disconnected; I agree there's no sense paying for a landline anymore."

Samara and her errands! The last time she'd used that excuse, Clair's house had been on fire.

"Get going; we don't have all day."

As Samara parked behind the bookshop, Clair said, "That's not right."

"What?"

"Don't you see? The back door isn't closed all the way." Clair could see it distinctly. Why hadn't her daughter noticed? The door protruded from the frame by almost an inch.

Up close, nothing except the door ajar seemed amiss. No scratch marks. No dents. Clair backed away, pulling Samara with her.

"No, this is not right," Clair said. "Don't go in. Call 9-1-1."

Samara pulled out her cell and did so. After hanging up, she said, "My nerves were already on edge from the Madoff news, but now I'm spooked. No way would I have opened that door without backup."

Less than a minute later, a cruiser pulled up behind Samara's car. Officer Giles Joyner got out. He'd patrolled this district since Samara finished college. Though his linebacker years ended a decade ago, his muscular build hadn't diminished. And none of that muscle had morphed to fat. After another minute, a second officer—nearly a twin—arrived.

"Both of you wait by your car while we check this out." They drew their weapons, turned on flashlights, and entered the building.

Precisely three minutes later, Officer Joyner walked out, his gun now holstered. "You *have* had a break-in. The shop itself looks undisturbed, but your office back here, well… Come in and see for yourselves." He held the door.

Samara flipped on the light and halted. Clair peered in from behind her daughter. The entire stockroom was in shambles. Stacks of cartons toppled over—most torn open—and new books strewn all over the floor. File drawers ripped out and dumped. What a nightmare! Only their desks had been spared.

Clair's heart rate spiked. She felt as if iron hands gripped her throat, cutting off all air. She retreated to the car.

****

Giles put a comforting hand on Sam's shoulder. "I can understand how tough this must be for your mother— the divorce, the fire, and now this at her shop—right before Christmas. I'll fill out the report, and she can sign it in the car."

Sam said, "I'm the one to sign that. I own the shop."

"I thought—"

"When Dad wrote his will, he never expected to pass at fifty-seven. He must have figured he'd die long after retirement, so it made more sense to hand the business directly over to me."

This was her standard explanation; the real reason was Mom's shortcomings. She did a terrific job juggling numbers and following Dad's step-by-step task lists, but when it came to the big picture, she had no idea how to strategize and make critical decisions.

"My mistake. I know it'll be hard in this chaos, but take a close look around. See if any valuables are missing. If not, it may be merely a case of vandalism."

Sam poked her head through the doorway into the bookshop itself and was reassured to see it undamaged. However, three college students, bulging backpacks tugging at their shoulders, pressed up against the front window and gazed into the darkened shop. With exams approaching, her "study nests" were in high demand.

She wrote "OPENING AT 3 P.M. TODAY" on a sheet of paper and told Giles she'd be back in a moment. When she taped the notice to the inside of the window, she mouthed, "Sorry."

They shrugged and walked away.

While Giles prepared the report, Sam phoned Mariah and gave her the news. Before Sam could finish asking her to help clean up, Mariah cut her off mid-sentence.

"You know I'd do anything for you—anything but murder Al." They both chuckled. Mariah always knew exactly what to say to lighten Sam's mood, although today Sam might have pressed her to eliminate the "anything but" clause after how he'd devastated her mom's life. Mariah added, "I'll be there in ten."

Soon after the police left, Mariah and Sam coaxed Mom back into the shop. The three of them contemplated the wreckage.

Sam picked up several books at her feet. "Looks like we'll have to get these out of the way before we can even move around the room. With all that we've sold in the last two weeks, we need to restock the shelves anyway. Let's have a book brigade. Mom, you can be stationed in the shop, and Mariah and I will sort these by where they belong. We'll bring them out to you one batch at a time, so you can get them properly shelved. Will that work for you?"

"Yes." It was her first word since she'd fled to the car.

Mariah put a CD in the shop's sound system, and the overture from "The Nutcracker" began. "We might as well enjoy a little Christmas music while we work."

"Not too loud. I don't like loud," Mom said as she picked up the first stack and went into the shop.

"Not too loud. I promise." Mariah closed the door.

With Mom out of earshot, Mariah said, "Brilliant. You got her out of the confusion and busy with manageable tasks." She gave Sam a high-five.

"I really did it to get her out of here, so I could bring you up to speed on the morning's events. But thanks. That did work rather well."

And it hadn't come from Aunt Patrice's manual for handling Mom. Maybe Sam could add a page or two of her own one day.

As they sorted stack upon stack of books, ferrying them periodically to Mom, Sam started with the scene in Mardigan's office.

Mariah rolled her eyes and grinned. "I wish I'd seen Al eat that fist."

Sam matched Mariah's grin. "And the look on Mardigan's face when his fresh white shirt was splattered—priceless. Al told me he flies to Hong Kong once a year for the sole purpose of getting them custom-tailored." Sam relayed the next stack to Mom and then returned. "But a couple of things struck me as odd. When I first opened Mardigan's door, before Al realized I was there, he was yelling something about '*they're* all gone' and 'I don't have *them*,' but when he saw me and continued shouting, it sounded like he was talking about only one thing—his lost investment. And why would he be so angry with Mardigan over something he brought on his own fool self?"

"Sounds like our poker player was running a bluff on you. But for what?"

"No telling with Al. While we're on unanswerable questions, how did our vandal get in here? You, Mom, and I have the only keys, and there's no sign of forced entry. Nothing was stolen that I've noticed yet. Why create this bedlam?"

"Do you think the mess could be payback from Al for embarrassing him in front of his precious fiancée? Or maybe Elena's the vindictive sort. Al carried a key before divorcing your mom, didn't he? Maybe he kept it. You should have changed the locks as a precaution, but it's too late now."

"I'll tell you one thing: I'm having them changed ASAP."

By the time three o'clock rolled around, the book carton disaster had been cleaned up, but papers were another matter. All three women were exhausted. Sam conceded defeat and changed the sign to "REOPENING SAT. DEC. 13 AT 10 A.M." After thanking Mom for a job well done, Sam told her to go home and relax.

"I'll go, but I have two questions. First, why did Al bite Duane's fist?"

Sam grimaced. How had Mom overheard the conversation with "The Nutcracker" playing?

"Mariah didn't mean it that way. She meant Duane punched Al in the mouth."

Her mom humphed. "And second, why did you try to keep the whole incident in the bank from me?"

Sam squirmed. "I don't know… I guess I was trying to protect you from any mention of Al."

"That brings up one more question." Mom planted fists on her hips. "Why do you think I need protecting? I'm a grown woman who was perfectly capable of protecting you as you grew up. Has something changed?"

Since when had Mom developed such self-confidence? Would it last? And if only it were that simple. She sidestepped the subject.

"At least you now know the bright side; Al's been fired."

"Yes, there's that. He deserved it."

After Mom left, Sam and Mariah tidied the papers into piles: ones for paid invoices, book distributors, leases, building maintenance, and a host of other categories. The final reorganization would be up to Mom and would probably take her until Christmas. The room's appearance had progressed from chaos to merely unkempt. Mom could deal with unkempt. Sam had given her lots of practice when she was a kid.

Mariah drove Sam home, and they split a hodgepodge of leftovers for dinner. For a Friday night oldies movie, Sam suggested the 1989 version of "Batman," but Mariah nixed it. They'd had enough of cleaning up after crime. Mariah chose "Mrs. Doubtfire."

They desperately needed the laughs.

****

On Saturday, the edge of a nor'easter churning along the Atlantic coast brushed by Ashland, keeping all but the hardiest shoppers away from Paperbacks. Although skies cleared by late afternoon, business didn't improve. Taking advantage of the slow, soggy day, Sam, her mother, and Mariah worked together on the sorting and refiling. They made a sizable dent in the task, but there was still a long way to go.

Sam set Sunday morning aside for putting up Christmas decorations at home. In all the commotion around Mom's mortgage mess, the fire, and the move, decorating had been the farthest thing from her mind. She wrestled three cartons down the narrow pull-down stairs from her attic. Now that Mom's stuff was gone, there'd be oodles of room for her paltry nod to the season.

Sam had never felt the need to fill her home with miniature snow-dusted villages, stuffed Santas, snowmen, or garlands of fresh-cut evergreens. She'd always celebrated Christmas at her parents' home, and they'd had those bases well covered, including all the multi-colored lights Dad used to drape over the bushes in front of the house, transforming the humdrum yard into a fairyland.

Since Dad had died, she'd taken over the task of stringing the lights but was never able to conjure up the magic. Now that homeplace was vacant. She really missed Dad's lights. And Dad. And Kyle, with his sunny outlook that had so briefly made her world glow.

When she looked at the box that held her four-foot pre-lit tree and thought of Mom's seven-foot one buried in the storage unit with all the rest of her collection, Sam realized perhaps she wasn't the only one sinking into the hollow holiday blues. She gave her mom a call.

"How would you like it if I brought over a few Christmas decorations for your new abode?"

"Why bother? I don't know where to put them. This apartment doesn't look anything like the old house."

Mom's Christmas notebook, filled with lists and diagrams specifying the arrangement of every decoration in the house, was also packed away. The only bright spot was that they both now thought of the house in the woods as the old house as if they'd started letting go of the past. Maybe if the present could be whipped into shape, the future wouldn't look so glum.

"I'll help you figure out a new plan. It'll be fun. I can be there in a few minutes."

"Doesn't sound like fun to me, but don't forget to bring the Sunday paper with you."

Fifteen minutes later, her three cartons sat in the middle of Mom's living room.

"Hey, Mom, on the way in, I noticed you've already started on the yard cleanup. It looks much better without all those dead branches. And you've cleared the old flowerbed and turned over the soil."

"It'll take a lot more work next spring. Friday night,

when I showed Zena what I'd marked in a seed catalog, she invited me to stay for dinner. She loves having lots of houseplants around, but they're in sad shape. It'll be all right, though. In addition to the outside gardening, she'll let me take care of her indoor plants, too." Her eyes glowed with delight.

How generous of Zena! A vision of Tom Sawyer whitewashing the fence came to mind. It was worth it, though, to see Mom happy for a change, but her joy evaporated the moment she opened the carton that held Sam's little Christmas tree. Mom shook her head.

"This will never work. I always put my big tree beside the fireplace, but there's no fireplace here. That tree is too small, anyway. There's no place it would look right."

Sam scanned the room. Options were few. The sofa, upholstered chairs, end tables, and china cabinet filled three-quarters of the open space, leaving a sort of corridor along one wall running from the door to the kitchen area. Where the walkway met the dinette, just to the left of the antique wall phone, stood the card table Mom was using as a desk, with a two-drawer file cabinet next to that.

"If you use the dinette as your desk for a few weeks, we could put the tree on the card table."

"That's stupid. That would leave me no place to eat."

"You could sit on the sofa and use the coffee table," Sam suggested.

"Do you expect me to subsist on coffee until Christmas is over?"

"Why are you always so negative? Flex a little. Coffee tables can be used for more than coffee, Mom."

It took an hour and a half to clear the card table, meticulously position every desk do-dad on the dinette,

117

set up the tree on the card table, and place all the decorations. Mom rearranged the tree ornaments several times to make sure that the various colors and styles were distributed evenly.

The whole time, Sam kept eyeing the second antique phone. The pair had come from her grandmother's family home and were among the few things she and Sam's father had brought with them when they moved to Ashland from, well, wherever they'd come from. For some unknown reason, he'd never shared a thing about his pre-Ashland days. Sam felt her dad's presence as if he were watching them from inside the phone's oak cabinet. She knew he'd be proud of her and grateful for her attempts to look after Mom, regardless of how little Mom valued her efforts.

As they stood back and surveyed their handiwork, Sam asked, "What do you think?"

The twinkling red, green, blue, and yellow lights warmed the room, just like the glow from a fireplace.

Mom sighed. "It's not the same."

"You're right; it's not." Anger tinged her voice. Maybe she was also right that Sam shouldn't have bothered. She threw her mother's own words back at her. "But I like different, don't you?"

Mom cast a blank stare at the wall. "It's change I can't tolerate. Nothing's been the same since Preston died. If he'd been here…"

"You think you're the last person on earth who'd rather things be the way they were? You lost one man you loved. I lost two."

A vision of finding the exquisite diamond solitaire ring Kyle had hidden inside a Fabergé-like egg ornament drew tears to her eyes. Bitter tears, not the same as on that

Christmas Day. If Mom ever stopped pushing her into the past, maybe she could escape it, move on. But *the way it used to be* was where Mom was stuck, and Sam's duty to watch out for Mom stuck her firmly by her side.

Sam willed away those tears before they could flow and muttered, "No use fighting it."

"Fighting what?"

"Never mind."

Sam fixed sandwiches for an early lunch while Mom read the newspaper. When Sam set plates and chips on the new dining table—the coffee table—Mom pointed to an article on the front page of the Metro section: FIRE DRIVES ASHLAND FAMILY FROM HOME. "This is about the Chaneskys' house. I haven't seen Duane since Al had poker nights at our house."

"I hadn't seen him for quite a while, either, before the scene with Al."

Over the years, Sam had seen more of his wife Amy, who periodically brought their two well-mannered boys into the shop. She slid the section across the table and read it. After Christmas shopping and a dinner out, the family had arrived home to find the cedar shake roof of their two-story colonial engulfed in flames. Fire trucks had shown up quickly, but not before the entire roof and attic were destroyed. Their holiday and beyond would now be spent in a hotel.

Replaying the HD memory of Duane breaking Al's nose, and then Al getting canned, Sam shuddered. Maybe this fire hadn't been accidental.

****

For the next several days, Sam scoured the *Times-Dispatch* for updates on the fire. Wednesday's paper paid off, confirming her suspicions. Al had been arrested and

charged with arson, but she was disappointed to see he'd
been released on bail after only one night in Pamunkey
Regional Jail. She would have loved the thought of him
spending more quality time with drunks, druggies, and
thieves in the county lockup. However, if all went well at
his trial, that fantasy could become his hell for much more
than a single night.

Hungry for more details than the paper could provide,
she phoned Ryan to see if he could join her for lunch at
Paperbacks.

"On one condition," he replied. "I'm buying. In the
fiasco at Thanksgiving, you ended up paying the whole
check."

"That was as it should be. After all, I invited you. But
if you feel you owe me, let me choose the place. Pick it
up from the café next door. Sometimes it's hard for me to
step out of the shop, even for a minute." She dictated her
sandwich order and, for good measure, added a slice of
pecan pie.

At noon, Ryan came through the front door. "Chow
time."

"Bring it back here." She'd set up a folding chair
behind the counter and put a flattened carton on top of
Phoenix's crate to use as a table. The puppy whimpered
for attention, but that would have to wait.

"Sorry, it's not exactly the Ritz."

"And when you brought me dinner, I was afraid *my*
Ritz might not be up to your standards." They shared a
laugh. Still smiling, he said, "I know why you asked me
to come today, but let's eat first. I'm starved."

When the sandwiches were gone, Sam reached into
the bag for the pie and found two boxes.

Ryan said, "I figured you'd rather not indulge alone,

so I bought two pieces."

"In that case, you're in for a treat. Their pecan pie recipe includes semi-sweet chocolate chips." Silence, except for "mms" and "aahs."

As Sam tossed the empty boxes into the trash, she said, "I'm sure you're right about my reason for calling you…"

"You're inviting me to a home-cooked Christmas dinner? I knew it." He grinned and raised his eyebrows that same innocent way he used to do after he'd pulled a prank. Then he opened the crate's door and picked up Phoenix.

The puppy, who finished his lunch before Ryan arrived, promptly snuggled up in his lap and fell asleep. Sam watched, a little jealous. He didn't fall asleep that readily for her.

"All right, wise guy, tell me what you know about the fire."

All signs of joviality disappeared from Ryan's face. "Of course, I wasn't there, so this is all second-hand. The ribs are getting better, but I won't be back on the schedule for another month. Those Chaneskys lucked out. Mechumps Creek runs right behind their house. Our engines hold only enough water for a few minutes, and there are no hydrants out there. The guys were able to pull more water from the creek, which was swollen from the recent heavy rains. And the cause, no question it was arson."

"How can they tell?"

Sam had to wait for an answer until she'd rung up two customers. Once they'd left, she sat down again.

"The arsonist made it easy for us. He'd tied knots in a bunch of bath towels—right in the middle—and soaked them in gasoline. Then he flung them up on the roof, followed by Molotov cocktails. All cedar shakes are treated with fire retardant, but Chanesky's were no match for this scenario. The roof was twenty years old, plus Duane hadn't cleaned pine tags and leaves out of the gutters. For added insurance, the perp tossed one of the Molotovs through a dormer window into the attic. The roof burned inside and out."

"How can you tell all that? Weren't the towels consumed by the fire?"

"The guy must not have known his own strength. One apparently sailed over the peak, rolled off the other side, and landed on the shrubs in back. A dark brown cotton towel with a red-stitched border. Ugly, if you ask me."

"Why do they think Al did this?"

"You'll like this part. After shopping, when Duane turned onto his street, he passed a vehicle going the other way—a black SUV. Al owns a big, black one, and after the dust-up at the bank, he was sure it had to be Al going for payback. Frankly, I'm surprised Duane would admit to the assault, but it makes for a hell of a motive for Al."

"Much as I hate to say it, the evidence sounds shaky. Not much more than seeing a dark car on a dark night."

"*But wait*, as they say on TV infomercials, *there's more!* Add a search warrant, an identical ugly towel in Al's trash can, and no alibi."

"That should do it. My fantasy come true."

He smirked, twitched his eyebrows twice, and cut a sideways glance. "Can you share this fantasy? With me?"

"Pick your mind up out of the gutter. I was picturing Al sharing a cell with a hulky, hairy, drug-dealing biker with an attitude and no girlfriend."

Ryan threw his hands up defensively. "Whoa! You don't care much for your ex-stepfather, do you?"

"From the day I met him, it's been a long ride downhill…to hell." She picked at a loose thread on her sweater.

"I think from now on I'll try harder to stay on your good side. The bad one is frightening."

"How's this for frightening: why don't you risk another holiday dinner with my family? Come to my place for dinner on Christmas Eve. We always have our special dinner then, so we can relax and munch on leftovers all day on the twenty-fifth."

"I knew it. That's really why you asked me here today, but is your mom still mad at me? At Thanksgiving, she didn't once look my way."

"I wasn't kidding before. She wasn't mad. She's not into eye contact with anybody, even me."

"That'll take some getting used to. I take it Al and Elena won't be invited?"

"Count on it."

"Then count me in. I'll bring the wine."

He eased Phoenix onto the pile of towels in the crate and latched the door. The whole maneuver was so gentle that Phoenix never twitched an ear.

Chapter 10

One look at the calendar told Sam it was her last day off to finish shopping. The following Thursday, she'd be off, too, of course, for Christmas Day. The main gifts for her mom, Aunt Patrice, and Mariah were already bought and wrapped; just some small additional ones remained to be found. Then she thought of Ryan. In case he showed up with a gift, she'd better be prepared with one for him.

What do you get for a man who has…? She had no idea what he had, needed, or wanted. After eliminating gifts that would be too personal, too impersonal, too expensive, too cheap, sized items, one-size-fits-all items, and "As Seen On TV" gadgets, her mental list of potentials was still blank until she thought of Two Frogs on a Bike. She knew she could find something unique and fun at her favorite antique store. She threw on her coat and drove toward Hanover County's courthouse complex.

The store, built around 1900, was an antique itself. Its deeply weathered siding hadn't been touched by the business end of a paintbrush in fifty years. In the past, it had been a general store with shallow shelves lining the walls and rooms for the owner's family upstairs. On the first floor, sheets of pale green stamped tin clad not only the ceiling but all the walls, as well. She and Dad used to drop by here once a month to see what oddities the proprietor, Jack Endicott, had recently acquired. It saddened her to realize the last time she'd set foot inside had been a year ago when she'd bought an oak quilt rack for Mariah.

No sooner had Sam entered than Jack welcomed her with a good-natured scolding for neglecting him. He sat where he always did, at a large L-shaped desk adorned with a hand-cranked register old enough to allow for prices up to only $9.99. After a ten-minute catch-up, Jack forgave the lapse in her visits when she promised to "hop in" more frequently.

Sam wandered the store, imagining her dad following along, explaining what some obscure item had been used for a century ago, pointing out what, with a modicum of imagination and elbow grease, could be restored for a new life.

Once, they'd found a green drop-front desk plastered with peeling decals. Chips in the paint revealed at least two prior coats of blue and white. Only by looking at bare wood inside a drawer could they tell it was oak. Dad sensed a gem under all that paint.

Some of her friends' fathers bought them used cars for their eighteenth birthdays. Sam's gave her a hands-on lesson in furniture stripping and refinishing. In his workshop, tucked in the basement just past the furnace room, they painstakingly removed all *four* layers of paint, then applied a warm brown stain, sanded the raised grain smooth, and rubbed in tung oil as a sealer. Throughout the process, he taught her the chemical properties of the solvents, stains, and oils and why they worked the way they did.

Strange for a man who claimed a degree in philosophy. Who knew? Dad was always full of surprises. Her friends' gift cars had been relegated to the scrapyard years ago. Sam's mission oak desk, its finish shiny when she dusted it, still graced her living room.

Twenty meandering minutes later, when three more customers walked in and shut the heavy door, Sam snapped out of her reverie and remembered why she'd come. What intriguing item would appeal to Ryan? She bypassed a duck decoy and brass candlesticks resembling deer antlers, then found a sure winner in a table-top display case. Ryan had been the pitcher on their high school's baseball team. In the case were two unopened packs of baseball cards from 1953. The price was reasonable, and there could be a rare card inside, waiting to be discovered.

When Sam interrupted Jack's lunch to pay, her growling stomach reminded her she'd skipped breakfast. She headed to Hanover Café, a quarter-mile down the road, right across from the courthouse.

The lunch special on the signboard read "Hot Turkey Sandwich w/ Cup of Tomato Soup." Perfect. Inside the small vestibule, Sam chose the room to the right, where a white carousel horse with roses painted on its rump stood mid-prance beside the doorway.

The next sight to greet her was Al, seated with Elena and a man in a suit and tie. Elena wasn't exactly overdressed this time, but her gold-trimmed black sweater dipped low in front, showcasing considerable cleavage. Empty plates littered their table, and they were talking in low voices, holding half-full glasses of iced tea. Sam about-faced and headed for the room to the left of the vestibule, but halfway there, she heard her name called. Sam turned to see Elena waving her over.

"Please join us."

Al glared at Sam, issuing an unspoken *don't-you-dare*. A dare like that was irresistible. Besides, her curiosity demanded an answer. Why would that woman invite Sam to dine with them, especially after her aunt had ruined their Thanksgiving dinner? Had Patrice gotten through to Elena? Sam backtracked to their table.

"I don't usually lunch with arsonists like your companion, but I'll make an exception since you so kindly invited me."

Though Sam hadn't raised her voice, everyone nearby in the small room turned to watch. Al reddened.

"You have no idea what you're talking about. He's been framed—" Elena said in a low voice.

"I advise you not to speak with anyone about this. Wait for the trial," the man beside Al said.

"No, I want her to understand. Mr. Prendergast, this is Samara McNeer, Al's stepdaughter."

"Former stepdaughter," Sam corrected.

Elena pulled out the empty chair. "Mr. Prendergast is Al's attorney. Please sit down, so we can talk."

Sam sat. With the excitement waning, most folks turned back to their meals.

"She's not going to believe the truth, Elena. Save your breath," said Al, staring at Sam.

"Both of you, stop telling me what to do. I'll talk if I want to talk." The men folded their arms and sat back, clearly annoyed with Elena's willfulness. "Samara…"

"Please, call me Sam." She was beginning to have some respect for the woman.

"All right then, Sam. I know you're devastated by the Madoff thing, but keep in mind that Al lost his savings, too. And it wasn't just what he put into it with Clair. He already—"

"Don't—"

"Shut up, Al. As I was saying, he'd already invested

127

a bundle of his money with Madoff, going all the way back to the early nineties, and doubled his investment in the first five years. He lost a whole lot more than Clair did."

Sam shook her head. "But Mom lost every buck she had. And he's pushed her toward foreclosure on her house."

"Don't be fooled by Al's defensiveness. He's truly sorry about your mom."

Al sat stone-faced, neither agreeing nor disagreeing.

"And about Duane's house—"

Prendergast broke in, "Not now, you may compromise our—"

"Let me finish. Why would he burn up his own belongings? He never had the time to pick up the things Duane stored for him after he moved out of Clair's house. He had family heirlooms in there. And he'd never be so stupid as to throw incriminating evidence into his trash can. As I said before, he's obviously being framed—an easy target after Duane bashed him and broke his nose and loosened some teeth."

No one spoke. What Elena said did make sense, but knowing Al, she couldn't trust it to be as simple as that. Looking from Elena to Al and back, Sam said, "Regardless of what he tells you, I advise you to get a prenuptial agreement before marrying that man."

"No need," she replied, a resigned look on her face.

"Just a word of caution, because—"

"I repeat, no need. Neither of us has anything worth protecting. We're both broke."

Sam couldn't imagine Al pursuing someone with no money to take. Did he know about her situation from the start? She couldn't think of anything to say. Al saved her the trouble.

"I'm leaving." Al, Elena, and Mr. Prendergast stood and put on their coats.

"Goodbye, Sam," said Elena. "Thanks for hearing me out."

As the three left, Mr. Prendergast picked up the check. Time was when Al would have grabbed it first and whipped out his American Express, making a show of his largesse. Were all his credit cards maxed out?

****

On Saturday, only five shopping days before Christmas, customers in Paperbacks were getting to the desperate stage in their gift-hunting. They demanded advice in selecting books, complained the bookshop didn't offer free gift wrapping like the big box ones did, and criticized the speed of checkout when there were two customers in the line. Both Samara and Mariah worked the floor and enlisted Clair's help at the register. Clair hated dealing with the public. She knew what was coming: snap judgment, rejection.

As one customer paid, he said, "That's a mighty pretty poinsettia in your front window. I've never seen the red flowers with white centers before."

Clair decided to risk starting a conversation. "That's one of my favorites. Its common name is Ice Punch." She handed him his bag and receipt. "What most people mistake for the flowers of poinsettias, part of the spurge family, are what's called bracts, leaves modified with bright colors to attract pollinators to the real flowers, the tiny cyathia in the center of each—"

"Uh, thanks." Turning his back, he sought out Samara to wish her a Merry Christmas and left.

During a lull in business, Clair called Samara to the

129

counter. "I tried to talk with a man ten minutes ago, but right in the middle of me speaking, he left. I was telling him about—"

"Maybe he was just in a hurry, Mom. He probably had a long list of errands to finish up." Samara went over to the Young Adult section to help a customer.

Why do people either ignore me or avoid me? The man wasn't too busy to find you, Samara, to wish you a Merry Christmas. And my own daughter treats me the same way. Is it because I'm different? What's wrong with being different?

After an exhausting day, they all went to Clair's apartment and pulled together a buffet of leftovers. Everyone was too tired for conversation over dinner, even the normally talkative Mariah, so they finished quickly. Clair rose to wash the dishes. When she reached into the cabinet under the sink for the dishwashing liquid, she came up empty-handed. She bent and looked in, then straightened and stuck hands on her hips.

"Samara, why did you put the detergent on the left the last time you washed up? You know I always keep it on the right."

"The last time I did the dishes was at least a week ago. Haven't you washed anything in the past week?"

"Well, then how can you explain the bottle on the left? I certainly wouldn't put it there."

As Samara came over to see, Clair bent down for a second look. There was the bottle on the far left. She was right-handed, so she kept it on the right. Then she gasped.

"Oh, no. The lid on my blue plastic box of cleaning cloths that I keep there in the back isn't latched down. Who's been messing with my things?" She latched the lid, then briefly lifted the box, and set it back down, reassured but still shaken.

"Mom, I have a bad feeling about this. Please check all your cabinets. See if anything else is in the wrong place."

One by one, Clair checked them. All the pots, pans, dishes, glasses, and food were fine.

"We should look in your loft, as well. Let's see what else might have been disturbed," Samara said.

"I'm coming, too," said Mariah. "This is weird."

Samara led the procession up the spiral staircase. Samara and Mariah watched as Clair methodically worked her way around the room. When she opened the second under-the-bed drawer, she halted.

"The front corner of that lid is torn." Clair pointed to her keepsake box, a Miller & Rhoads gift box that once held a winter coat.

"Open it, Mom."

Clair lifted the lid. Inside, a bunch of papers was jumbled with dried flowers, photographs, letters, a rabbit's foot, some pieces of ribbon, and lilac-scented soaps from The Homestead, where Preston had taken her for their twentieth anniversary. She collapsed into a heap, covering her face with her hands.

"Nothing's missing, is it?" Samara asked.

"How will I know until I sort it all out?" she snapped.

"I'll set the box aside." Samara helped Clair to her feet. Their hands shook. "You can straighten it in the morning. Let's go downstairs. I'll make us a pot of decaf. We have some figuring to do."

When Samara lifted the open box out of the drawer and set it on the floor, it revealed a folded sheet of pale green notepaper that had been under the box. It read, "To Samara." She reached for it.

"No. That's not for now." Clair said.

"Why not? You addressed it to me."

"Now is not the time." Clair hoped it would be no time soon. She closed the drawer, put the lid on the keepsake box, and headed to the stairs. "Come on. Coffee."

Soon Samara and Mariah were settled on the sofa, and Clair had sunk into what they called "the comfortable chair." All three of them cradled hot coffee mugs in their hands.

"Things happen for a reason. When the shop was trashed, it looked like vandalism—maybe by Al or Elena. But two break-ins so close together, I doubt vandalism's the answer," Samara said.

"If you're implying the two are linked, why would one place be so messy and the other barely disturbed?" asked Mariah.

"No clue. Maybe instead of looking at differences, we should see what they have in common."

"Boxes," Clair stated flatly. *Why can't they see the obvious?*

"That's mostly true, Mom. Whoever did this trashed boxes in the storeroom but they also dumped the files from the drawers. Yet in here, it was just two boxes and detergent, which they probably moved to get to the cleaning cloth box. Any other ties?"

"Me. My work and my home."

"It seems to boil down to someone searching boxes. Your boxes, Clair. Do you have any idea what someone could be looking for?" Mariah chimed in.

Clair stared at the antique phone on the wall. She wished for Preston's steady guidance again. The room was so quiet she could hear a crape myrtle branch scratching the garage's clapboard siding.

"No," she answered.

****

Early Sunday morning, Clair had no luck getting Samara to answer her cell. She tried the antique phone, and the response was immediate.

"I'll admit, this phone is a bit jarring, but it does the job. I was getting to the last of the newspaper when the phone's bells jangled. It made me spill coffee on the comics."

"It's all because you don't answer your cell."

"Sorry. I must have left my phone in silent mode again. What's up?"

"We might be wrong about the break-ins. I found more evidence. Come see." Clair hung the earpiece on its hook, slipped on her coat and boots, and then stepped out her door.

Two inches of snow had fallen overnight. Zena's yard was pretty enough for a greeting card, but Clair held no hopes for a white Christmas. With the brilliant blue sky and temps warming toward the forties, this light snow would be gone before sunset. The tree-sheltered path to Samara's house showed just a dusting of snow. Clair met her daughter at the edge of Zena's backyard.

"Stop here. Look at the shed behind my apartment."

Samara looked. "Nothing wrong with the door; it's shut tight. But I see footprints in the snow, one set leading to the door and a second leading away, nearly overlapping the first. Someone's been in that shed. Could it be Zena?"

"It wasn't Zena. It was me. I went to get a bag of ice-melt to put on the walkway. I'd seen some when I put my gardening things there. Now come take a look." Clair led her inside and pulled a chain to turn on the utility light.

Her shovels, rakes, hoes, plant stakes, and hedge trimmers stood at attention on the right side, a hodge-podge of Zena's implements leaned against the back wall, a lawnmower stood in the center, and on the left was half-empty shelving. The shelves held paint cans, insecticides, weed-killer sprays, bins of worn-out gardening gloves, and more, alternating with blank spaces. On the floor below sat several cartons with closed but unsealed flaps.

"Those used to be on the shelves. I asked Zena about it. She told me she'd not been out here since she helped me make room for my things. It's about boxes again, but this time they're hers, not mine. Something else must be going on."

"Yes, but a stranger wouldn't know whose belongings were whose. If someone were hunting for something of yours, they wouldn't overlook any box. Apparently, they haven't found whatever it is because they're still hunting. Maybe my house will be next. It creeps me out."

"Samara, they must have searched here at the same time they searched my home."

"What makes you say that?"

"Only my footprints in the snow. Yesterday, when we discovered what they did inside my home, there was no snow on the ground. Whenever they came into this shed, it wasn't last night."

****

Late that afternoon, after a tornado of twin toddlers had blown through the bookshop an hour before closing, Sam and Mariah were straightening displays when the phone rang. Sam stretched across the counter to pick up.

"McNeer's Paperbacks by the Tracks. How may I help you?"

"Sam, this is Elena." Her voice sounded heavy like she was coming down with a cold. "I wanted to tell you before you hear from the police. Al's gone." Her voice cracked. "He's dead."

Chapter 11

Dead? Impossible. Al was too conniving to let death hold the winning hand. "What on earth happened?" Sam asked.

"I wish I knew more. Al was so agitated last night, pacing around my house, muttering to himself. He never does...uh, did that. He said he was going somewhere else for a drink. When he didn't come back, I thought he'd gone to his place to sleep it off." She sniffled. "Give me...a minute."

"Take all the time you need." As if parroting a TV script, she added, "I'm sorry for your loss." *But you'll be much better off without him.*

"Who died?" Mariah quietly asked.

Covering the phone with her hand, Sam whispered, "Al."

Mariah's jaw dropped.

"When did you find out?" Sam asked Elena.

"About eleven this morning. I phoned him, and it went to voicemail, so I drove to his house. Two police cars were parked in front. His front door stood ajar, its jamb splintered. I figured someone must have broken in... Oh, I can't believe this!" Elena broke down again.

"Surely, they didn't make you identify him right there, did they?" Sam asked.

"No, not then. I ran up, but when I tried to step inside, an officer said, 'This is a potential crime scene.

You can't come in.' He grabbed my arm to lead me away. I shook loose. I told him, 'I'm Al's fiancée. Did whoever broke in hurt him?' He pointed to his car and said, 'Let's have a seat in there, where we can talk out of the cold wind.' There he said the *police* were the ones who'd forced the door. He told me…he told me Al's body had been discovered in the James River." She choked.

"Were they sure it was Al?"

"I just returned from the morgue in Richmond." It sounded like she was trying to muffle her sobs.

Although Sam had taken an immediate dislike to Elena when they met on Thanksgiving, she'd since developed grudging respect for her. She'd seen Elena stand up to Al's bullying in a way Sam's mom had never managed to do. "Is there anything I can do for you?"

After a couple of hiccups and a long pause, Elena said, "Not really, I suppose. Maybe something later. Bye." Mid-sob, Elena hung up.

A woman Sam hadn't noticed tapped her shoulder.

"If you don't mind me interrupting your personal conversation, isn't anybody going to ring me up? What are you waiting for, Christmas?"

Though tempted to match that snarky comment, she couldn't afford to lose customers. In a small town like Ashland, ticking off one customer could result in losing ten more once the tendrils of the gossip grapevine spread.

After the woman left, bag in hand, Sam curled into her comfy chair behind the counter and hugged herself. A mish-mash of emotions whipped her stomach into a froth. She wouldn't miss Al and couldn't count the number of times she'd wished the man dead. And short of death, she'd fantasized about him being on the receiving end of all sorts of nasty business. But she felt sorry for Elena losing someone she loved, even if it was Al.

Mariah came behind the counter, and Sam filled her in.

"Did Elena say anything about how he died?"

"Not much. Only that his body was fished out of the James. I imagine we'll find out more when the police call."

"Your mom's not next of kin anymore, and you never were. Why would the police call you?"

Sam gave a quick shrug. "Elena said she wanted to tell me before I heard from the police. She said that to get into Al's place, the police had to force the door. I'd say they suspect suicide or murder. I want no part of this."

When the door to the stockroom slammed closed, they both flinched. Sam's mom approached with an armload of books to shelve.

"Why are you talking about suicide and murder?" Clair asked, frowning. "That's not an appropriate topic with Christmas only four days away. Customers might overhear you."

Just then, a man with three grade-school-aged children came in. While the dad rifled through cookbooks, likely on the hunt for a gift for his wife, the kids fanned out and started playing hide-and-seek in the aisles.

Sam asked, "Mariah, are you okay by yourself for a few minutes?"

"Yeah, I've got this. Go."

Clair set down her load of books, planted rigid arms on the counter, and stared at the ceiling, shaking her head. "Aren't you going to answer me? I said, 'Why are you talking about suicide and murder on a day like this?' It's a simple question."

"Mariah will shelve those books. Let's go in the back. I need to talk with you."

Clair scowled, trailing at a distance after Sam.

Sam rolled her office chair up to her mom's desk, and they both sat. Sam told Clair the facts, the few she knew. Clair's reaction to the shocking news was exactly what Sam had expected: an empty stare. Her mom began rocking, a metronome keeping a silent beat.

Sam gave her five quiet minutes to process what had happened, then asked softly, "What are you feeling now, Mom? It helps to talk about it."

Clair stopped rocking. "How am I supposed to feel? What I *think* is that the man deserved to be dead." She looked like she was going to say more but didn't.

"It's getting on toward five o'clock. Would you like me to take you home early and let Mariah close up?"

"Yes."

No knee-jerk resistance to changing the routine? Sam's mom must be muddled to the core. But she could only guess at what really went on behind that stony façade.

After depositing Clair at her apartment and helping her start her dinner, Sam hurried around the block to her small rancher and turned on the TV to catch the local news. Among the show's teaser rundown of the top three stories was, "This morning, the body of an Ashland man was discovered in the James River. More in a moment." It was torture to endure over ten minutes of other stories and inane commercials before coverage of "more" resumed.

"Today, an early morning jogger on Riverside Drive spotted a body snagged on debris at the head of a small island in the James River, downstream from Huguenot Bridge. The victim has been identified as Albert Hobson, most recently employed at Ashland Community Bank." A photo of Al flashed onto the screen, the kind of headshot that might have appeared in the bank's annual report. "Richmond Police are treating this as a suspicious death. No further details have been released, but we will keep you updated as they become available."

Sam hit "off" on the remote. She'd been stuck at the disbelief stage, but the sight of Al's photo and name on the screen suddenly made it real. This was the kind of thing that happened to people you never heard of, not to your mother's ex, not to someone you hated.

She wasn't simply relieved that she'd no longer have to steer her mom around chance encounters with him, like the explosive one on Thanksgiving. There was another emotion mixed in. Could it be pity? Maybe. Even a rabid mongrel deserves a gentle death.

****

Richmond's TV networks seldom covered events of interest to Ashlanders, so Clair rarely watched the news. This night she tuned in. She sat still, stick-straight, hands in her lap. When the picture of Al appeared on the screen, she thought it didn't do him justice. Justice would have mandated that he be in a prisoner's jumpsuit.

What he'd done to her should have been against the law. He'd lied to her more times than she could count. He'd conned her out of what was rightfully hers. Clair's parents always said that if people didn't behave properly, sooner or later, they got what they deserved. Her parents were right.

She smiled as she turned off the TV and picked up a seed catalog that had arrived in yesterday's mail, pleased to see the company was offering several hard-to-find varieties of heirloom tomatoes.

****

Monday morning, twenty minutes after Paperbacks opened for business, Officer Giles Joyner came in.

"Sorry to bother you at this busy time of year, Sam. Can we talk in the back?"

"Sure." *This can't be good.* She escorted him toward the office.

As Sam opened the door, Clair almost ran into him. "Excuse me. I need to shelve these books."

"Hello, Mrs. Hobson. Please hang on a moment. I'm here to pass on a request. Richmond Police would like to talk with you both today. It's about Albert Hobson's death."

"No problem," Sam said. "Just give me the number and with whom to speak. We'll give them a call right away."

"I wish it worked like that, but they need you to come in person."

"Isn't there another way? Or another time?"

"Only an escorted half-hour ride in a police car, I'm afraid."

Taking option number one, they drove into downtown Richmond. What an awful time to leave Mariah alone in the shop!

Sam had never entered a police station, not even Ashland's small one. All she knew of the inside of a station was what she'd seen on crime shows. After passing through security, Sam gave their names at the desk, and the sergeant directed them to a waiting area. They stewed for a half hour before a detective finally opened a door.

Elena Fairchild, eyes red and swollen, walked out, her coat draped over her arm. As she shuffled by Clair, she looked at Sam and mouthed an almost imperceptible, "Sorry." Whatever did Elena need to apologize for?

The detective leaning against the door jamb called out, "Clair Hobson?" When Sam and her mom stood and picked up their purses, the detective asked, "Are both of you named Clair Hobson?"

"No," answered Clair flatly, "This is my daughter, Samara McNeer. We were told you wanted to speak with us both."

"It would be better together," Sam added. Her mom's awkward communication skills often led to misunderstandings.

"You'll have your turn, Ms. McNeer. One at a time, please. Come with me, Ms. Hobson."

Before Sam could object, he ushered Clair from the waiting room. The metal door clanked shut behind them. This could not go well. Sam's hands were freezing. She bought a cup of coffee—a caffeine and hand-warmer combo—from the vending machine and returned to her seat. To keep her mind from visualizing the worst, she pulled a booklet of Sudoku puzzles from her purse and started one rated "Fiendish."

Ten minutes and four filled-in numbers later, she flipped the pages back to a "Medium" one, letting it draw her into something solvable. Thirty-five minutes, two more coffees, and two puzzles later, the door opened. Her mom headed straight to the chair beside Sam, sat, and started her metronome swaying. Definitely not good.

"Your turn, Ms. McNeer," announced the detective.

The man stood a menacing six-five or six-six, no hint of a smile on his broad, flat-nosed face. He looked like the Ashland officer who had come into her shop several times a few years back. That guy would hang around the shop, leering at her, until she offered him a free cup of coffee. He'd thank her and leave. Never bought a book.

The room resembled a typical cop-show interrogation room with that intimidating one-way observation window, but it felt smaller, stuffier. And on TV, you don't get the ambiance created by harsh industrial cleansers mixed with various odors emitted from stressed human bodies. Sam took a seat at the table opposite the detective. He pushed a button on a recorder of some sort. On the ceiling in one corner, she saw what must be a camera encased in a gray plastic bubble a little smaller than a tennis ball. Did that button turn on both sound and video?

"This conversation is being recorded. I'm Detective Paul Patillo. It's 11:37 a.m., Monday, December 22, 2008. Please state your name." He looked up from an open folder in front of him.

"Samara McNeer."

Yes, Patillo had been the name on the coffee-mooching officer's shirt. Sam was awful at recalling names but readily recognized them when she saw or heard them again. She decided not to say anything. Not now.

After covering the rest of the particulars—address, occupation, relationship to the deceased, etc.—he asked for her Social Security number.

Sam frowned. "That's personal. Why do you need that?"

"Strictly routine. We do background checks on folks we question. Your number?"

Though the room was chilly, Sam felt a light sweat breaking out on her forehead. She gave the number.

"Did you see your mother on Saturday?"

He suspected her mom? Patillo's questioning of her mother must have been a debacle. The walls of the room felt like they were closing in.

"Yes, Mariah and I had dinner at Mom's place, and after dinner—"

"That would be Mariah who?"

"Mariah Gabrielli. She's the assistant manager at my bookshop. After dinner, we discovered evidence of a break-in at Mom's, and this wasn't the first break-in recently. The first—"

"You should take break-ins up with Ashland Police. Moving on, what time did you leave your mother's place?"

Sam was miffed by his brush-off but anxious to get this circus over with. "It must have been about nine. We were so shaken by the break-in—"

"Where did you go after you left?"

"Home."

"Is there anyone who can confirm that?"

"No. I live alone. Why would I need an alibi? You think *I* killed Al?" Sam rolled her eyes.

"Did you?"

"Of course not."

"Why did your mother divorce Mr. Hobson?"

He clearly hadn't gotten the story straight. Whatever had Elena told him?

"That's backward. Al is the one who dumped my mom, but not before fleecing her of her life savings."

He looked Sam in the eye. "Ms. McNeer, is that why your mother killed Albert Hobson?"

"She wouldn't!" Sam's heart hammered. "You've got to be kidding."

She felt like she might pass out. From her dad, Sam had inherited the duty of easing her eccentric mom over the potholes in life. This wasn't a pothole. This was the

Grand Canyon.

"Murder is certainly not a joking matter. When I asked your mother if she killed him, she smiled, staring at the ceiling, and shaking her head. Then she said he only got what he deserved. That's nearly a confession in my book."

"My mother doesn't have a mean bone in her body. It's just that she reacts differently from most people. I'm pretty sure she has—"

"You'd be surprised what I know about how people react. Guilty people, that is." The corners of Patillo's lips tweaked up a hair into a smug grin. "She has that same blank stare I've seen a million times. Guilty folks won't look at me. They know I'll see right through their lies. All your mother did was sit there like a stone, her hands clenched together, giving me one-word answers. She's looking good for the deed."

Shock and fear morphed to caffeine-and-adrenaline-fueled anger. Her inner "Aunt Patrice" attitude bubbled up. She rested her crossed arms on the table and leaned forward.

"First off, my mom never lies. Not even white ones. Second, she doesn't look anyone in the eye, including me. That's part of what I meant by *different*. Third, what makes you think my mom had anything to do with Al's death? Fourth, do you even know if it was murder, or was it suicide? And fifth—"

"Easy, easy, Ms. McNeer. Let me ask the questions, please. You're very protective of your mother, aren't you?"

"Who wouldn't be?"

"It seems there are others who protect her, too. Ms. Fairchild told us about the personal attack on

Thanksgiving, launched by your mother's sister in front of a room full of patrons at the Iron Horse. What's your aunt's name? Ms. Fairchild didn't recall it."

"Patrice Givens."

He wrote it down, along with her contact information.

"What do you want with Aunt Patrice?"

"Not your concern." He shuffled through a few pages of notes. "Tell me about the meeting at the bank. You know, the one where Duane Chanesky punched Mr. Hobson in the face. Ms. Fairchild told me you said you wished you'd done that."

"She wasn't there. How does she know what happened?"

"Mr. Hobson had related every detail to his concerned fiancée. So, what made you mad enough to break his face?"

"I didn't break anything. Al did. He's why my mom is broke. He talked her into investing her savings with that ginormous pyramid scheme that crashed, the one run by Bernard Madoff. Al ruined her financially. She's the victim here."

"Let's see if I have this right: you and your aunt are hyper-protective of your mother, whose life savings have just been wiped out by Hobson's doing. Chanesky lost out big time, too. You're all extremely pissed off. Sounds to me like each of you has a primo motive for murder. I suggest that you not leave the area. That goes for your mother, too." He closed his folder, stood, and opened the door. "Thank you for coming in."

And Merry Christmas to you. Sam shoved her seat away from the table. It made a spine-chilling screech, but nowhere near as piercing as the shriek echoing in her skull.

On the drive back to Ashland, she wanted to hug Mom and tell her everything would turn out all right *and* yell at her for behaving so stupidly. Sam couldn't do either. Her mom didn't want to be touched when she was upset, and Sam couldn't yell at her mother. She felt stupid for giving the detective Aunt Patrice's name and dropping Mariah's name, as well.

Now she understood why Elena said "sorry" when she left. She'd also been led into sharing too much.

Damn.

Chapter 12

Clair's Monday afternoon had been most unproductive. Her mind wouldn't focus on paperwork. The evening proceeded the same way. After a half-hour of trying to plot out a landscape diagram for Zena's garden, she gave up. The page was nearly blank.

Why hadn't Detective Patillo believed her? As always, she'd been swear-to-God honest in every answer to his questions. She told him she never lied. Even after Samara told him the same thing, he'd still not believed it. Why? It made no sense.

****

Monday evening, all Sam wanted to do was hole up at home and douse her flaming nightmare with wine, a sure-fire sedative to knock herself senseless. She had no tolerance for alcohol.

As she uncorked the bottle, the *thunk* of her front door closing sounded from the living room.

"ISC Convention." By the time Mariah entered Sam's kitchen, she'd already shed her coat.

"Bad timing, Mariah, unless you agree to drink and not talk. I've done too much talking to police today, and it all backfired." Sam filled her wine glass, the largest she owned, nearly to the rim.

Without a word, Mariah took a glass from the cabinet and filled it halfway. "Permission to speak?"

"As long as it has nothing to do with today's

disaster."

"Since you're sharing the wine, I'll share this spinach and feta pizza I brought from Ukrop's." She retrieved the box from the living room, set it in the middle of the table, and opened the top.

"You sure know how to mess with my plans," Sam said, getting out two plates. "With a full stomach, it's going to take more wine to do me in. Hope I have enough. Now, no more speaking."

Silence, pizza, and wine reigned supreme for the next ten minutes.

Sam's glass registered one gulp from empty. When she reached for the bottle, Mariah grabbed it first, corked it, and stashed it in the fridge.

"Hey, I need that. Bring it back." Sam shot a commanding glare at Mariah.

Arms crossed, leaning back on the fridge, Mariah matched her glare, then raised it to new heights. "First, don't you think you owe me the courtesy of letting me tell you how my session with Detective Patillo went since you were so kind as to drop my name in his lap today? Just because I joined you and your mom for dinner Saturday night?" Mariah sat down across from Sam.

That punctured Sam's ballooning despair. And replaced it with guilt.

"You know I'm sorry about that."

Mariah wrapped up the leftover pizza slices and put them in the fridge.

"So, do you want to hear about my afternoon or not?" she asked.

"Yeah, I do owe you that. Then more wine, okay?"

"Detective Patillo let me chill in that waiting room for an hour and a half. Boy, did I regret not bringing along a book! When he finally called me in, all he wanted was for me to confirm having dinner with you and your mom Saturday night and to describe Clair's typical demeanor. I was out of there in under ten minutes."

"No other questions?"

"There was one. He told me Al's car had been found at Eastminster Presbyterian Church by Ashland's police. He asked me if I knew any reason why Al would have gone to the church, and I said I didn't think he attended any church."

"Bingo! That must be why the police are assuming he'd been murdered. What person bent on suicide leaves his car a dozen or more miles from where he jumps off a bridge?" A siren sounded in the distance, a *ta-da* to her deductive powers.

"Okay, your turn, Sam. Tell me about your questioning. When you got back this afternoon, you were high on dudgeon but low on details. How can I help you if I don't have a clear picture of what happened?"

Sam raised her empty glass. "More wine."

"Not a chance. I want to hear this before you start conking out."

Sam huffed out a breath and rested her head, already fuzzy, on the table. The wine had dulled the fight in her. "Whatever." She sat up and started shredding her napkin, bit by bit. "Where do I start?"

"How about with Patillo's first questions?"

"Okay. Right off the bat, he asked if I'd seen Mom on Saturday, which threw me off-kilter. I couldn't believe he'd have suspicions about Mom. I told him about our dinner, you included. When I tried to tell him about the break-in we discovered that night, he blew me off, telling me to take it up with Ashland Police. And when I said I left about nine, he asked if anyone could confirm that I was at home all night. I said no, then he had the nerve to ask me if I'd killed Al!"

"Sounds almost as if he has it in for your family. His tone wasn't anything like that with me. Any clue why?" Mariah began shredding her napkin, too.

"Nada. Next, he asked why Mom had divorced Al. He had it backward, I told him. Al had dumped Mom like a used paper towel, but only after mopping up her life savings for himself. Then Patillo came out with the bomb of a question—asking if that was why Mom had killed him. Apparently, Mom had smiled when he asked her the same thing. He read her reaction as close to a confession. I told him she reacts differently and that she wouldn't hurt a fly, but he ignored me, promising he was going to…to nail her," Sam said, stumbling over the words. "That's when I lost it."

"It's not like you to break down."

Mariah laid a comforting hand on Sam's clenched ones. Sam shook it off.

"Not losing tears, girl. Losing my temper. I peppered him with a stack of comebacks and questions. He just he rolled his eyes and told me to cool it, that it was his job to ask the questions." Sam grabbed a fistful of napkin bits and let them snow down on the table.

"Hey, you were totally within your rights. You were only setting him straight. If you don't stand up and protect your mom, who will?"

"Protect. That was his keyword. He latched onto it and flipped it on its ear. He said others protect her, too. Elena told him about Patrice's scene on Thanksgiving at the Iron Horse. Next, he asked about the confrontation in Mardigan's office. You know, the one where Duane

151

Chanesky punched Al in the face. He said Elena learned from Al that I'd said I wished I'd done that. Of course, that led to the Madoff fiasco. Then he lumped it all together, saying Mom, Patrice, Duane, and I all were pissed off enough to murder the man."

Mariah sat back. "Damn. But surely they can't arrest anyone on mere motive, without a shred of evidence, can they?"

"*Now*, more wine?"

"Definitely."

****

Despite nursing a pounder of a headache, Sam was relieved to be occupied with everyday business at Paperbacks the next day. Mom finally finished refiling the papers that had been dumped but was behind on paying invoices. No worries. She'd get caught up quickly. Neither of them had been arrested. It was a good day.

The local nightly news carried an update on the investigation into Al's death. "And in a new development in Albert Hobson's death, we have an exclusive interview with George Speers, a bartender who witnessed an altercation Saturday night between two of his regular customers, one of whom was the deceased." The camera cut to a fellow standing by a neon sign touting, *Someplace Else—Come in when you need to get away*.

So Al had told Elena precisely where he was going: to Someplace Else for a drink, not "somewhere else," as she'd put it. If Elena hadn't made that mistake when she told Sam, she would have recognized it.

"Mr. Speers, tell us in your own words what happened." The reporter thrust the microphone up to the bartender's pudgy lips.

"Well, Al came in at about ten, and a couple minutes

later, Duane—uh, that's Duane Chanesky—comes in, and the two of 'em start arguing and pushing each other around. Al grabs a beer bottle and breaks it, and ends up cutting Duane's hand. I'm getting ready to toss 'em both out, but another regular gets to 'em before me and talks 'em into drinking up and leaving. Soon I hear engines gunnin' and gravel grindin'. That's the last time I saw Al, rest his soul."

The reporter added, "We have it on good authority that Duane Chanesky is now being detained for questioning."

Football scores came on, and Sam hit "off."

Duane sure showed an ugly side when he punched out Al, but to her mind, that was fully justified. Duane was a steady husband and an attentive father. He even coached Little League. No way he'd risk it all by murdering somebody. Who were the police going to call in next—the rest of Al's poker buddies? His co-workers? His mailman?

The only good news in the awful situation was that Patillo was throwing accusations at everyone.

Chapter 13

Sam was more interested in enjoying her holiday than wringing every last dollar out of her customers. As she did every year, she closed the shop at two o'clock on Christmas Eve. Aunt Patrice would be arriving by three, giving Sam plenty of time to prepare their big dinner—by picking up the complete meal she'd ordered from Ukrop's Super Market.

Ukrop's was packed with shoppers like her who'd pushed essential shopping to the last minute. As she passed a display of poinsettias, it reminded her the only festive things in her house were the Christmas cards lined up on the mantel. All her decorations were at Mom's. She selected the biggest poinsettia of the bunch and added it to her cart. It would make a great stand-in for a tree, something to surround with gifts.

At home, she removed a trailing ivy plant from its tall stand and put it on the right corner of the mantel. She trailed the ivy across the mantel like an evergreen garland and used brass candlesticks with red candles to hold the ivy vines in place. With the poinsettia on the plant stand, moved to the left side of the hearth, and her colorfully wrapped gifts below, the scene didn't look half bad for a jerry-rig.

She picked up the morning paper from the coffee table. She'd not had time to read it earlier. On page two, halfway down, was the headline, "Chanesky Charged with Murder." How could they do that? They had just as much on Duane as they did on anyone who knew Al, motives aplenty. Like Mariah had said, they couldn't arrest anyone on a mere motive. Sam read the short article.

Tuesday evening, Duane Chanesky was arrested for the murder of Albert Hobson, whose body was recovered from the James River last Sunday morning. Although details of the autopsy report have not been made public, the death has been ruled a homicide.

In addition to Mr. Chanesky's two altercations with the deceased, the most recent one taking place the evening before his death, police found physical evidence in a search of Chanesky's property.

Sam was in shock. Instant, dizzy-headed shock. She flat-out couldn't believe Duane was a killer. He certainly had reason for rage—losing his investment with Madoff, then losing half his house to fire—but murder? It had to have been someone else. Sam simply had no idea who.

A light rain had begun falling, along with the temperature. A white Christmas might be in the cards after all, and she would be hosting the celebration shortly. After a few deep breaths to settle her spinning head, she finished tidying up, then set out a dish of nuts and some cheese and crackers. It was a quarter to four, and Aunt Patrice hadn't arrived. As she picked up her cell to get a progress report, her aunt's car pulled up. When Patrice started unloading gifts and luggage, Sam went to help her bring them in.

"Traffic must have been tough," Sam said as she wheeled a suitcase into the guest bedroom.

"No problem with traffic. I've been at the Richmond Police Station since two." Patrice deposited a stack of wrapped gifts on the bed.

"Why didn't you tell me?"

"I didn't want you getting upset, it being Christmas Eve and all. You've been through enough." Patrice wrapped Sam in a hug. "It's my own damn fault for going off on Al in front of half of Ashland. I was so pissed I don't even remember half of what I said. Did I really threaten to kill him?"

"No, but you came close. What did they think you said?"

"The quote was 'I'll make sure you never marry again.' They heard it from several diners and Elena, so I must have said it."

"Good thing they didn't ask me. Your exact words were, 'I'll make *damn* sure…' "

Patrice winced. "Clair always warned me to edit out the cuss words. I should have listened to my baby sister."

"Why would they ask you in for questioning when they've already arrested Duane?"

"Hell, ah, heck if I know. Sorry."

"Let's go into the living room. I have an article from this morning's paper to show you."

Patrice grabbed the stack of gifts from the bed and followed Sam. After one look around the living room, Patrice commented, "I like what you did around the fireplace, but where's your tree?"

"I put it up at Mom's. All her decorations are still in storage, behind a barricade of heavy furniture. Take a look at this." She opened the paper and handed it to her aunt.

Patrice skimmed the article. "The police phoned me Monday and wanted me to come sooner, but I told them I couldn't, and they said today would be okay. Even with a suspect in custody, I guess they need to make sure they follow up on every lead. Frankly, in light of this article, I'm peeved they went ahead with the appointment. You'd think they'd cut me a break on Christmas Eve, but no. As soon as I told them I'd been leading my book group's discussion that night, they lost interest. Then I figured if they wanted to waste their time chasing down everybody who had it in for Al, I'd give them one more."

"How's that?"

"You should have seen Patillo's face when I told him about Al's first wife, Gail."

"You didn't! Why cast suspicion on someone you don't even know? Don't you think she's suffered enough on account of Al?"

"Not to worry. I'm sure she's been safely snowed in up there in Connecticut. It won't cost the detective any more than a phone call or two to confirm it." She reached for the cheese and crackers. "I'm starving. Do you think you could find a bottle of wine to go with this? I'm more than ready to relax."

"Can't argue with that. I could use a little loosening up myself."

As darkness fell, the rain switched over to sleet, not snow. Mariah and Mom arrived, and Sam brought them up to speed on recent developments, then Patrice insisted they change the subject.

"Murder doesn't mix well with merriment," she said.

To set a cheerier mood, Sam offered to turn on the gas fireplace, but Mom delivered a lecture on how heat would dry out the ivy and the poinsettia. As the next best, Sam turned on the TV and popped a DVD into the player. On-screen, a match was struck, and a beautiful fire was soon crackling while Christmas music played in the background. Amazing how the mere sight of dancing flames could warm a room and everyone in it.

The doorbell rang. Sam wasn't prepared for the sight that greeted her when she opened the door. Santa Claus stepped in.

"Ho, ho, ho! The jolly thin man's here." Ryan's red stocking cap, white beard, and mustache looked the part but muffled his words. He opened his sack—a white plastic trash bag with a red cinch—reached deep and handed Sam a tall, skinny gift bag. "Put this in the refrigerator for now."

The commotion of Ryan's arrival woke Phoenix, who'd been napping in his crate. A closed bedroom door was no match for his plaintive whimpers.

Ryan looked down the hall. "Hey, what's the puppy done to deserve solitary confinement?"

"Same thing all puppies do at his age. He's not totally housebroken yet, so I bring him in here only when I can keep an eagle eye on him. He also loves the taste of wrapping paper and cardboard, as in those gifts over there. He can visit with us after dinner."

Ryan inhaled like he was getting ready to speak, then looked away. Sam peered in the gift bag.

"These two bottles of wine you brought will be more than enough for five of us, especially considering the one we've already opened. I've not seen this kind before. What's Conundrum?"

"You mean, aside from our friendship?" He grinned, and one corner of the mustache slipped down an inch. "Hope you don't mind if I take this thing off. I don't know how the mall Santas put up with it. As for the wine, it's one of my favorites, an intriguing blend of several varieties. If you like wine that's fruity yet refreshingly dry, you'll love it."

Conundrum—a puzzling problem, intriguingly fruity—a most appropriate definition of their friendship. If she could work around the puzzle part, the intriguing part could be quite delightful.

Ryan removed the beard getup, along with his stocking cap and heavy black parka, revealing a red V-neck sweater, white shirt, and a tie decorated with nutcrackers. "Merry Christmas, everyone."

The others returned his greetings. Patrice said, "You can put Santa's sack over here by the poinsettia. We saved you a fireside seat." She pointed to a chair beside the TV.

He scanned the last-minute decorations. "I must say, Sam, you always did have a creative streak." When he propped the bag against the fireplace's marble surround, its contents shifted and clunked over with a crinkling sound. Everyone's eyebrows shot up. "Don't worry, folks. Nothing breakable."

They discussed Ryan's mostly healed ribs, Sam's unique approach to holiday trimmings, Mom's new apartment with one picture—Van Gogh's *Starry Night*—now on her living room wall, and the progress on repairing the fire damage to her house.

When the topic segued to the options for kitchen countertops, Sam asked, "Speaking of kitchens, I smell savory goodness wafting from mine. Anyone hungry?"

She didn't have to ask twice. Soon the five of them were seated around the oval dining room table, enjoying Ukrop's best. The buzz of conversation punctuated with light laughter, the clink of silverware on plates, the aroma of turkey with sage stuffing, the flicker of candlelight. All was perfect.

Over dessert, Mom contributed a blessedly short monologue on poinsettias, which she called *Euphorbia pulcherrima*, and the various species of ivy, in the genus *Hedera*. Sam basked in the jovial spirit, but other images came unbidden. Duane in a jail cell. His wife Amy and their sons in a small apartment without him. Al in a morgue. And Elena, with an engagement ring, but no fiancé.

Ryan must have noticed her somber mood. "A penny for your thoughts."

"I was just thinking about some who are much less fortunate. I don't often stop to appreciate my blessings." She put on a faint smile and added, "Who has room for more pie?"

Everyone groaned. Once plates were cleared, they gathered in the living room.

When Ryan came in carrying Phoenix, Sam warned, "You might want to rethink that. Better take him outside first. I'll go with you."

They stepped out the back door. The sleet had stopped. Clouds scudded past a nearly full moon.

"Careful," Sam said. "These steps are slippery." She showed Ryan where to set the pup down.

Phoenix immediately squatted and did his business. When he started padding off toward the yard, Ryan scooped him up and rubbed his head.

"Coming along on your training, aren't you, boy?" he said, scratching him behind the ear. "You know, you never did tell me what you named him."

"Let's get back inside, or I'll have to rename him Frosty." Back in the warm kitchen, Sam said, "Mariah came up with his name. It's Phoenix."

"I like that. Say, when are you going to wash off all

this soot? He's still black." He held him up nose to nose and was rewarded with a puppy kiss. "Let's go see what's in Santa's sack."

"Don't we have to wait till tomorrow?"

"Not unless you want to."

He put Phoenix on the living room floor and claimed his seat by the "fire." The puppy, his whole hind end wagging, scampered to greet everyone. Phoenix lingered the longest at Sam's feet and Mariah's but wriggled away from any attempts to be picked up as he explored every corner of the forbidden territory. When he discovered the gifts on the floor, he went straight to the white sack and started gnawing on one corner.

"Oh, no, you don't." Sam jumped up to stop him, but Ryan was quicker.

He retrieved both the sack and the puppy, who wouldn't let go.

"Looks like we're opening these now. Phoenix is already enjoying his." Ryan pulled out a puppy stocking stuffed with chew toys, treats, and a squeaky reindeer.

Sam was touched that he'd thought to bring something for Phoenix.

"You might as well open yours, too. Sorry if the wrapping smells like dog biscuits," he said, handing Sam a present.

She hefted it. "This has some weight to it." All she could think was that it weighed a hundred times more than those baseball cards.

She ripped off the green ribbon and the red-and-green plaid wrapping paper, opened the cube-shaped box, and found a clock. Its slightly yellowed six-inch face was ringed in brass and set into a rich brown wooden case. Elegant in its simplicity.

"This is beautiful. It'll look perfect on top of my bookcase, but you went overboard. I don't know what to say, but thanks so much."

"It's not all that old, but it came from that antique mall on Staples Mill Road. Time never goes out of style." His eyes twinkled, just like Santa's.

She ran her fingers over the silky woodgrain then stole a glance at the pile of presents under the plant stand. The wrapped baseball cards had become hidden behind gifts the others had brought. His generosity called for drastic action, painful as it would be.

Sam steeled herself and turned to Ryan. "What do you think of your present?"

He put a hand on his belly. "I already ate it, every last delicious bite."

"Not that. Your real present."

"You have to give it to me first."

Sam picked up the green ribbon she'd discarded, went over to Ryan, and looped it around the puppy's neck. "You're holding it. All you have to do is unwrap it, or should I say him."

This drew a slight gasp from Mariah and an "ooh" from Patrice.

Phoenix sealed the deal by licking Ryan's hand.

He stammered, "Uh, you know how I can't resist this little guy, but...but he's yours. You must be so attached to him after all these weeks of mothering him night and day."

"You don't have to take him if you don't want to." *Oh, how I hope you don't want him!* Sam fought back the prickle of threatening tears. "I know it's a big commitment to take on a pet. But soon he's going to grow too big to bring to the shop, as I've been doing. Since you work from home, you can keep him company all day. Too bad he's not a Dalmatian, or he could ride with you on the fire truck, too."

This brought the grin back to his face. "Are you *sure* you can part with him?"

"On one condition: that I can see him every once in a while." Sam beamed him a broad smile.

It would hurt like hell. She and Phoenix had become best buds. Her plan to take him to the animal shelter had disappeared, though she couldn't say precisely how long ago.

"In that case, thanks. How did you know that every year I asked Santa for a puppy, and every year I got a stuffed one?"

"Lucky guess." *Bingo! But why'd I have to go and do that?*

After Ryan, Mariah, and Mom said their goodbyes, Patrice helped Sam with the dishes, then retired for the night. With the DVD long since over and everyone gone, the living room emanated an empty stillness. She dug out the package tagged "To Ryan" from the pile, unwrapped it, and looked from the baseball cards to the antique clock. Intended or not, Sam felt like they'd just started something. Time would tell.

She stashed the cards in a drawer, thinking they might serve as a birthday present… if she ever learned his birth date.

****

On Christmas morning, Clair awoke early. She stretched across Preston's side of the bed and picked up his framed picture from his nightstand.

"Merry Christmas, Preston." She kissed his picture then hugged it to her chest. "You understood, didn't you?

163

Different was okay with you." She carefully replaced his portrait on the nightstand.

After selecting her clothes for the day, she carried them downstairs and showered. She slipped the silvery-white turtleneck sweater over her head and looked at her reflection in the bathroom mirror. Preston had given the sweater to her for Christmas nine years ago. He said he loved the way it was a perfect match for her beautiful hair. She'd worn it every Christmas since. It warmed her.

Before leaving for Samara's house, she went to the antique phone. She ran her finger over the small brass plate on the phone's oak cabinet: Stromberg-Carlson Telephone Mfg. Co. "Yes, you loved me as I was, different and all." She zipped up her coat and went out the door.

Mariah was already at Samara's. Since her parents had died, Mariah had spent most holidays here. If Mariah's brother ever tired of going to his in-laws' house in Atlanta, the day might come when she'd celebrate with him. Samara had told Clair that would take some of the "merry" out of her Christmas.

Patrice prepared a big breakfast, including her specialty, fried oysters. Mariah passed on the oysters, but she made up for it by eating almost a third of the freshly baked cinnamon coffee cake and a double helping of scrambled eggs.

After the frenzy of opening gifts died down, Samara took out two decks of cards for the family tradition of Decking the Halls, a marathon of playing Michigan Rummy. As lunchtime rolled around, one player after another scrounged a snack of leftovers from the kitchen and brought it back to the dining room table, but play never ceased.

At four o'clock, Mariah stood and stretched. "This doesn't seem to be my day. The card elf scrimped on his gifts of wild cards, at least for me. If you don't mind continuing with just the three of you, I'll think I'll go home to sleep off this last piece of pecan pie."

Patrice added, "Now that you mention it, I'd better be getting on the road. I should head home before traffic gets thick and the temp drops. And in case you hadn't noticed, Mariah, the only one who's been winning consistently, wild cards or no wild cards, is that card shark over there, my sister."

"It's your own fault," Clair said. "I don't understand why the rest of you keep making poor choices for your discards. All you have to do is remember which cards the others are collecting."

Patrice shrugged. "I have enough trouble remembering which blouse I wore yesterday. And I don't have fifty-two blouses."

"If you used your memory, you wouldn't—"

"Come on, sisters. Break it up. Should I send you to your rooms?" Samara chided. "You're too old to be arguing."

Patrice chuckled. "We're never too old. That's what sisters are for. But should anyone other than family hassle us, watch out."

Samara smiled but raised an eyebrow. "Yeah. We all saw that in spades on Thanksgiving."

****

When everyone left, all the joy drifted out the door with them. The vacuum threatened to suck Sam into a dark place, so she busied herself separating recyclable wrapping paper from ribbons, blister packs, and shrink wrap. Not with visions of sugarplums, but of Mom's

165

traditional turkey noodle soup, she sliced off as much turkey as she could, then plucked the remaining "niblets," as Dad had called them, from all the little crannies on the carcass. About every fourth moist niblet disappeared into her mouth.

This greasy chore used to be Dad's, the only difference being he snuck every fifth chunk to their dog Mookie, who patiently stood on his hind paws, a front paw propped on the lower cabinet door. Mom's protests did no good. Dad blamed the "accidents" on slippery fingers. Sam caught herself readying a niblet for Phoenix. Though he'd only been with her six weeks, his absence left a gaping hole in her life.

After wrapping meal-sized packets of turkey for the freezer and saving the bones for soup, Sam scrubbed down the entire kitchen. Then she warmed a plate heaped with sweet potato casserole and stuffing, picked up the tin of cookies Mom had baked—all carbs get a free pass on Christmas Day—and watched *A Christmas Carol*. By the time Scrooge joined his nephew's family for Christmas dinner, she'd absentmindedly eaten all but three of the cookies.

Settling into a nest of pillows on her sofa, she made the mistake of opening a book. The next thing she knew, the thump of her book hitting the floor startled her out of a vivid dream—dripping-wet Al was dropping two big boxes on her home's doorstep. But that front door wasn't hers. Behind jail bars, Duane sat on what passed for a bed, his arms wrapped around knees pulled up to his chest.

A spectral Al and a destroyed Duane—two unnerving images rolled into one nightmare. Sam shuddered but couldn't shake off the foreboding scene. Was Al, like

Marley's ghost, trying to tell her something? What did Al have in those boxes? Was there anything she could do to help Duane?

She made herself a big mug of decaf coffee, started the DVD of the blazing fireplace, then double-checked that she'd locked the front and back doors before sitting down with her book. She'd always savored solitary times like these, a chance to recharge her introspective batteries. Yes, it was a silent night, but this silence set her nerves on edge.

Since fires, break-ins, murder, and Duane's arrest had hijacked her attention, *alone* had become the last thing she wanted to be.

Chapter 14

Over the weekend, Mariah helped customers find the books they'd hoped to get as gifts instead of the ones they'd received, and Sam handled exchanges at the register. It seemed too spacious behind the counter with no crate to step around. Quite a few of their regulars asked where the cute puppy was. They missed him, too.

Five minutes before closing time on Sunday, Duane Chanesky's wife came in with their children. Austin, the older boy, took after Duane with the same sturdy, square face, brown hair, and startlingly pale blue eyes that beamed like headlights. The younger fellow, Ethan, was a clone of Amy, all except for gender. Their rail-thin builds, warm brown eyes, and sandy blond hair made them look vulnerable, pushovers if challenged. But the firm set of their lips said otherwise.

Amy told the boys to keep their voices down and stay in the Young Readers section. They trotted off, and she watched to make sure they complied. More customers should follow her example. Too many parents treated shops like Sam's as playgrounds and expected the staff to supervise their kids.

"Sam, do you have time to talk? I know you're closing, so I won't take long." Amy's face had aged five years since Sam had seen her two weeks ago.

"Certainly. We can take all the time you need." Sam locked the front door, asked Mariah to drop Mom off on her way home, and then set up a folding chair behind the counter. "Come have a seat."

"Duane didn't do it. You know that, don't you?"

"I'd never seen him so furious as when he stormed into Mardigan's office, but I can't bring myself to believe he'd do such a thing. What in the world did the police find in the way of evidence?"

"They turned our apartment inside out, then went to the big trash bin for our building and bagged the entire contents. They told us they found an empty packet with residue from a date-rape drug."

Sam frowned. "How could that tie in?"

"The autopsy showed the presence of the same drug. They think Al was drugged before being thrown off Huguenot Bridge."

"The stuff must have belonged to one of the other tenants. How can they stick that on Duane?"

"Which of the other tenants would you pick: seventy-four-year-old Mrs. LaRouche, the lesbian couple, or the retired teacher, Alice Caudle?"

"The evidence had to have been planted."

"That's what Al kept insisting about our fire and the incriminating towel in *his* trash. We were so sure Al set it out of spite, but now I'm inclined to believe his story."

Amy stood for a moment to look toward the Young Readers section. She needn't have worried. Glancing up at a security mirror, Sam could see both boys sitting cross-legged on the floor, thumbing through books.

"Is there anything I can do to help?"

"Just knowing you're on Duane's side is a boost. When it comes to trial, I'd like you to be a character witness."

"Of course, but I wish there were something I could

do now. I still owe both of you a huge debt. Without you two taking charge of shutting down the cookout and doing all sorts of other stuff right after Dad and Kyle were killed, I don't know how Mom and I would have made it through those awful days. If you think of anything— anything at all I can do—don't hesitate to ask."

Amy helped her boys shelve the books they'd pulled out.

"Aw, Mommy, I want that one. Please?" pleaded Ethan.

"Not now, honey." She pulled up his coat's hood and secured the strap under his pouting chin.

"Wait," Sam called. "Which one did you like?" He sheepishly pointed to *The Knight and the Dragon.*

"And what about you, young man?" Sam asked Austin. "Which was your favorite?"

"That one." He pointed to *The Everything Kids' Science Experiments Book.* "I'm gonna be a scientist when I grow up."

Sam picked up the two books and studied them, front and back. "That's strange. I've never seen these two books before. They must have fallen out of Santa's sleigh. You'd better take them with you. If Santa comes back looking for them, he'll never find them in the middle of all my books."

Amy's eyes filled with tears. Sam's responded in kind.

As Amy slipped on her coat, she paused, a contemplative look on her face. "There is one thing you could do for me, but I know it's a lot to ask."

"Ask away."

"I'll be visiting Duane on Tuesday afternoon. It's so hard to see him in that awful place. And the judge won't allow bail for a murder charge. He's stuck in there for God knows how long." Her tears began in earnest. "Would you consider going with me, a little moral support?"

"When do you want to pick me up?"

She let out her breath as if she'd been holding it. "Thank you so much. Leaving at twelve-thirty will put us there by one when the afternoon visiting hours start. At three o'clock, they'll kick us out, so I'll have you back here by three-thirty."

"No problem. Glad to do it."

White lie. As the thought of entering Richmond's overcrowded hell-hole of a jail sank in, Sam was scared shitless.

****

On Monday, when Sam retrieved her turkey sandwich from the fridge in the shop's office, Mom said, "Wait. I need to talk with you."

One look at her fidgeting with a stack of envelopes on her desk, and Sam's anxiety level jumped. "What's up?"

"Squire Mardigan's secretary called. She said I have to meet with him tomorrow at four-thirty, but she wouldn't tell me why. I don't like that man. I asked if you could go instead, and she said no, but we both could go. Will you go with me? Please?" Mom's hands trembled.

Sam wasn't sure she'd ever find being her mother's protector a comfortable role. It was supposed to be the other way around. Well, if she could weather a visit to the Richmond City Jail, dealing with Mardigan again should be a piece of cake.

"Of course I will. Maybe it's good news. He could have found a way for you to keep your house."

She caught Mom actually looking at her, probably trying to read if she was telling the truth. Good thing she'd never been able to do that.

****

Business had slowed to a crawl by Tuesday, so Sam didn't feel too guilty leaving Mariah alone all afternoon to handle customers. At the café next door, Sam bought her a slice of their amazing pecan pie for a little snack and an apology for imposing yet again on her easygoing nature.

"After Amy's visit, I've not stopped thinking about Duane," Sam said. "Stewing in jail while Amy is struggling to hold things together for their boys must be tearing him up. I dread going into that place, but no way could I turn her down when she asked me to go."

"Have you ever been inside a jail?" asked Mariah. "Sounds creepy to me."

"Not as awful as it must be for Duane. Did you see the *Times-Dispatch* features a couple of years back about conditions there? They cram 1,600 inmates into a facility designed for about half of that. A barracks-style room built for fifty men holds a hundred and fifty at times, so some unlucky ones are forced to sleep on the floor. A major bummer for an innocent man."

"Are you sure he didn't do it? I don't know him like you do, but the police have found all three biggies: motive, means, and opportunity."

"No one ever knows exactly what goes on inside another person's head. I'm not a hundred percent sold, but I'd give it ninety-nine. I hope I get a reason to push it to a hundred when I see him face-to-face."

Amy arrived fifteen minutes early. Sam wasn't as anxious to get there as Amy apparently was, but she sucked it up and put on her coat.

Walking into the jail didn't confirm Sam's worst fears. It replaced fear with revulsion. The echoes of heavy doors clanking shut somewhere, the rigid industrial look, the smell, the cold faces of those who worked there and those who couldn't leave—all had a hard edge. Amy gave a guard Duane's name, he scrutinized their IDs, and then they waited.

With each passing minute, Sam's hands became colder and colder. After twenty minutes, they were shown to a cubicle in the visitors' room, near the middle of a line of other cubicles. Low voices melded into white noise.

Duane slouched on the other side of the glass. His face looked pinched, all sharp angles as if he'd taken on the hardness of the place already. Like a burned-out bulb, the light had gone out of his pale blue eyes. As soon as he caught sight of Sam sitting down beside his wife, he shook his head.

"Hi, Sam. What brings you here this fine day?" His tone dripped with sarcasm, almost anger.

"Duane!" said Amy, the air going out of her like a pricked balloon.

"That's a heck of a way to greet me," Sam said. "Are you this welcoming to all your visitors?"

"*All* my visitors?" He locked his gaze on her. "You must be referring to the S.O.B. representing me. He's been here a grand total of two times—once to introduce himself and hear what I had to say, then once to see if I wanted him to work toward a plea deal to spare my life."

Sam was tempted to leave, but she imagined being caged with criminals might have nasty effects on the best of folks. "Cut the crap, Duane. Take a good look through the glass. Right now, you could be glaring at one hundred percent of the people who believe you're innocent."

His shoulders drooped, and the tough demeanor crumbled. "Sorry… How could one man destroy me so completely from both sides of the grave? He took my money, my house. Now he's after my life." He slumped back, deflated.

"Money? Yes. House? No, that will be repaired. And life? Let me help you fight that one."

As soon as the words fell out of Sam's mouth, it felt like she'd stepped into quicksand. She was neither a lawyer nor a P.I. It wasn't like a shop full of paperbacks could give her an instant education. But she couldn't let Duane rot in jail while the real murderer roamed free. Might as well start at the obvious spot—the beginning.

"Tell me what happened at Someplace Else that night."

"When I walked in, Al was at the bar, sipping his whiskey and chatting up the bartender, hooting like it was the comedy hour. That snarky laugh of Al's pissed me off. So I asked him, 'What do you have to laugh about— the arson charge for torching my place? It won't be so funny when you get a horny cellmate unless you're into that sort of thing.' He told me to fuck off, that having his ex-wife call to gloat was enough for one day."

"Clair called him?" Sam couldn't envision that happening. Her mom hated using the phone, even to speak with her sister.

"Must have. He only has one ex."

"He'd never mentioned someone named Gail?"

"Who's Gail?"

"Wife number one. From Connecticut." She gave him a brief rundown of what she'd learned from Aunt Patrice.

"Son of a bitch. Just like on our poker nights—no tells. Anyway, I offered to rearrange his face some more,

174

and he broke the neck off a beer bottle and gashed my hand. I grabbed another bottle to defend myself and who should jump between us but that asshole he worked for, Mardigan. He played it all high and mighty like he always does. Called us *boys* and told us to go home before the cops came. I saw the bartender behind Al, talking low on his phone, and decided leaving might be a good idea. But Al wasn't buying it, so Mardigan grabbed his wrist and smashed it into the bar, knocking the broken bottle out of his hand, slicing Al's thumb in the process. At least Mardigan evened the score for me; we were both bleeding like stuck pigs. He told me to clear out, handed Al the rest of his whiskey, ordered him to drink up and do the same."

"Did that put an end to it?"

"Yeah. When I pulled out, Al was unlocking his car. I should have gone to the ER to get my hand sewn up, but I didn't need the bill. And I didn't want to face you, Amy—you'd already chewed me out for breaking Al's nose—so I drove around half the night until I knew you'd be sound asleep. There's not a soul who can vouch for me. I'm totally screwed."

Not much to work on. Where could she go from here?

"I don't know what I can do, aside from finding you a better lawyer or something."

"Don't bother. I can hardly afford my cheap one. Better try for the 'or something' part."

"I'll be in touch. There must be a way out of this." Sam hoped her words sounded more confident to Duane than they felt to her.

"Not that I can see." He cast a pained look at Amy.

"Well, let me give you two some private time. Your wife didn't bring me here so I could hog the

175

conversation."

Sam found a seat at the edge of the room and spent the next hour and three quarters with her nose buried in a mystery. Maybe she could glean some tips from another sleuth. If only this case could be solved as neatly as the fictional one.

"Time's up," announced a guard.

The mics shut off, interrupting goodbyes mid-sentence.

Though the ride home covered the same miles as earlier, the trip passed twice as fast without anticipatory dread dragging out the sense of time. Amy dropped Sam off at the shop, where she spent a half-hour bringing Mom and Mariah up to speed.

Leaving Mariah alone to cover the shop yet again, she drove Mom to Ashland Community Bank. When they entered Mardigan's office, Sam couldn't stop herself from stealing glances at his desk and carpet, checking for overlooked droplets of blood. None found.

"Come in, come in. Make yourselves comfortable." It sounded like a canned script. "I'll give you the disappointing news first."

When he looked toward Clair, Sam laid a cautionary hand on her lap. *Don't rock.*

"I was hoping we might be able to offer you a loan modification and waive some of the penalties, but I hit a roadblock. When the clerk tried to pull your file, he couldn't find it. The paperwork on your home equity loan seems to be missing. We have digital records, of course, but we'd need all the originals before we could proceed with anything."

Why weren't digital records enough? And what kind of financial institution loses its files? "Did the clerk look in offsite storage?"

"That was the first place he looked. We only keep the previous two years of records here. And before you ask, yes, he checked here, too. Your file may be with a few others we've not been able to locate—probably misfiled." He sped through the last two words as if he didn't like the way they tasted.

"However, putting that issue aside for the moment, I do have some news you'll like to hear." A Cheshire cat grin spread over his face, exposing a mouthful of perfectly aligned white teeth. "I don't know if you realized it, Clair, but Al had a term life insurance policy as an employee benefit, paid up through the end of this month. And you are the sole beneficiary." He sat back, folding his hands in his lap, waiting for the news to sink in.

Sam was incredulous, to say the least. "Mom, did you know about this?"

"Yes. I saw it on his W-2 when I gathered our papers for tax time. Because of the high amount of the policy, part of its cost was considered taxable income. It doesn't matter now. We weren't married when he died."

Mardigan folded his hands and leaned forward on his desk. "Apparently, he didn't change the beneficiary after the divorce. Maybe he forgot about it, or he could have planned to change it to Elena after their wedding. But all this speculation is moot. The fact is, Clair, you will be receiving a check from the insurance company for…one hundred and twenty thousand dollars."

"When?"

"The executor of his estate will need to send the company a death certificate. Then it's up to their standard procedures. I don't know what they do in the case of murder; it may take longer than usual."

"Will it come in time to save my house?"

"It might. You'll have to wait and see. If we could find the original loan paperwork, it could give us more options. I don't like talking ill of the dead, but before I fired him, I suspected Al might have taken the files for some reason… Well, to be honest, I did more than suspect him. I accused him of it."

The nasty scene in this very office flashed through Sam's mind. "So that's what you were arguing about when I came in to confront Al. I knew there was more to it than the news about Madoff. What did he say?"

"You heard the man yourself. He said he didn't have the files. He said they'd been burned."

"Did he mean in our house fire?"

Mardigan crossed his arms. "I've said too much already. This is an internal matter. However, if you happen to come across any of our files, please return them to the bank. You can send them to my attention. It could save your house, Clair."

On the drive back to the shop, Sam's emotions were in turmoil. The insurance money could rescue her mom's house, and then some. Did Al really steal the files? Why?

Mom broke into Sam's thoughts. "Al stole those files. They didn't burn."

"What?"

"That must be what was in the boxes by my front door. Al carted them away right before the fire. Remember? We saw an even layer of soot everywhere, including where those two boxes had been. If the boxes were removed after the fire, there would have been clean spots under where they'd sat."

"Why would he take files of old loan paperwork?"

"I have no idea why people are dishonest."

"Well, even if Al's insurance payout doesn't arrive in time to save your house, you'll have a great start on rebuilding your savings."

"Yes, there's that." The corners of Mom's lips curled up into a rare smile.

Usually, Sam welcomed the sight of those smiles, but this one looked devious. The vibes from her upturned lips didn't match her expressionless eyes. If she didn't know better, she'd suspect her mom had had a hand in Al's death.

No wonder Truitt and Patillo reacted to her the way they did.

Though Sam now knew her quirky reactions were typical of someone with Asperger's, she wondered if her mother neglected to tell her something important.

She never lied, but she also didn't volunteer unrequested information.

Unless it had to do with plants, of course.

Chapter 15

That night, as Sam stretched her legs out on the sofa and reached for a book, her phone rang. She brightened when she saw the caller ID: Ryan Bennett.

"Hi, Sam. Do you have any plans for tomorrow night? You know, New Year's Eve?"

"What do you have in mind?"

"I was planning to go out with the guys, but that fell through. I wondered if you'd like to come over tomorrow night, watch the Times Square thing on TV, and ring in the New Year."

Shades of his last-minute invitation to their senior prom. "Do I understand you correctly? I'm your backup plan? For New Year's Eve?"

"I didn't mean it like that. It's just that I thought you might be free and—"

"Open mouth, insert foot. Now you're assuming no one else has invited me to a New Year's celebration." Did he think she was still so unpopular? Admittedly, her social circle was rather small—okay, tiny—but that's fine with an introvert.

"This isn't going to happen, is it?"

"Nope." She hung up. *Now, why did I have to do that? Stupid. Stupid. Stupid.* What was it about Ryan that triggered her senseless defenses?

****

On New Year's Eve, Sam wondered why she'd

bothered to open the shop at all. Randolph-Macon students had fled the campus for the holidays, and Ashland residents must have been cruising the malls for big end-of-year discounts. Mom stayed home to cook the traditional turkey noodle soup simmered with the bones from the Christmas bird. Sam let Mariah go before lunch, so she could take off early for Fredericksburg to visit her uncle and his family.

At three o'clock, after a half-hour of no customers, Sam posted "Happy New Year! Hope to see you on January 2nd" and locked the door.

The aroma of the soup at Mom's place was so tantalizing that Sam convinced her an early dinner was justified. Afterward, Mom contented herself spending the rest of the day and evening alone, reading the new gardening books she'd received as gifts.

Sam contemplated going to a movie, but there wasn't a single one that appealed. If she hadn't let her pride rear its vile head, she'd be seeing out a miserable old year by opening the door to new possibilities. *Too late now.* The best she could do toward preparing for a fresh year was to vacuum and dust her house. As she took out the canister vac, she chuckled to herself. *Once a year, whether it needs it or not.* Somewhat of an exaggeration, but not far from the truth. She'd even posted a sign on her living room wall: "Please don't write in the dust. That's my job."

If she'd been into noisemakers and silly hats, there were plenty of cafés and sports bars where Sam could get lost in a like-minded crowd, but that had never been her thing. Imbibing any amount of alcohol was a lost cause. Even one glass of wine could send her to the nearest sofa for a nap. Some party animal. She preferred to build a roaring fire and watch the flames dwindle to neon embers while sipping one or two root beer floats. Not an option now, given her current gas-log fireplace.

The image of glowing embers segued to house fires, then to Al and the news clip showing the garish neon sign for Someplace Else and the bartender's interview. Someplace Else would be rocking tonight. Duane? No celebrations there. She had to do something to give him a thread of hope. Maybe the bartender could fill in another detail or two. Surely the whole staff would be there tonight.

As Sam pulled past their parking lot, she saw she was right. The nearest available parking space was a block down the street. A biting wind made the short walk miserable, but once inside, the heat of so many bodies forced her to shrug off her coat. Every barstool was taken. Patrons stood several deep, pressing toward the bar. The cacophony of voices, blaring music, and flashing white lights on a big ball hanging from the ceiling set her head to throbbing. From the rope-and-pulley apparatus strung from the ball to the bar, the intention was clear—a mini Times Square countdown would play out at midnight.

It took her ten minutes to wedge her way to the front, where she could finally see three bartenders hustling to keep up with orders. And one of them was the same pudgy man Sam had seen on TV. She couldn't remember his name until the guy next to her called out, "Hey, George, over here." That was it—George Speers.

After drawing a beer for the fellow beside her, the bartender asked, "What can I get to put you in a party mood, little lady?"

Sam resented the "little lady" bit but played along. "A screwdriver, please." At least she'd get her quota of vitamin C. While he mixed it, she asked, "Say, didn't I see you on TV about a week ago? You're George Speers, right?"

"Yup. That's me. Filmed me from my good side, don't ya think?" He posed for a side shot, which only served to emphasize his prodigious paunch. "Here you go. That'll be five bucks, or you can run a tab. What'll it be?"

"I'll pay now," she said, laying six dollars on the table, "and I'd like to hear more about that wild fight you saw."

"Sorry, little lady, time is money, especially tonight," he said, looking down the bar.

"Will this help?" Sam slipped out a ten and laid it beside the six. He looked at it, pensive, expectant. She dug behind a flap in her wallet and pulled out her emergency twenty. This was a lot more awkward than it looked in the movies.

"What would you like to know?" He grinned and pocketed the thirty bucks, leaving six by her napkin.

"You mentioned that another regular broke up the fight. Do you know his name?"

"Sure. Mardigan, the dude who thinks he's a squire."

"Had Al been with Mardigan before Duane came in?"

"How should I know? Do you realize how busy we are on Saturday nights?"

"What happened after Duane went out the door?"

"Like I said, Al left, too."

"Right away?"

"Yeah, he drank up, making like he was gonna take his time, but rushed out the door when he heard a siren in the distance. I'd faked calling the police, and wouldn't you know it, a siren went off anyway. He took off so fast he didn't even wait for his change. I felt bad about that, but it doesn't matter now, does it?"

"How much did he leave?"

He leaned closer, lowering his voice. "A fresh Franklin. Hell of a tip."

"A hundred, wow!"

A group at the far end of the bar started belting out "Auld Lang Syne." To make sure the man only two feet away could hear her, Sam had to shout her next question.

"Did you tell all this to the police?"

"Of course, exactly what I told that reporter on TV, every bit."

"I didn't hear you say anything about that tip."

"What? You think I'm nuts? I've got a family to feed." He cast a glance at Sam's measly dollar tip for the drink, then a pleading one at her.

"Sorry, I have EWS."

"What's that? Hope it's not contagious."

"Empty Wallet Syndrome."

His belly jiggled as he laughed. "In that case, soon as you drink up, get outta here before you infect the others."

The wind was just as chilling on the way back to her car, but it didn't feel so bad. Sam's spirits were buoyed by the hunch that she'd learned something useful. It was either that or the alcohol. Regardless, what was Al—flat broke and jobless Al—doing with nothing smaller than a hundred-dollar bill?

The huge ball must have dropped in Times Square, but Sam didn't see it. Ten minutes after turning on her TV, she drifted asleep on the sofa. Her tolerance for alcohol was nil. The main benefit was she rarely consumed enough to bring on a hangover.

As the first rays of 2009 streamed through Sam's

living room window, she stretched. Before opening her eyes, she tried to grab hold of a fading dream, but it leaked through her fingers like water. Something about her mom and red lights—or was it fire—and Ryan running toward her with little Phoenix trailing behind. Whatever it was, she was glad that not all dreams come true.

She started coffee brewing, then made a beeline for her toothbrush. Somehow her teeth had grown icky fuzz overnight. Next, she exchanged last night's sparkly silver sweater and black slacks, now well wrinkled, for maroon sweatpants and an oversized sweatshirt from San Francisco. Its graphic of cars snaking through hairpin turns down Lombard Street mirrored her life lately, twisty and steeply descending.

While waiting for the Rose Parade to begin on TV, she read the paper. Those creative floats always fascinated her, all the more so because when she was a child, Mom had never let her watch the parade. It's criminal to raise all those magnificent flowers just to kill them, Mom had ranted.

As she rose for a second cup of coffee, the doorbell rang. Mariah never used the doorbell, and her mom came by the path to the back door. That left Ryan. Sam looked in the mirror over the hall table. Well, coming by on no notice, he'd have to take what he got—a woman in sweats and disheveled hair, and bags under the eyes, to boot. Maybe she'd look to him like a morning-after party girl. *No, don't go overboard again, you idiot.* She ran fingers through her curls to coax them into some semblance of order.

She opened the door. No one there, but on her doorstep sat a dish garden overflowing with an artistic mix of shiny green foliage accented by a plant with showy leaves. Deep veining textured each symmetrical leaf into a pattern, like feathers laid edge to edge. Silvery stripes cupped each side of the central dusky green vein. She brought the dish inside and set it on the kitchen counter.

The card, stuck on a little plastic stick, read:

Sam, can I please take a make-up test, since I failed the pop quiz? Ask your mom about the variety of pilea known as panamiga. Wishing you a Happy New Year, Ryan (and Phoenix)

A golden opportunity to use the Mom Phone. Sam lifted the receiver, turned the crank, and waited.

"Please use your cell, Samara. The bells on this thing are loud enough to wake Zena. And I think she's going deaf."

"These old phones just seem so appropriate. I'm not calling from my playhouse for an umbrella, but I could use your help. Ryan sent me a dish garden with a plant I've never seen before. He wrote on the tag that it's *pilea*, also called panamiga, and that—"

"Of course, the genus *Pilea* is the largest in the nettle family. The species *involucrata* is referred to as 'panamiga' in Central and South America, where it usually grows. If he already identified it on the tag, what's your question?"

"I don't really have a question, but he wrote that I should ask you about it."

"Maybe so you won't neglect the plant to death like you often do. Panamiga loves a moist environment, so keep it well-watered and spritz it lightly with a mister every day because the air in your house is so dry in the winter. Why did he give you a dish garden?"

"Well, at the last minute, he asked me over for New Year's Eve." How could Sam put this without betraying her idiotic behavior? "I'd already made other plans, so I turned him down. And this morning, the dish was delivered to my doorstep."

All went quiet on the other end. Just as Sam suspected the connection had somehow broken, she heard her mom laughing. "For once, I see symbolism. He's saying he wants to be your friend."

"I don't get it."

"You would if you knew that panamiga is commonly called the friendship plant. Don't forget to bring me the Sunday paper when you're done with it. Bye."

Every time Sam had slammed the door in Ryan's face, he'd reopened it. She felt flattered; he must think she was worth all the trouble in spite of her renewing their former acquaintance by nearly causing his rapid demise. Then she'd given him so much grief when he was just kidding around after the lost watch ploy. Though he wasn't Kyle—nobody could ever be Kyle—Ryan was a rather enticing example of a living, breathing man. A man interested in her. A new year called for a resolution:

Be nice to the man. Don't have a hissy fit when he puts his foot in his mouth. Make it up to him when you do flip out.

No time like the present to start. She picked up her cell.

"Hey, Ryan, thanks for the beautiful dish garden. You didn't have to do that. I was the one acting like a dufus."

"No, I should have asked you at least a week earlier. Planning is not my strong suit."

"How about we call it a draw? Would you like to

come over to watch the Bowl games?" Sam hated football. *Ah, the sacrifices one makes to keep New Year's resolutions.*

"That sounds terrific, but I have a better idea. If we hang out over here, you can get in some quality time with Phoenix."

"Fine. I'll bring pita chips and hummus. Is one o'clock okay?"

"Sure. See you then."

Her first resolution was working so well that she considered making more but decided not to press her luck.

****

When Ryan opened his door, Phoenix dashed out, yipping, wagging, and jumping all over Sam's feet. Dribbles of pee dotted the concrete. Ryan swiftly picked him up and deposited him on the grass. Phoenix did his thing, then resumed his dance around Sam. She had to carry him inside to keep from stepping on his paws.

"I think he's missed me, but he sure hasn't missed any meals."

"Right on both counts. And if he grows into those big paws, I'm going to have a lot of dog on my hands."

When they sat on the sofa, Phoenix tried to jump up but couldn't quite make it, so Sam boosted him. He bounced from one of them to the other and back, licking and nuzzling, then plopped down between them and rolled over for a tummy rub. They both reached for him.

"This pup chose a prime spot, where he gets double the attention," Sam said. "I'll take under the chin, and you can have the tummy."

While Ryan was absorbed in the game, Sam's gaze wandered around the room, noting clues to the man he'd become.

Furniture from Early Attic Period. Practical or short on cash.

No diplomas displayed. Not pretentious.

No ashtrays, so no smoke smell, either. Non-smoker.

Lots of well-used books. Avid reader.

Desktop orderly. Neat.

All trash in wastebasket. Better aim than hers.

Computer with mega LCD monitor. Techie or visually challenged.

Crumb-covered plate on table. Not obsessive about neatness.

During TV commercials and timeouts, she steered the conversation toward Duane's predicament, her visit to the jail, and the few bits of info she'd gathered. She asked if he had any suggestions for how she could help Duane.

"Don't you think you should leave all this to the police?" Ryan asked.

"Haven't you been listening? Now that Duane's in jail, the only thing they're looking for is more evidence against him."

He shrugged. "No ideas here, unless you want to investigate the others who hated Al: you, your mom, and your aunt."

"There have to be other suspects. I just have to find them," she declared.

"And how do you do that?"

"Okay, Mr. Skeptical. For your information, I already have one in mind: Gail Hobson."

"Touchdown," he shouted, throwing his arms in the air.

Phoenix saw it as a game and began jumping after the waving arm-toys.

189

"I thought you were listening to me," she grumbled.

"I was *listening* to you and *watching* the game. Multitasking. So tell me, what makes you suspect Gail? See, I've been paying attention."

When Sam brought up her visit to the bar, he interrupted. "You know, that place down on Route 1 was a favorite of mine and my buddies when we were underage. When my parents asked where I was going on Saturday nights, I'd tell them, 'Just Someplace Else. Don't worry; I can take care of myself.' No lies needed. Then the bar killed our fun and probably half their business when they replaced their little hand-painted sign with that neon one, big enough for all the world to see."

Sam snatched the remote and muted. "Focus on this: at the jail, when Duane talked about arriving at the bar, he told me Al greeted him with a few choice words and then added that he'd already put up with enough for one day. His ex-wife had called to gloat, too."

"Why would your mom phone Al?"

"She wouldn't. It must have been Gail, his first wife. And Duane didn't recognize Gail's name when I mentioned it. Al had never told him about her."

"That's pretty thin. Not much suspicious there."

"Before Patrice contacted her, she hadn't been in touch with him for years. She hadn't even known where he'd disappeared to after their divorce. All I'm saying is that the phone call shows she's still pissed at him."

"Sorry, but going from being pissed at an ex to committing murder is a bit of a leap. Any other ideas?"

"Here's where my new friend George, the bartender, comes in. He confirmed what Duane told me about the fight. But George neglected to tell the police one part of the story. He said Al was in such a hurry to leave that when he paid his tab, he didn't wait for his change. He paid with a one-hundred-dollar bill."

"Now there's something worth looking into."

"That's what I thought. If Al were as broke as he claimed, I'm guessing he'd just come into a pile of cash. How would that happen to a penniless banker who's jobless?"

"Blackmail?"

"If it was, I'll bet Al was great at hiding the goods. At the Iron Horse, he accused Aunt Patrice of ransacking his place before Thanksgiving. Maybe the blackmail victim was looking for the damning evidence. Now that I think of it, the victim might have searched our shop and Mom's apartment for the same reason. Since Al had been a big part of Mom's life for two years, the person might think Al had stashed it with her."

"Wait a minute. You never told me about someone searching your shop and the apartment."

Sam filled in the gaps.

"This puts the whole picture in a different light. You must go to the police with this. If you're right, you're already on this person's radar. If you do too much snooping around, it could put you in the crosshairs." He covered her hand, still holding the remote, with his. "Please tell me you're not going to be stupid about this."

The gentleness of his touch sent a warm ripple through her.

"Okay…I don't trust them to follow through, but I'll tell them."

He snatched back the remote, rested her hand on Phoenix's head, and unmuted the TV. "Do that. I'd hate to lose you before I even get the chance to ask you for a date."

"This doesn't qualify as a date?" she asked, dipping a pita chip into the hummus.

"You called me, remember?"

Chapter 16

Every crime show on the planet said a murderer couldn't resist showing up for his victim's funeral, so Sam figured she had nothing to lose but a couple of hours in the bookshop by seeing who appeared for Al's big day.

She didn't bother asking Mom to go. No sense even broaching the subject of Al; Sam told her mother she was getting an oil change for her car. Mom questioned why she was wearing good black pants instead of jeans to a filthy auto shop. After Sam claimed all her jeans were in the laundry hamper, Mariah backed her up, pointing out the wise choice: black doesn't show grime.

"All right, you two," Mom said. "You can stop with the lies. You know these walls are thin. And I know you're going to Al's funeral. Why didn't you just tell me the truth?"

Sam's face heated up. "I didn't want to even mention his name to you. I know how much any thoughts of Al upset you."

"There you go protecting me again. Did it ever occur to you that I might think it proper for me to go? After all, I was married to the man. I certainly don't love him now, but once, I thought I did. I should pay my respects to the dead." Mom pressed her lips into a thin line.

"Sorry, but that's the last way I thought you'd see it." Her mom never ceased surprising her. "Mariah, will you be okay here by yourself?"

"Sure. Clair, I'm sorry to have covered for Sam, but my thinking was the same as hers." Mariah took Mom's coat from the hook and held it out. "Here, let me help you."

No memorial service preceded the graveside ceremony. Sam drove them directly to Woodland Cemetery, which dated back to Civil War days when Ashland served as a hospital center for the Confederacy. A fitting place to lay a Connecticut Yankee to rest? He was about to become a Northern peg planted in a Southern hole.

They arrived twenty-five minutes early, giving Sam plenty of time to study folks as they straggled in. Elena came alone, followed by two cars full of bank employees, then Mardigan and his wife, three guys Sam remembered from Al's poker nights, and two couples she didn't recognize. Oh yes, there was Detective Patillo. Maybe he thought there was truth behind those TV scripts, too. She certainly hoped he wouldn't note that her mom was here. Then again, maybe Sam shouldn't have come, either.

Five minutes before eleven, a black limo pulled up. The chauffeur stepped out, opened the back door, and stood at attention. Everyone at the graveside halted conversations and craned necks to watch the unexpected spectacle. Anticipation built for a full minute. At last, an elderly gentleman emerged. His shoulders stooped, but he strode confidently toward the gathering and seated himself on a folding chair to Elena's right. From Sam's place standing behind the group of about twenty, most of what she saw was the back of his full head of impeccably groomed white hair.

He pivoted slightly toward Elena, said a few words, and shook her hand. Introducing himself? That couldn't be her father. Was it Al's dad, the ballyhooed judge? Mardigan, who'd taken seats on Elena's left for himself and his wife, leaned forward and appeared to say something to the newcomer. Aside from glancing Mardigan's way, he made no response.

Reverend Quarles, Randolph-Macon's chaplain, conducted the simple service: low on substance where Al's life was concerned, high on the standard "dust to dust," and over before nippy January air froze Sam's toes. He'd probably never met the man.

Their obligation to the departed complete, most folks moved more quickly when leaving than when arriving. After Mardigan gave Elena a comforting hug and then escorted his wife to their car, Sam approached dry-eyed Elena and offered condolences. Clair hung back, watching.

The white-haired stranger was writing a check. When he ripped it out of his leather-covered checkbook and handed it to Elena, Sam noted his black pen's cap was crowned with a distinctive snowy white star—the trademark of the epitome of pricey pens. He tucked away both pen and checkbook, then turned to go, nearly bumping into Sam.

She made good use of the moment to introduce herself, omitting her former relationship to Al.

"I'm Michael Hobson, the deceased's father."

Elena picked up a small piece of paper from the ground, cast one last look at the open grave, then at Sam and Mr. Hobson, and walked away without a word.

"I'm sorry for your loss, Mr. Hobson. It must be difficult to see your son pass away before you."

"No son of mine," he said with a *humph*. "We adopted him at age five after my brother and his wife died. From the outset, he never measured up. We gave him everything, even the same Exeter education we provided for our own son. Then he disgraced us by dodging the draft." He glared at the grave and spat. "You'll find my real son's name on the Vietnam Memorial in D.C. As far as I'm concerned, Albert died the day he snuck his cowardly butt over the border into Canada."

"If you feel that way, why did you go to the trouble of coming here?"

"Who do you think paid for this plot and the marker that will be cut? I believe in dealing face-to-face on important matters. Can't allow a half-assed job with *any* stone bearing the respected name of Hobson, even if the man never lived up to it. Besides, how would the media play it if word leaked out that I hadn't attended his funeral?" He frowned at his watch. "I've got a plane to catch." No goodbye. He simply left.

Sam felt a desperate need to walk over to her dad's gravesite, a mere dozen yards away. Taking off her right glove, she traced the words "Loving Husband and Father" with her index finger. No one gets to choose their fathers, but she'd definitely won in the luck of the draw. Al had lost big time.

"Dad was a good man through and through." Sam glanced over her shoulder. Her mom stood there, rocking gently.

****

"I want to see the place Al died," Clair stated. She didn't know why, but she needed to see. "Less than an hour has ticked by since we left the shop. As long as Mariah is covering, let's make the most of it. Drive to Richmond."

"I've wondered about that, too, Mom."

Huguenot Bridge, spanning a half-mile of river and lowland, connected Richmond's upscale West End to like neighborhoods south of the James River. Twenty-five thousand cars and trucks rattled over the bridge's potholes and patches every day. With one lane each way, no shoulder, and a narrow sidewalk on each side, there was no place to stop without blocking a lane. Samara drove to the south end, parked on the off-ramp's gravel shoulder, and they trudged back to the middle of the bridge. January's freezing wind pierced every layer Clair had bundled in.

They stood in that mid-way spot, silently studying the frigid river for five minutes. From their vantage forty feet above the shallow river, it was almost impossible to spot any sign of the city, upstream or down. Trees and twiggy brush lined both banks, obscuring the steep rises on each side. Lovely homes perched far above any risk of floodwater, but she could barely see a one. The natural beauty of Richmond's oft-ignored gem of a river never failed to instill a gentle peace in her soul...until today. This time she saw it as a weapon.

After midnight, about the time of the murder, traffic would have been sparse but not nil. With a heavily drugged victim barely able to walk, or unconscious, the killer couldn't have parked a quarter-mile away, where Samara had. In a move that was either bold or foolhardy, he must have risked stopping here for at least several minutes to lug Al out of the car and maneuver him over the high railing.

"How could one person have hoisted Al over that railing? It's up to my shoulder."

"Whoever it was must have been mighty strong. Al

was over two hundred pounds, wasn't he?"

"Yes. It would have been a lot easier if the murderer had help."

"You know, the police never did release the actual cause of death," Samara said. "If the fall from this height didn't immediately kill Al, I couldn't guess which would have sealed the deal first, hypothermia or drowning. Maybe Al was too wasted from drug-laced alcohol to suffer. I hope that was the case. Any man who'd been raised in such a miserable family shouldn't have to come to his end in agony, too."

"Any time I start thinking my parents were too tough on me," Clair said, "I'll remember Al's father. At least my parents told me, again and again, they loved me. No matter how frustrated they were by my behavior, they never gave up on me."

They hustled back to the car, then drove down the off-ramp to Riverside Drive and turned east, downstream.

At first, the dense forest of Huguenot Flatwater Park blocked all view of the river, but after a quarter-mile, only a narrow grassy strip separated the road from the south bank. In clear view from the road, Clair spotted an island a third of the way across the river, just as the newspaper had described. The point at the skinny island's head had collected a huge pile of logs and brush washed downstream in floods.

"Do you think Al's is the first body that island has snagged?"

****

That evening Sam cranked up her laptop and sifted cyberspace for background on Al's bastard of a dad. Sure enough, Michael Hobson proved to be a prominent lawyer turned appellate court judge. Not only that, but one article claimed he was short-listed to fill a vacancy on the Connecticut Supreme Court. She couldn't believe it, Al's father, a real high muckety-muck. For once, Al had spoken the truth. Still, his dad seemed to be a prime example of the arrogant lawyer everyone loves to hate, reminding her of an old joke. What do you have when you've buried a dozen lawyers up to their necks in sand? Not nearly enough sand.

The promise of a new year was supposed to inspire fresh starts, yet Sam found this impossible when weighed down by last year's unpacked baggage. Her days in the shop allowed her to immerse herself in the one place she'd always felt secure, but nights brought out the demons. Images of prisons, fires, ransacked rooms, bloody fights, and bodies in the James wrangled their way into her dreams.

Monday morning made things worse. A little bomb dropped. Richmond Police phoned, asking Sam and Clair to come in for more questioning. Another day asking Mariah to cover everything. Another time having to defend Mom. Sometimes life reeked. The only upside was Sam would have the chance to pass on the info she'd gathered like she'd promised Ryan.

Today Detective Patillo questioned them together. Much better, Sam thought at first.

"It has come to my attention, Mrs. Hobson, that you will be receiving the death benefit from Albert Hobson's life insurance. Is that correct?"

"Yes," she answered with her strange half-smile.

"And you were aware that he had this policy?"

"Yes." She sat stock-still, hands clasped in her lap.

"That money will improve your finances in a big way, won't it?" Patillo matched her expression.

"Yes, of course."

"You found a quick way to get that money, right?"

"It might not be quick, but I expect it won't be too long," Mom said.

Sam jumped in. "I see where you're leading, Detective Patillo, but—"

Patillo held up his hand. "Was your daughter always this impatient to have her turn when she was a child, Mrs. Hobson?"

"Yes, she was."

The two of them made Sam feel like an impertinent kid at a grownups' party. Patillo didn't even bother to look at her before continuing the conversation.

"The insurance money will help balance the scales of justice. He lost your money and jeopardized your house. Now it's only right that you should recover what was lost. Don't you think so?"

"Yes. What he did wasn't right, and now he's paid for it." She smiled again.

"And you made him pay, didn't you?"

Sam reached for her mom's hand but drew it back after a sharp look from her. "Don't answer that. He's trying to make you say—"

"Answer the question, Mrs. Hobson."

"He's not paying me. The insurance company will pay me $120,000," she said, still smiling.

"I can see you're quite pleased with that, aren't you?"

"Yes." Mom sat straight and motionless, gaze downcast, but answering without hesitation.

"And you conspired to kill him to get that money, right?"

"No, he died in the river."

"Oh, so the river killed him? Did you just push him

in?"

"Which part do you want me to answer?"

"The whole thing. You pushed him in, and the river killed him, correct?"

"That's two things. They have different answers. No, I never pushed him anywhere, and yes, the river killed him."

This time Sam smiled. Her mom seemed to be handling the situation quite well. *Thank goodness for her precision.*

Now Patillo turned to Sam. "Oh, this amuses you, Ms. McNeer. Do you enjoy getting away with murder?"

"The only person getting away with murder right now is the real killer because you've got it all wrong, Detective."

"This is how I see it. You and your mother and Chanesky and maybe even your aunt figured out a way to make Hobson reimburse you for the lost investments. What was Chanesky's cut for doing the dirty work?"

"Wrong. All wrong." Sam shook her head.

"And I suppose you'll tell me you have a better answer." He flicked an invisible speck off the table.

"I don't have the final answer, but at least I've been asking a few of the right questions."

"Were you getting your stories straight when you visited Chanesky in jail?"

"Instead of questions based on nothing but conjecture, ask a few based on facts for a change. Why don't you ask Gail Hobson why she phoned Al the day he died? Why don't you find out where dead-broke Al came across the hundred-dollar bill he paid his bar tab with?"

Patillo's brows twitched. At last, a trace of reaction.

"Why have there been three break-ins at Al's place,

our shop, and my mom's apartment?"

For the first time since this circus started, Patillo fell silent. He scratched a few notes. "Have you been withholding evidence?"

"No, just waiting for the chance to give it to you. You've been doing most of the talking."

"Chanesky already told us that Clair phoned to harass Mr. Hobson that day." His grin turned into a smirk. "You're disputing the man you're telling me is innocent?"

"When Al said in the bar that someone called to gloat, he didn't use a name. He said, 'ex-wife.' Duane heard this and assumed it was Clair. He didn't know a thing about Al's first wife."

Patillo no longer smiled. "Where did you hear about a hundred-dollar bill?"

"From George Speers, the bartender at Someplace Else."

"What are you doing questioning these people?"

"Simply trying to find the truth."

"That's my job, not yours." Patillo stood, towering over his desk, and motioned them toward the door. "That'll be all for now."

Sam clenched her teeth to keep from blurting out a zinger of a comeback.

****

The fact that Sam and her mother worked the same hours, combined with Mom's homebody habits, had left zilch in the way of opportunities for her to snoop in the apartment. Sam itched to read the note addressed to her she'd seen weeks ago under her mom's keepsake box. Her powerful curiosity might be her undoing one day, but that had never stopped her. Though the waiting tested every inch of her flimsy restraint, she'd bided her time until an opportunity to read the note presented itself.

After dinner Wednesday evening, while Sam finished washing the dishes, Mom gave her the perfect opening by driving to Virginia Center Commons Mall to shop for curtains.

Five minutes after Mom went out the door, Sam wound her way up the spiral stairs to the loft. Taking pains not to let the contents of the keepsake box shift, she lifted it out of the under-the-bed drawer and set it on the floor. That folded green notepaper lay in the same spot. In spite of seeing *To Samara* written in her mom's neat lettering, her sense of right and wrong stopped her. For a full minute, she weighed the choice, yea or nay. The chance that the note might reveal something about Dad's hidden background tipped the balance. Yea. She opened the single sheet.

The date at the top stunned her. *May 12, 1986.* Her mom had kept this hidden for over twenty-two years. Sam had been only ten years old then.

Dear Samara,

If something happens to me, there are a few things I want you to do. First, take good care of your father. He worries a lot, but he laughs the most when you're around. Laughing is better than worrying.

Second, remind Patrice not to get so angry with people. Some people did stupid things to me, but maybe they couldn't help it like I can't help the way I am. Maybe if I'm not around, she won't need to get angry so much.

Third, I know you like hugs. Sorry, I can't give them to you myself, but anytime you want one, wrap your arms around yourself and know it's from me.

Love always,

Mom

By the time Sam finished reading, tears threatened to splotch the note. Mom had said she loved her always, expressed in unmistakable terms. In a note she wouldn't let Sam see. Would she ever understand this enigma of a woman? Not completely. That spiral staircase she'd just climbed brought to mind the spiraling nautilus shells on Atwood's book cover. She'd just seen inside one hidden chamber. How many more were there? But now Sam knew Mom truly loved her, in her unique way. That was more than enough.

She gave the words a second look. The note revealed one answer but raised more questions. Patrice's hair-trigger anger apparently evolved from watching her sister being badly mistreated, yet this note also showed Mom's concern for the impact on Patrice.

What made Dad worry so much? He must have been good at hiding his feelings; Sam had rarely noticed the signs.

Why did Mom think something would happen to her? What "something?"

What prompted her to write the note in 1986?

Why hide the note for decades?

About those self-hugs: no need to test it out. Sam learned at an early age how to fill her bottomless hug tank without Mom's assistance, starting with the open spigot at Mariah's house. Although her dad had provided energetic Wow!-You-did-it! hugs and milder So-sorry embraces, Mrs. Gabrielli's hugs had a pillowy softness no male could ever achieve. What would Mom's be like? She might never know.

Until reading Attwood's book, she'd attributed Mom's lack of physical contact to coldness, or maybe an extreme defense of personal space. Then she'd learned it stemmed from hypersensitivity to touch. Many people with Asperger's perceive even a light touch as too intense, a tidal wave of unwanted sensation.

The best demonstration of Mom's tactile sensitivity was her clothing. Not a single garment she wore still had a sewn-in tag. Some even sported holes where she'd cut through seams to rid the things of every last shred of irritating tags. She'd also routinely cut them out of Sam's clothes. She grew up thinking everyone removed tags from new clothes, like taking off price tags.

Though Sam wanted to tell her how much the words she wrote meant to her, that would require admitting she'd gone against Mom's wishes. Shame for sneaking behind her back wrestled with the joy of discovery and the prickle of unanswered questions. Shame won out. With the note positioned precisely where Sam had found it, she replaced the box and went home.

As she was getting ready for bed that night, her cell phone rang. Seeing Mom's number on the display chased away any weariness. She never called at this hour.

"Samara, I've had another break-in. Come see."

"What did you discover out of place this time?" The guilty devil in her wanted this to be a real yet harmless break-in, while the imperfect angel prepared to come clean.

"I found a sign of tampering. Please, help me do a complete search."

"Did you set some kind of trap?"

"Exactly. I stuck a fine sliver of clear tape across the opening of each under-the-bed drawer, off to one side where it was nearly invisible. The tape on my keepsake-box drawer is now hanging loose. Nothing inside seems amiss, but the drawer has clearly been opened. How soon can you get over here?"

Confession time. "Relax, Mom. I opened that drawer."

"Why?" Her voice dropped low, a sure sign she was mad.

But what could Mom do? Ground her adult daughter?

"To read the note you wrote me."

"I told you not to do that. I don't care if you are thirty-two. You shouldn't disobey your mother."

"I let my curiosity get the better of me. I'm sorry. But I'm grateful for what you wrote, especially the part where you said, *Love always*. It means the world to me to read that."

"How could you not see it all these years? Surely you knew."

"With all you've done for me, totally. You've kept a home as well-tended as your garden, provided me with all I needed to grow up healthy and strong. I always knew you weren't the touchy-feely type when it came to showing your love, but I desperately needed to hear the words."

"You should have told me. How can I be expected to know what you need if you don't tell me?" she said, her tone fraught with frustration.

"That's okay. From now on, I'll tell you." From what she'd read about Asperger's in Attwood's book, Mom's lack of insight into emotional needs—her own or anyone else's—was classic, a key difference between someone with Asperger's and 'neurotypicals.' "Most people learn to recognize what others need, Mom, by watching them and reading their body language."

"That whole deal about body language makes no sense to me. 'Language' means words. I've never heard a body talk, only a mouth."

"Maybe I can teach you. Think of it like you're a deaf person learning to read lips, only you'll be learning to read anger, joy, embarrassment, sadness, surprise, loneliness…" Sam sensed a grimace through the phone line. "Change of subject. After reading your note, a few questions came up. First off, what made you write it?"

"Preston talked me into going with him to New Orleans for the American Booksellers Association's annual conference that year."

"Yeah, I remember. I stayed with the Gabrielli family while you were gone. With how much you hate the idea of flying, I was surprised you went."

"I almost didn't. After he bought my plane ticket, I tried to back out. I worried that if something happened to me, you'd be left alone, not knowing what to do without me around to guide you. He told me to write you a letter, listing the most important things I wanted you to know, then put the note in a safe place. He was right; that helped. I was still terrified when I stepped onto the plane, but not worried about you."

"Mom, that was twenty-two years ago. Why haven't you tossed that note?"

"You never know when something unexpected will happen. That's why they call it 'unexpected.' You might need that note one day."

"Since I've already read it, would you mind giving it to me to keep?"

"I suppose it's okay. I'll bring it with me in the morning. Good night."

Now Sam would have a treasured keepsake of her own, proof positive of her mother's love. However, Mom left her with a lot to chew on. Why had she never asked her mom for what she needed most—to hear the words *I love you*? How badly had Mom been bullied? It must have been awful. Patrice still turned into a mama beast whenever Mom was mistreated.

How could Sam teach her about body language when she doesn't look at people? It would be like trying to teach a child to read when the student refuses to open the book.

Chapter 17

One blessed week passed with no fallout from the unsettling session with Detective Patillo.

Amy called to ask if Sam would pay a solo visit to Duane this week. She'd come down with a nasty case of the flu but didn't want her husband to go too long without seeing a friendly face. Sam agreed to provide the face-of-the-week, though she wouldn't have much to offer him in the way of uplifting news.

While enduring the rigmarole of getting to the visitor room, Sam was too busy rehearsing what she'd say to Duane to pay attention to the depressing atmosphere. Duane hadn't lost the wan, pinched look, but this time he was glad to see her face through the glass.

"Thanks for coming back. After the reception I gave you last time, I couldn't blame you if you never wanted to see this ugly mug again."

"Not to worry. It sucks to see you languishing here, and I'll do whatever I can to help you fight this."

When she'd finished her report of the talk with the bartender and the latest interview with the detective, Duane commiserated with her.

"Yeah, Patillo often plays the 'bad cop.' I think they're just harassing you to see if you'll divulge something that incriminates me. One bright light, your mom is going to get bailed out of her crunch with all that insurance money."

"Yes, if the wheels ever start turning. Mom still hasn't heard from whoever is administering Al's estate. He'll be the one who can order a copy of the death certificate to send to the insurance company."

"That *he* was supposed to be *me*. Al put me down as administrator, just like he was gonna be mine. In my case, I didn't want to lay that burden on my wife, and besides, she has no head for figures. In Al's, I guess he didn't have anyone else to ask. Anyway, I'll certainly not be dealing with Al's estate from here. By now, the court must have assigned someone else. You better call the courthouse if you want to see the money anytime soon."

"Speaking of money, do you have any notion where Al would have gotten a hundred-dollar bill?"

"Even when he was flush, I never saw him take out anything bigger than a twenty. Not like Mardigan. Mardigan was always all about the flash. It could have been him. Hey, look, I really appreciate what you're trying to do," Duane said, leaning toward the glass and lowering his voice, "but don't get in over your head. Pass your info to my attorney. Let him deal with it. Maybe he'll earn whatever he gets paid."

"What's your attorney's name?"

"Markus DeVaughn. One more thing—Amy told me about the books you gave my boys. Thanks for looking out for them. That means a lot." Duane's eyes filled with tears.

"It's the least I can do."

Her gesture now felt so inadequate. Surely she could contribute in a more substantial way.

****

DeVaughn's law office didn't look anything like Sam had expected. The man worked out of a small ranch house

210

like hers. A fiftyish woman greeted her at the door, then led her to a conference room that still resembled its former life as a dining room, complete with chair rails circling the walls and a polished table large enough to seat eight. The woman left and returned a minute later with a steaming mug of coffee. DeVaughn came in, they exchanged pleasantries, and he shut the door.

He was a young man, maybe mid-twenties, with boyish good looks, which would inspire more in the way of female interest than the confidence of someone with his life on the line. But a framed diploma behind him indicated he'd earned his law degree from Duke, a strong school that had also produced a U. S. President, even if it was Richard Nixon, a.k.a. Tricky Dick.

"You say you have some information that may prove useful?" he asked, picking up a pen. "I hope you do because nothing much has turned up thus far."

"I've got two names you might want to dig into. The first is Gail Hobson. I learned that she'd phoned Al—"

"Pardon me for interrupting, but no need to waste time on that one. From the materials passed to me by the district attorney, I know they've established she'd been nowhere near Virginia. She's a workaholic putting in sixty-hour weeks for a computer consulting company. She was on call the fateful night and had to go in to fix a system crash. Next?"

Sam's hopes started deflating. "The next is Squire Mardigan. Did the police question him?"

"Only to get his take on the incidents when Duane broke Al's nose and when those two scuffled at Someplace Else. I don't see how he'd have anything more to add to the case."

She told him about Al paying a hundred dollars for a

ten-dollar tab, her suspicion that it could have come from a blackmail payoff he'd just collected, and Duane's comment about Mardigan carrying hundreds.

DeVaughn said, "A report of personal effects on Al when they pulled him out of the James said his wallet only had a fiver and several maxed-out credit cards. If there'd originally been more bills to match the big one, the killer must have pocketed it. No way would he dispose of a body without removing a wad of cash first. And blackmail would be an interesting twist." He checked some paperwork in front of him. "This is something I can work with. I'll be deposing George Speers in two days. A perfect time to get confirmation of the huge tip and see if there's anything else Speers hasn't told the police."

Sam left the meeting with renewed optimism. Although DeVaughn looked like he'd just taken the training wheels off his bike, he seemed genuinely interested in doing his best to help Duane. It better be enough.

At home that evening, she phoned Mariah with the news then called Ryan. He sounded relieved she was being sensible and turning over the legwork to professionals. She started wrapping up the call.

"Don't hang up yet," he said. "I was just getting ready to give you a call. This being Monday, is it too late to ask you out for dinner and a movie next Saturday?"

"An official date? Sweet! The answer is yes...no, I mean no, it's not too late, and yes, sounds like fun."

"Glad you clarified that. You had me worried. I'll pick you up at six. Don't get in any trouble between now and then. Bye."

"Bye." She hung up and immediately redialed Mariah.

"More breaks in the case already, Sam?"

"No, but I caught a break. Despite the way I've treated him, Ryan asked me on an honest-to-god date for Saturday night."

"Don't tell me you forgot."

"About what?" A momentary tremor of panic tinged Sam's voice.

"About your date with me. I was going to teach you how to make cannoli." Mariah chuckled. "Gotcha. The cannoli lesson can wait."

"I'm so glad you didn't make me choose. I'd hate to hurt your feelings," she poked back.

****

On Wednesday, all Sam could think about was that DeVaughn would be taking Speers's deposition. Were there any other tidbits of information the bartender had neglected to share with the police? Just before closing the shop, the phone rang. The caller ID was Marcus DeVaughn LLC.

"Hi, Mr. DeVaughn, this is Sam. How'd the deposition go?"

"Hey, just call me Mark. I hate to be the bearer of bad news, but Speers denied receiving a hundred dollars from Al."

"But he told me Al left 'a fresh Franklin.' Those were his exact words."

"When I asked him if he told you that, he said yes, only he was exaggerating for effect. He laughed, saying, 'You should have seen the little lady react to that!' Speers said Al did leave without his change, but he'd laid a twenty on the bar."

"That lying bastard." Sam recalled Speers's sly expression when she'd asked him if he'd told the police about the huge tip. Mom couldn't read body language, but Sam sure could. "I'm positive he spoke the truth when he told me. He's just afraid someone will make him give the money back, for fingerprints or something. Were you able to get anything useful out of the man?"

"Not much. Both Mardigan and Hobson had been there a while before Duane arrived because they'd each come up to the bar a couple of times to order drinks. But he couldn't say if they'd shared a table at any point."

"That might be the break we need. Another patron could have seen them sitting together." Her heart raced as she clicked the pieces in place. "If you could find a witness and somehow get Speers to tell the truth, it would point to motive—being blackmailed—and opportunity, the perfect setup to spike his drink with a drug. I'll bet anything it was Mardigan."

"Unfortunately, this isn't a football pool. It takes a lot more than odds to pin murder on anyone. Are you forgetting about the drug residue found in Duane's trash?"

"Easily planted in an outdoor bin. You know, that's where evidence was found—a towel in the trash—that pinned arson on Al. He claimed that was planted, too. That can't be a coincidence. I always thought the unburned towel in the back bushes was too sloppy for anyone but the dumbest criminal. Besides, the arsonist would have needed one heck of an arm to lob it clean over Duane's two-story house, without it hitting the roof or getting hung up on the gutter."

"What do you do for a living, Ms. McNeer?"

"I run the bookshop on Center Street. Paperbacks by the Tracks."

"Do you read the mysteries you sell?"

"Totally. Why?"

"I'll bet you solve them halfway through the book."

Sometimes it felt like her whole life was a bag of mystery novels. Dad's past, his and Kyle's deaths, Mom's weird behavior, the break-ins, Al's murder… Maybe that's what drew her to reading so many, trying to learn how to make sense of it all.

****

Saturday's book signing event was a great success. The free cookies weren't the only things being snapped up; three local authors sold a total of twenty-six of their books. Mariah offered to take care of closing time and then give Clair a ride home, so Sam could leave a few minutes early. At a quarter to five, she raced home to get ready for her date.

How long had it been since she had dated anyone? The answer depressed her, seven empty years since Dad and Kyle died in the car wreck. Seven years in which she'd been so preoccupied with grief, taking over the bookshop, and grappling with how best to mother her mom. She'd dropped her gym membership and stopped attending events with a solos' group she'd joined out of desperation. At least the latter wasn't a sacrifice; it felt like a meat market. And she'd brushed off any flirty guys who tested out their pickup lines in checkout lines. No male had come close to matching Kyle's magic. Or maybe she'd not allowed anyone close enough to try.

What to wear? Sam's approach to clothes had always been comfort over fashion, and her boring closet showed it. Couldn't go wrong with black. She selected a pair of tailored black slacks, a frilly white shirt, and punched it up with a red cashmere cardigan and glittery red earrings. How much makeup? Maybe a little extra eye shadow?

Her lipstick had gone missing long ago, so she slathered on some cherry-flavored lip balm that could pass for gloss. No perfume; flowery scents made her sneeze. Her hair? Well, the curls did their own thing; she let them be.

The doorbell rang at 6:02 p.m. Not that Sam was watching the clock or anything. She slipped on her coat and opened the door.

He grinned. "I see you're not going to keep me waiting for twenty minutes like you did for the prom."

"I only did that because Mariah told me it was Standard Operating Procedure to keep your date cooling his jets for a half hour. On prom night, I cut you a ten-minute break."

"And the S.O.P. has changed?"

"No, I'm just hungry. I'm good to go. Where are we going?" She tried to keep any eagerness well hidden.

"Do you like Thai food? There's a nice little place in Richmond, not far from the theater."

"That'll be great." She'd never been to a Thai restaurant, but it was probably like Chinese. She loved Chinese.

In the car, neither of them spoke for the first minute. Sam wracked her brain for small talk other than the weather—cold and dreary—and came up empty. Ryan came to the rescue.

"Did you hear anything from Duane's lawyer?"

"Yes, and it's mostly good." The rundown of her Wednesday conversation filled the next five minutes. When she got to DeVaughn's comment about her penchant for solving mysteries, Ryan chuckled, then turned serious.

"There's a big difference between fictitious murderers and real ones, though. The ones in novels can't hurt you. Keep your distance from Mardigan."

"No worries. The only time I ever see him is at the bank for business. Say, would you help me with a little experiment later? I'd like to see if you can toss a wet towel over your townhouse. Your place has two stories and a roof profile similar to Duane's."

He gave two exaggerated nods. "Sure. I can't think of a more romantic way to wrap up our evening."

She would've jabbed him in the ribs but wasn't sure if they'd still be a little tender. "Come on; we can find out how strong your pitching arm is and how well healed your ribs are."

"The ribs haven't been bothering me in the gym, but I don't see how this will help Duane. With Al dead, they consider Duane's house fire a closed case."

"That's the point. If we can show that the towel evidence was all a setup, they might reopen it. And maybe rethink the drug evidence found in Duane's trash. Both items could easily have been planted."

"I'll give it a go, but first things first. We're here." After Ryan parked, Sam reached for the door handle.

He said, "No, not yet," and ran around to open the door for her.

"My, aren't you the gallant one?"

"Just S.O.P., according to the dating manual."

Dinner went smoothly, except for Sam gasping at the burn when she tasted Ryan's "Thai hot" Pad See Ew. How anyone could eat a whole plate of the molten stuff was one mystery she'd never solve. He claimed it came in handy for a firefighter to have an asbestos-mouth. The movie they saw, *The Curious Case of Benjamin Button*, left her unsettled. It seemed so wrong to see a person born old and die at birth. So futile to watch a man live life in reverse, always saying goodbye before saying hello.

On the ride back to Ashland, Ryan talked about his years between college and Mom's house fire. A year after graduating from Virginia Tech, he'd followed his older brother into the Army and was stationed in Wiesbaden, Germany, with the medical corps. He credited the Army for broadening his language skills. Not limiting himself to German, he learned to cuss in six other languages. He recited one Arabic curse but couldn't remember the precise translation—something to do with camel spit and mothers.

When his active-duty enlistment was up, he returned to Ashland. His degree in accounting led to a job with McMurtry & Williams in Richmond, but he burned out quickly with almost a hundred percent of his consulting assignments out-of-town. So Ryan hung out his shingle in The Center of the Universe—Ashland—and starved for a year before his business took hold. With a schedule he could control, he was able to volunteer as a firefighter. And that brought Sam up to date by the time Ryan parked in front of his townhouse.

"Come into my lair, fair lady," he said in his most enchanting tone. "Upstairs, to the right."

He trailed after her. The last time he'd used that corny *lair* line was in the tenth grade, in a play he'd written for the drama club. That knight-corners-maiden scene in his mash-up of *Romeo and Juliet*, *Monty Python and the Holy Grail*, and *My Fair Lady* drew cheers from the guys and jeers from the girls.

"If you're thinking…"

"The linen closet is behind the bathroom door."

She was both disappointed and relieved.

Suddenly Phoenix came bounding into the small

bathroom. His tail thwacked against the linen closet door with every wag. He did his happy dance around Sam's feet, then Ryan's. Good to see she still came first in his affections. Ryan picked him up and started downstairs.

"While I take him outside, you see to the test towels."

"You've got blue, blue, blue, and three more blue bath towels in here. All a bit threadbare."

From the bottom of the stairs, he said, "Threadbare is good; the lighter, the better. Grab three of them, your choice of color. If I don't make it within three pitches, your theory wins."

Once they'd finished their respective duties, they regrouped in the kitchen. He firmly knotted each towel in the middle, soaked them in the sink, and wrung them out. "To the pitcher's mound."

Ryan stood about fifteen feet from the front of his townhouse and handed Sam two of the wet towels. Her bare hands, already chilled, were now about to grow icicles. He said, "Step back...a little more. I don't want the towel to hit you when I swing it."

He whirled it overhead like a lariat, throwing off a spray of droplets.

"Hey, wait! You're soaking me."

"Sorry. Back up more." He wound up again and hurled it in a high arc. The towel landed with a splat about three feet below the peak of the roofline.

"Ball one."

"The aerodynamics suck and, besides, I'm out of practice. I know I can do better than that. Hand me another."

He moved forward a couple of feet, whirled the towel faster, and let it fly. Another splat, this time one end of the towel draped over the peak.

"Ball two."

"A close one. Last shot… Maybe we should have brought four towels." Ryan grabbed a deep breath, wound up again.

The towel flew over the peak and hit the roof with a splat, thump, thump, thump.

"What? No call?"

"It disappeared behind the plate."

"Let's see if we can find it." He led her in the front door and, after grabbing a flashlight from a kitchen drawer, out the back.

His neighbor cracked a door and yelled, "What's all the racket?"

"Just doing a little experiment," Ryan called back.

"At eleven o'clock in the middle of January? Are you whacked?" The door slammed shut.

"He has a point," Sam said. "Let's find the towel quick, so we can go inside where it's warm."

"You got me into this."

Ryan played the flashlight over all the bushes and grass to no avail. Looking up from the downhill slope of his backyard, the viewing angle made it impossible to see the roof beyond the gutter. He scanned the edge of the gutter, then focused the beam on one spot where a few inches of towel draped over the edge.

"Now that I tossed them up there, any bright ideas about how to get my towels down?"

"Firefighters always have ladders. Where's yours?"

"Attached to the fire truck. Looks like I'll have some roof ornaments for a few days until I can borrow a ladder. Time to get inside."

Ryan heated water in the microwave, mixed two mugs of instant hot chocolate, and then added generous splashes of peppermint schnapps. "Greatest warmer-upper ever made," he said, passing Sam one.

Between the sugar crash and the alcohol tranquilizer, she'd sleep well tonight.

"Based on our experiment, I have no doubts. The gas-soaked towel didn't end up in the bushes behind Duane's house by an accidental overthrow."

"I agree. The scene looks intentionally staged to create a link with the matching towel discovered in Al's trash. Would you like me to speak with the fire investigator, Don Truitt?"

"I'd appreciate that." She had no desire to ever see the man again after the way he'd spoken about her mom. *Mentally challenged, indeed!*

Ryan drained the last sip from his mug. "Sorry to cut the fun short, but I'd better get you home. I have to be at the firehouse by seven a.m. sharp." He put their mugs in the sink and took keys out of his pocket.

When he pulled to the curb in front of Sam's house, she said, "Thanks for a great evening, Ryan. And thanks for sacrificing your towels. Don't bother to get the door. I'll just dash in the house."

"Before you do, let me get that runaway curl out of your eyes." He softly tucked the strand behind her ear then cupped his hand behind her head, drawing her close. His kiss was light and lingering, sincere with a promise of so much more. "Stay safe and warm."

No problem with the warm part.

Chapter 18

When Mariah came to work on Monday, Sam's mood was still buoyed by the date with Ryan.

"Sam, when you didn't call yesterday, you made me think the date was too awful for words, but that's clearly not the case."

"I must have been a little preoccupied. It was great." Heat rose in her cheeks. "He even went along with an experiment I cooked up."

After Sam gave her an abbreviated version of the movie night, up to and including the towel caper, Mariah asked, "How will reopening the arson case help? Duane was the victim in that one, not the accused."

"No way did that gasoline-soaked towel accidentally end up in the bushes behind Duane's house. If that was a setup, they might reconsider the drug packet they're using to pin the murder on Duane. In both Duane's house fire and Al's murder, the only physical evidence was found in outdoor trash bins. Also, if both were planted, it makes sense that the same person could be guilty of both crimes: Mardigan."

"Why would Mardigan burn Duane's house? They hardly knew each other."

"Duane's whole house didn't burn, just the attic. I asked myself, why would someone go to all the trouble to set the attic on fire instead of starting it on the first floor? I think he wanted to make sure the attic was destroyed before the fire could be put out."

"What difference would that make? And you didn't answer my question, why Mardigan?" Mariah flashed her one of those will-you-ever-get-to-the-point looks.

"During that confrontation in Mardigan's office, Duane demanded that Al remove all of the junk he'd stored in Duane's attic. Maybe Mardigan thought Al had stashed blackmail evidence there—perhaps the missing loan files—where Mardigan would never think to look. Duane's house fire was set one night later, then pinned on Al for good measure."

"What do you figure was in those files that could be worth murdering Al?"

"Who knows?" Sam shrugged. "Maybe Mardigan was falsifying applicants' financial data so his customers would qualify for loans that otherwise would be too risky to sell on the secondary market."

"What a tangled web you've woven!" Mariah shook her head. "You've forgotten one thing. If the files burned up in the fire, there'd be nothing left as fodder for blackmail. Why would Mardigan then kill Al and implicate Duane?"

"Oops. I thought I had it all worked out." Sam flopped back in her chair, defeated. Both of them stared into space.

"I know what must have happened," said Mom, appearing from behind a bookrack.

"How long have you been back there?" Sam was glad she hadn't gone into more detail about her date night.

"I've been shelving books for about ten minutes. What a silly thing to ask Ryan to do, throwing wet towels onto a roof."

Sam groaned. Mom hadn't missed a thing. "So,

what's your theory?"

"Isn't it obvious? The files never were in Duane's attic. They were in the boxes that disappeared from the foyer before my fire started. Al stored those boxes in my attic and left them there as long as he could. Then he moved them to another location, certainly not in his own house or a friend's. All you have to do is find that spot."

Mom was correct but exasperating. "And how do you suggest we do that?"

"Mardigan has already shown you where *not* to search—if he was the one who ransacked Al's house, this bookshop, my apartment, and Zena's shed. Then he burned Duane's attic, all for naught. It's like that silly saying, 'Things will always be in the last place you look.' Of course, they are. When you find them, you stop looking. I suggest you start looking. They'll be in the last place."

How could Mom simultaneously clarify an issue and take away all hope of resolving it?

Someone tapped on the front door's glass. Mom scolded, "You forgot to unlock the door again."

****

Did she push Ryan too far with the towel-tossing escapade last Saturday? Here it was Wednesday night, and he hadn't called or dropped by the shop. Then again, it was tax season, an accountant's busiest time. Well, did it matter? Sam turned the clock back a decade and a half to their relationship throughout high school. Today she couldn't say what any of those heated arguments had been about, but the irritation they'd caused still felt as fresh as a new mosquito bite. If she was going to reenter the dating pool, he was probably the last person she should choose to test the waters with.

She burrowed under a throw on her sofa and was soon engrossed in a book.

When her phone rang an hour later, she thought, *aha, at last,* but was disappointed to see Elena's name on the screen.

"Sam, I hope I'm not calling too late."

"No, I don't go to bed this early. It's only ten o'clock."

"I finally heard from the court. They've assigned a firm called Reliant Financial Services to administer Al's estate. I know you'll need a death certificate to file the life insurance claim. Would you like me to add one for you when I ask Reliant for the ones I'll need for some joint accounts we'd set up?"

"Thanks so much. That would save me a lot of trouble." She grabbed a discarded envelope from the trash and jotted down "Reliant Financial." Now she'd know who to contact if they needed anything more than the death certificate.

"One more thing. Reliant will be cataloging Al's debts, and I'm afraid there will be creditors lined up around the block. The administrators will probably auction off his belongings to pay them but still come up short. Before they get a chance to inventory the house contents, bring your mother by to see if there's anything she'd want to take, maybe something they acquired during their marriage. It may be illegal, but frankly, I don't care. It's the least I can do, considering the awful financial shape he left her in."

"How do you have access to his house? Didn't they seal it or something?"

"It's my house I'm talking about. He'd moved in with me after Thanksgiving, bringing about half his things. The lease on his house was up December thirty-first."

"Sorry, my mistake. Tomorrow is our day off. Is there a convenient time to come by?"

"How about nine in the morning? My students never sign up for that time. I tutor Randolph-Macon freshmen who need help with English composition."

"I appreciate this, and I know my mom will, too. That'll be great."

What a turnaround! Elena had gone from defending Al a few months ago to admitting he'd screwed up Mom's life. Maybe Aunt Patrice had gotten through to Elena in that ugly scene at Thanksgiving.

Five minutes later, Sam's phone rang again. She thought Elena might be calling back to reschedule, but the caller ID showed Ryan Bennett.

"Hey, Sam. I know it's late, so I'll keep this short."

"Not to worry. I never turn in before eleven."

"I wanted to see if you'd like to try another dinner and movie on Saturday. There's only one condition: no towel tossing."

"Wasn't that fun?"

"Easy for you to say. You didn't get a sore arm, ribbing from your friends when you needed a ladder, and an extra load of laundry."

"I promise. No towels. Did you pass along the results of our experiment?"

"Yes, but it didn't do much good. All Truitt did was make a notation in the file. It's still on the back burner."

"Why is it that every promising step I take goes nowhere? Maybe tomorrow will be different. Elena just called and invited Mom and me to look through Al's things. I'd thought he bought a house when he left Mom, but all he did was rent one and then moved into Elena's."

"Are you planning to do what I think you are?"

"Absolutely." She recapped Monday's discussion with Mariah and Mom. "Maybe I can find what Mardigan couldn't."

"If you keep this up, I'm going to have to start calling you Sam Spade. Just keep in mind even real detectives sometimes land in trouble."

"Not to worry. Here's lookin' at you, kid."

"Right actor, wrong movie. That quote was Bogey playing the part of Rick Blaine in *Casablanca*, not Bogey as Sam Spade in *The Maltese Falcon*. Keep your characters straight."

Why did he always have to correct her? "I knew that. I was just seeing if you knew." *Lie... Damn. I even tell them to myself. Mom's right; I shouldn't be telling lies.* Of course, he knew. He was nearly as big a classic movie fan as her dad had been.

"Right. See you at seven on Saturday."

In the last couple of decades, the memories must have become scrambled. By the time Sam turned ten, her dad had her hooked on watching old shows with him, their own "date nights," complete with popcorn and root beer floats in tall glass mugs. Bogart was Dad's favorite. He'd played one of those black-and-white movies so many times that the VHS tape broke. Personally, she liked Groucho Marx, and his *You Bet Your Life* show the best.

A box in the attic still held Dad's collection of VHS tapes, along with a VCR player she'd never tried to connect to her flat-screen TV. Next best thing…she went to the bookcase. She found what she wanted on a bottom shelf and blew the dust off *The Maltese Falcon*. She needed to brush up on her namesake. Couldn't let Ryan keep one-upping her, as he did years ago. No telling what would happen if he got a lock on the upper hand now.

****

No wonder Al had chosen Elena to be his next wife. Her house displayed all the status symbols: classic architecture, manicured landscaping, and a prestigious location only a short walk from the college. Probably worth a princely sum. Clair's heart hammered as Samara rang the bell. The vision of Al and Elena ruining her lovely Thanksgiving dinner at the Iron Horse wouldn't leave her head.

Elena welcomed them in. A small half-round foyer table looked lost in the huge entry. A crystal chandelier cast glittery light on the ten-foot ceiling trimmed with dentil crown molding, but no pictures adorned the walls.

"Sorry the place looks so barren, but I'm moving out shortly. I've found a full-time teaching position at a community college in Charlotte. I've sold most of my furniture. Don't worry; I only packed up the stuff we brought with us."

"We? But you said this was *your* house," Samara said.

"Mine and my deceased husband's. When we arrived from Amherst, this rental was going to be temporary until we bought a house. He taught for two semesters at Randolph-Macon before he became too sick to work. Lung cancer, six months from diagnosis to death. I'd told him smoking was going to get him, but the craving for nicotine was stronger than his willpower."

"I'm so sorry," Samara said.

Though Clair busied herself taking stock of the house, she paid close attention to her daughter's conversation with Elena.

"Life goes on. I don't mean to rush you, but I have a student scheduled for ten."

Samara asked, "One question first. Isn't Al's dad, Michael Hobson, going to want some of his things?"

Elena stifled a laugh. "No love lost there. As soon as we stood up after the funeral service, he said that if he ever heard another word about Al or Ashland again, it would be too soon."

Elena led them around the nearly empty rooms. She was all business, pointing out item after item of Al's. A motley collection. Eight models of old sailing ships, poker chips and decks of cards, odds and ends from his bank office dumped into a carton. An old phonograph and a few dozen worthless records. Clair had hated the scratchy music. He'd played it hour after hour to drive her to the opposite side of her old house.

"And this was his," said Elena, brushing some dust off a dented two-drawer metal file cabinet.

It was the same one Al had put in Clair's basement, along with his rag-tag collection of ship models. Samara riffled through Al's personal papers. The dozen folders contained only credit card statements, receipts, pay stubs from the bank, warranties for things he probably didn't own anymore, and the like.

Samara turned to Elena. "Frankly, I expected this to be packed to the hilt. Don't bankers usually squirrel away every piece of paper that crosses their desks?"

Perhaps Samara was hoping for the same thing Clair did, that Elena might divulge the location of more papers, the missing loan files.

"Funny you ask. I'd assumed he left the bulk of his older paperwork with your mom since she had all that storage space in her attic."

Clair flinched when Elena tapped her shoulder to get her attention. It felt like a big spark of static electricity.

"Didn't mean to startle you, Clair. Any chance that when you moved out of your house, some of his old papers ended up in your storage unit?"

"No," Clair answered flatly. "I'd never take something that didn't belong to me."

Elena backed up a step, then shifted foot to foot. "Let's move on."

They found Al's closet, full of mostly business clothes, all except for a pair of navy blue sweatpants in mint condition. No sign of the ragged black pair Samara said he'd worn the day of her fire. Had he ditched those? If so, the odds that he'd tangled with the stray dog would skyrocket. Clair fingered the blue sweatpants and nudged her daughter.

Samara eyed the pants. "Say, Elena, looks like you talked Al into getting rid of those threadbare black sweatpants. I don't see them in here."

"It wasn't easy," said Elena. "Why he loved that pair, I'll never know. Men. But when they literally started falling apart, he agreed they were beyond fixing."

Coincidence? More likely, evidence of an encounter with a protective dog.

Once Elena started talking, it seemed she couldn't stop. She told them Al had lied about losing heirlooms in Duane's fire. The investigators sifted the remains of things like hockey skates and fishing poles out of the ashes. Nothing of value to anyone. Elena confessed she'd lied, too. She'd let Al believe she owned the house to impress him. With a rent she could barely pay on her part-time work as a tutor, Elena had hoped marrying a banker would solve her financial woes. It wasn't until the confrontation on Thanksgiving Day that she realized what she'd gotten, someone out for easy money, just like her. When Al lost all he had in the Madoff scandal, Elena pitied him, but not enough to marry him. She'd planned to call off the wedding after helping him fight the bogus arson charge.

As Elena admitted the truth of her relationship with Al, Clair began to smile but quashed it after Samara put a firm hand on her shoulder. Though she was both glad Elena had suffered for her lying and proud of her sister for exposing Al's deceit, Samara was right. It wasn't proper to smile at someone else's misfortune.

Going through the whole house, upstairs and down, took twenty minutes. The only item Clair selected was the granddaughter clock—a scaled-down version of a grandfather clock—five-eleven high, the same height as Samara, and only about thirty pounds. Al had given it to her upon their engagement in lieu of a ring, with the excuse that she still wore the diamond from Preston. Then he reclaimed the clock when the marriage dissolved. While Clair and Elena carefully carried the clock to the car, Samara tumbled the SUV's back seats flat to make room.

"Thank you for my clock," Clair said. "It was the only thing I liked from my marriage."

"Tell your sister she did me a favor when she woke me up to what was going on," Elena replied as Clair put on her seatbelt. Elena turned to Samara and lowered her voice. "To put it bluntly, the world will be better off with one less Al. Well, I should get those death certificates by next week. You want me to bring your copy by the bookshop?"

"Yes, thanks," Samara said. "Glad to see you're

moving forward with your life."

"Like I have a choice. This is one chapter I'm glad to put behind me."

As soon as Samara pulled away from Elena's place, she said, "You embarrassed me back there, Mom."

"Why? What did I do wrong?"

"Here Elena was doing everything she could to help us, and you had to take a simple question about having some of Al's things in your storage as a personal affront."

"Well, she so much as accused me of keeping something that didn't belong to me. I didn't like that."

"Like it or not, at least Elena dodged a matrimony scam and seemed grateful for the lesson learned. Personally, I think it's too bad she's leaving. She's reached out to me several times, and I would have liked the opportunity to help her make that fresh start."

"No, she *should* struggle by herself. She's not honest, and she's getting her due. I don't like her." Clair folded her hands in her lap.

No more words were said until they'd backed into Zena's driveway and unloaded the clock.

"Where do you want this?" Samara asked.

"Between the door and the base of my spiral staircase. It'll look good on that wall."

They eased it down. Clair stepped back and then directed her daughter to move it an inch to the right.

"It's not running. How do you get this thing going?" Samara asked.

"All you need to do is wind it up and start the pendulum. There's a key inside the case."

Samara opened the tall door on the base and fished out a key ring that lay on the bottom. "I assume the one like a big wing nut is the winding one, but what's the little

232

key for?"

"It's to lock that tall door to protect access to the pendulum."

"Nope. It doesn't come close to fitting." She handed the ring to Clair.

Clair held the small key up to the light and saw *Master Lock* etched into the silver metal. "This fits a padlock. It must be a key to the last place, where you'll find the files."

"What makes you think that?"

"The best place to hide a little key is in place of another little key. Maybe Al threw out the key to the pendulum door on purpose, so no one—not even Elena— would think the padlock key didn't belong with the clock. Most folks never lock that door anyway."

"Sounds promising, but this little key won't get us very far. The matching padlock could be on a locker at a golf course, a gym locker, a storage unit, a tool shed, one of those giant toolboxes you see in the back of pickup trucks. No telling."

"You'll figure it out." Clair handed the ring back.

****

Sam wished she could share her mom's confidence. One key and no lock. *Oh, well.*

And while she was at it, she added one more wish— that she could move on to a new chapter, like Elena. Sam was stuck on the page where the wrong guy was in jail, the real culprit was free, and the protagonist was determined to make things right but couldn't figure out how to do it.

That afternoon, she paid another visit to Richmond City Jail, this time accompanying Amy, still pale but mostly recovered from the flu. Duane was growing more despondent by the day. His lawyer had told him it would be about a year before his case would go to trial. And with any charge that could result in a life sentence or worse, Virginia courts wouldn't consider bail. News like that would depress anyone, optimistic or not.

From the way his jumpsuit hung loose, he'd lost at least ten pounds. As Sam relayed current developments, he snapped back with angry remarks.

To the report from Elena about Al's burned sporting goods in the attic, he said, "I could have told you that. I helped him haul that crap up there."

After Sam asked him if he knew of a location where Al might have used a padlock, he snarled, "How the hell should I know?"

Even though he and Amy had supported Sam with unending patience as she'd worked her way through depression after Dad and Kyle died, Duane's grouchy attitude pushed her close to losing her cool. She felt nothing but relief when visiting time was over.

Friday night, Ryan called to cancel their date. Two of the volunteers were down with the flu, and he needed to cover the Saturday shift at the firehouse in addition to his regular Sunday one. When he promised to make it up by taking her to a more upscale restaurant next time, she said she'd look forward to it and understood completely.

What she understood was that, on every front, she'd been taking one step forward, one step back—a two-step to nowhere.

234

Chapter 19

Tim, one of Sam's regular nesters, was knee-deep in his notes, studying for a test in Medieval Lit, so she let him keep at it when closing time arrived. His cohorts had cleared out before dark, heading to dinner. He'd certainly be no bother while she updated Paperback's window displays.

Winter-themed books and her meager collection of stuffed snowmen no longer caught anyone's attention. Even though February, just around the corner, often brought Virginia's worst snows, she was *so* over cold weather and freezing precipitation. With Valentine's Day coming, she figured books about love, chocolate, and the love of chocolate would be more appealing. Mariah would go bonkers over this.

After Sam positioned a heart-shaped box of chocolates—its contents stashed behind the counter—next to romance novels with bright red covers, she stretched to rearrange three vases of red, white, and pink silk roses. Her elbow bumped the pedestal holding a ceramic plate stacked with fake but yummy-looking brownies. The pedestal tottered, sending the plate—brownies and all—toward the floor.

"No!" she yelled.

She twisted around, lunged for the plate, and caught it but lost her balance. Both she and the plate hit the floor. The brownies skittered over the floor but survived. Not the plate. An explosion of pain burst from her ankle.

"Shit!"

Her shout brought Tim and Mom hurrying to her side.

"Ms. McNeer, are you all right?" Tim's brows scrunched together with concern.

"What happened to my left foot?"

"Here's the problem," her mother said. "It's caught in the toe kick below the display window. That's no excuse to use foul language." Mom reached to free her daughter's foot from its awkward position.

"No! Help me sit up first," Sam said.

Tim lifted her shoulders, and she sat. Leaning sideways, she was able to ease her foot out.

"Whoa, it's already swelling," said Tim. "Where's some ice?"

"I'll get it." Mom disappeared into the office.

"Let me help you to a chair," Tim said.

By the time Mom returned with a baggie of ice, Tim had Sam nestled into a study chair, both feet propped in a neighboring chair drawn close. Clair gave her the baggie.

Sam winced at the initial sting of the ice pack, but it soon brought numbing relief.

"I'd offer to take you to an ER," Tim said, "But I don't have a car."

"No problem," Sam said. "My car's out back. Mom can drive me."

Three hours later, they finally made it to Sam's house.

"Thanks, Mom. I appreciate you keeping me company at the doc-in-a-box."

"I only did what a mother does. And I wish you'd call the place by its real name—EmergiMedic Clinic."

"Sorry. I can't say that with a straight face. It sounds like something they'd sell in an infomercial for only $19.99—a Veggie-matic!"

Mom helped her get comfortable on the sofa, propping her foot on pillows. "Now tell me, so I won't have to guess. What do you need?"

"The TV remote, the book from my nightstand, a fresh baggie of ice, a glass of milk, and a bowl of instant oatmeal. We never did get any dinner. Join me if you want to."

Mom brought her a lap tray loaded with everything she'd requested, plus a box of brown sugar.

"Thanks. Exactly the way I like it. You're not having any?"

"I've got some leftovers at home. Need anything else before I go?"

Well, Sam had promised that next time she'd ask for what she really needed. Why was this so hard for her? "How about a kiss to make it better, like Dad used to do?"

Mom looked away, absorbed in thought. Then she kissed the fingertips of her right hand and rested the hand on Sam's injured ankle. Though a black plastic-and-Velcro boot encased her foot, ankle, and most of her lower leg, the light pressure felt every bit as healing as when Dad did the same for his little girl.

It's never too late to learn. For both mother and daughter.

Once Mom left, and the oatmeal bowl was empty, Sam considered phoning Mariah, but tomorrow would be soon enough. If she called now, Mariah would fly over to play nurse until o-dark-thirty. What about calling Ryan? No. He'd be a lovely distraction, but she felt embarrassed to be laid up by such a silly accident.

She didn't dare let him see her as vulnerable.

****

Back in her apartment, Clair pulled the bedcovers up to her chin. Seeing Samara in pain, needing her, had triggered a cascade of fears. Not only this whole business with house fires, break-ins, losing all her savings, Al's murder, getting accused of killing him…

But her daughter, taking on a role where she had no business being… What was she doing, entangling herself in a murder investigation? Samara could easily find herself in a much worse fix than having a sprained ankle, a fix Clair would be helpless to rectify. Preston had shielded them both from the evils in the world. Now it was up to her alone to protect Samara.

She clenched the edge of the comforter tighter. She couldn't stop her brain from dwelling on the frightening scene. If only Samara, with her blasted curiosity, had taken to heart what Preston always said: What you don't know can't hurt you.

She sat up, opened her tree encyclopedia, and started reading. But the words refused to build their soothing pictures in her mind.

****

The next day Mom drove Sam to work. Then Mariah drove her crazy, fussing over her as if she'd broken both legs.

Ryan phoned. 'Just to chat,' he'd said. *Sure. Right.* Mariah had tipped him off. Sam told him the bare bones of the accident but said she was doing fine. Mariah had already dished out all the sympathy she could stand. Any more, even from Ryan, and some dam inside her would break, unleashing a torrent of…she didn't know what.

"Stick to rice, and it'll heal faster," he suggested.

When Sam gave no response, he added, "That's r-i-c-e: rest, ice, compression, and elevation."

"Got it." She knew that—*not*. The acronym was familiar, of course, but she hadn't recalled what each letter stood for, except for the *ice* part.

All she wanted was to get lost in work, yet Mariah wouldn't let her lift a finger. When she came to the brink of lifting one particular finger to her best friend, Sam hobbled back to the office, in the guise of helping Mom place book orders, and took refuge.

"Mariah said it, and I'll say it: you look awful, Samara. The dark circles under your eyes make it look like mascara has run, but you never wear any."

"I didn't get much sleep last night." Mom had noticed her eyes. Amazing. Not exactly body language, but in the right neighborhood.

A tap at the door kept Mom from pressing the matter any further.

"Come in," Sam said, welcoming the interruption.

Elena opened the door halfway and leaned in. It might have been that Sam was seated and she was standing, but Elena seemed a couple of inches taller, like a weight had been lifted from her shoulders.

"I hope I'm not catching you at a bad time. The woman out front told me I could come back here."

When Mom realized who their guest was, she swiveled her chair around and began filing papers. Did she fear Elena would ask her to return the granddaughter clock?

"It's fine. We were just chatting." Sam was glad her booted foot was hidden behind the desk. She'd had enough of *Oh, you poor thing!* for one day.

"I know you're anxious to get the claim filed for Al's

life insurance, so I came right over after today's mail arrived. Here's the death certificate you need. Good thing it came through. I'm out of here in a little over a week." Elena handed her the form, and Sam glanced at it.

"That's funny; I've never seen a Social Security number starting with a zero," she said. Of course, she'd only seen a handful, those of her family and some students who'd worked part-time in the bookshop years ago.

"You've lived here in Virginia your whole life, right?"

"Yes."

"You've probably never seen the number of a person from Connecticut. Those first three digits indicate the state that issued the number."

"Hmm. Interesting." Handing Elena a Paperbacks by the Tracks bookmark, she said, "Our email address is at the bottom. Let me know how things go for you in Charlotte. And if you need help with any loose ends here in Ashland, get in touch with me."

"Thanks. After our first encounter at the Iron Horse, you're the last person I would have expected to wish me well. Same goes here, though. I hope you and your mom find your way out of the troubles Al dumped on you. Bye."

Elena looked like she wanted a hug, but Sam didn't want to struggle to her feet. Instead, she extended her right hand, and when Elena shook it, Sam added the left. Elena did likewise.

Once Elena left, Sam wasted no time enclosing the death certificate in an envelope with the completed insurance claim form, then asked Mom to take it directly to the post office. The sooner Mom received her check, the better the chance she'd have of saving her house if that's what she still wanted.

Yet she'd not only become accustomed to the garage apartment but seemed content. Maybe the smaller *different* space in town nearer her daughter suited her needs better than an isolated house with rooms she never used.

Whatever she felt about her old house, Mom would dread the thought of more change.

Chapter 20

On Friday, after two inches of snow top-coated a quarter-inch of ice, all schools were closed. Sam never failed to open on days like this. Some of her customers would take the road conditions as a challenge to prove their skills behind the wheel and insist they desperately needed to shop. Others who didn't want to tempt fate on the roads walked to her store. This translated to a moderately good sales day because once they survived the treacherous trip, they had to prove they'd made it by buying at least one book. She called Mariah and told her to enjoy a snow day; she and Mom could cover the shop.

Folks kept calling to make sure the shop was open before venturing out. At eleven o'clock, the phone rang for the umpteenth time.

"McNeer's Paperbacks by the Tracks. Yes, we're open and have a fresh supply of muffins and hot coffee."

"This is Jennifer Roberts calling from Jefferson Mini-Storage in Charlottesville. May I speak with Clair Hobson, please?" The woman sounded annoyed.

"This is her daughter, Samara. May I ask what this is about?"

"I suppose you'll do just as well. I've sent notices to Albert Hobson, but they've come back stamped 'No Such Address.' Then I tried phoning his cell, and the number's no longer in service. When I called his work number and asked for him, a woman told me I ought to speak with a family member and gave me this number. All this to track down a deadbeat. Tell him, wherever the heck he is, that if he doesn't pay the last two months' rent for his unit, I'll cut the lock off and auction the contents to pay his bill."

Sam's mind raced. The woman had the "dead" part of deadbeat right. This could be it. *Don't blow it.* "He never was very good at keeping up with his bills. How much is due and by when?"

"The only payment he ever made was in late October when he rented it. That money covered the partial month plus November, so it's a hundred and ninety dollars, including late charges. If I get it by the end of business today, that is. Next Monday is the second, and February's rent would get tacked on. Our auction is on the second Monday of every month, so he'll have one more week before he loses it."

"Could I get the money and bring it by on Sunday? I work retail. Now that the holidays are over, it's the only day my shop's closed."

"Sorry, honey. The business office is closed on the weekend. You should tell that man to grow up and learn to take care of his finances, instead of laying it on his family to cover for him."

"I'm afraid it's too late for that." The words slipped out, a reflexive reaction.

"It's never too late. Just give him the message."

Not without a séance. Sam could hear her rustling some papers. Was she getting impatient to wrap up the call?

"Wait. I'll give you my credit card number and recover the money later. Let's get this taken care of right now."

"I hope he's better at paying you than he's been with

me, but it's your dime."

With the transaction completed, Sam asked about access hours.

"Twenty-four-seven entry for renters. All they need is a gate security code."

"And what's the code?"

"Like I said, it's for renters only."

Improvise...improvise... "If you tell me the code, I can threaten to take his stuff hostage in return for the money I just paid you."

"I like that. You're not the patsy I took you for. The code we assigned him is, let's see…eight-four-six-seven. You know, you forget one thing. Don't you want the unit number?"

"Oops. Yeah, that would help."

"It's number one-nineteen in Building C. Got that?"

She thanked the woman and hung up. She'd never gambled with money in her life, not even on a lottery ticket, and now she'd bet $190 that a certain key would fit that lock. And she'd have to wait until Sunday morning to see if she hit the jackpot.

Sam could have burst with the news but didn't want to discuss it with her mom—or with Mariah or Ryan via phone—in front of customers. At the end of the day, as soon as she'd locked the front door, she limped back to the stockroom and sat at her desk.

"Ah, it feels so blessedly good to sit down! Mom, the most amazing thing happened." Sam related the whole out-of-the-blue scene.

"But what will you do if it's the wrong key? Your money and your gas would be a total waste."

Sam pictured the scenario and thought back to the phone conversation. "I could use bolt cutters. The same

244

thing the lady at the storage facility would use."

"You don't have any bolt cutters, Samara," Mom said.

"You're right; I don't. But I know who would."

Arms tightly folded across her chest, Mom planted herself smack in front of Sam's desk. "Wait. This is all wrong. Here you go again, chasing after trouble. It sounds illegal, maybe dangerous. No telling what's in that storage unit. Give the key to Patillo and let him handle it. Everything having to do with Al is his job, not yours."

"Come on, dangerous? I'll just unlock the unit and see what's there. What could be simpler?" Sam shook her head in frustration.

"Are you forgetting this is the property of a *murdered* man? It could show why he was killed. If you put your hands on it, maybe you'll get killed, too."

Were those tears shining in Mom's eyes? "Don't worry, Mom. I'll be fine. I'll take Mariah with me."

"And get her in trouble, too. Isn't there something I can do to talk you out of this?"

"Like I said, Mom, we'll be fine."

The ride home was yet another simmering silence.

Talking with Mariah on the phone that night bolstered Sam's confidence that she was right on target.

"It makes perfect sense. No blackmail victim would ever think of searching in Charlottesville. Even if they could, they'd have to get through the gate, then break into every storage unit to find which one was his. Al would never go to all that trouble to stash his stuff in Charlottesville unless he had something significant to hide," Mariah said.

"Would you go with me on Sunday? Be my cohort in crime?"

"You know I'd do anything for you, anything but murder Al… Oops. Guess I need a new line. How about anything but strangling Patillo? That should do it."

"Works for me. So you can go?"

"Wish I could, but my brother bought me a ticket to the Richmond Symphony that afternoon, so I could join him and his wife."

"No worries. I'll call you as soon as I get back."

After her next call, all preparation would be in place.

"Bennett Accounting Services, Ryan Bennett speaking."

"Hi, Ryan. It's Sam. I've got a little favor to ask."

"As long as no towels will be harmed, shoot."

Sam envisioned the smirk that must be on his face.

"Could you find a pair of bolt cutters to lend me for the weekend?"

"We always carry those on our fire engine. There's bound to be a spare somewhere. What do you need them for?"

She passed along the exciting break in the hunt for the boxes and the trip to Charlottesville on Sunday.

"Let me stop you right there. Even if the key fits, you're talking about stealing. I know the man's dead, but whatever is in there is still his property, not yours. It should be passed along to his next-of-kin, his dad, Michael Hobson."

"Yes, but—"

"No buts about it. It would be boldfaced theft. I can't be complicit in that. No way, Jose."

His sharp words cut her. "Do you expect me to watch Duane get convicted of murder because no one's found any evidence to the contrary? When I know there must be something suspicious in that unit? What else could I do?"

"How about giving the key to the police and letting them check it out?" He was nearly shouting into the phone. "It's their job, not yours."

"That's the same thing Patillo told me, but I simply don't trust him. He's likely to twist any evidence he finds into convicting Duane, not clearing him. He's laser-focused on putting nails in the coffin in front of him. Don't you see that?"

"We never had this conversation." He hung up without a goodbye.

Her budding relationship with Ryan was in danger of becoming a one-date wonder. And she hadn't even gotten to the part about asking him to go with her on Sunday.

If those boxes were there, she'd never be able to carry them to her car. Bearing her body weight on that booted left foot was pain enough.

No way could she handle the Charlottesville trip on her own.

Chapter 21

Though Samara claimed only her left foot was out of commission, Clair had insisted on driving. Samara had called late the night before, pleading with her to go along on the Sunday escapade. Clair knew her stubborn daughter well. If she hadn't agreed to accompany her, Samara would have headed into danger all by herself. A true mother could never let that happen. And with Patrice, three would be better than two, which is better than one.

The highway to Charlottesville was clear, but the streets near Patrice's house offered the dual challenge of steepness and ice. She'd never understood why her sister had chosen Charlottesville. Just because Patrice had graduated from the University of Virginia didn't mean she had to stay near there for the rest of her life, abandoning her nice, flat hometown of Ashland. And her sister.

Turning into Patrice's drive sent Clair's car skittering sideways. After she tooted the horn, Patrice gingerly inched her way down the slick walk and climbed into the back seat.

"Ready when you are, ladies. There's a shortcut to the mini-storage, but not a good one for today. I'll show you the route with fewer hills."

"Is there such a thing in this town?" asked Clair.

"It's all relative."

Ten anxious minutes later, they pulled up to the

security keypad. The code numbers did their job, and the gate slowly retracted. At Building C, Clair parked near a door marked 101 – 120. When the three of them got out, Patrice couldn't help but notice Samara's ungainly boot. Samara gave her a short version of the accident while they walked down a dimly lit hall to the padlocked door of Unit 119.

"Can you see well enough to tell if it's a Master Lock?" asked Patrice.

Samara said, "No. We'll know in a moment. Hold your breath…"

A cold sweat broke out on Clair's forehead. Samara inserted the key. After some jiggling, it snapped open. She removed the lock and opened the door. The meager light from down the hall illuminated the first two feet of an empty concrete floor. A whiff of mildew almost made her sneeze.

"Surely there's a light, but I can't find a switch on the wall. Oh, here's a chain." Samara pulled it, and a bare, overhead bulb cast a dim light on the five-foot by eight-foot space.

Against the back wall, Clair saw two unmarked cartons, nothing more. "Those are the same ones from my house, but they're stacked in the opposite order," she said. "The one with the black scuff on the upper edge used to be on the bottom, and the one with the mashed lower corner was on top."

Samara and Patrice looked at one another, shaking their heads.

"I wish I knew how you do that, Mom."

"I've told you so many times; it's just a matter of paying attention."

"Well, let's see what we've got. Mom, do you want

to take the first peek?"

"I guess."

They gathered around as she opened the tucked flaps. Inside were fat manila folders, standing as if the box were a file drawer. The dangling light bulb couldn't have been over twenty-five watts, useless for reading.

"Aunt Patrice, do you mind if we take these to your home, so we can see what we're looking at?"

"Fine by me. This place is not only dark; it's frigid. Let's get out of here."

Patrice picked up one carton, and Clair took the other while Samara shut the door, replaced the lock, and clunked after them.

Back at Patrice's, they put the cartons on the kitchen table and settled down to work. Each folder, neatly labeled with a date and a surname, held a sheaf of loan paperwork. The folders weren't filed in any discernable order. Clair shuddered.

"Let's sort these by date and see what time period we're dealing with."

All were two to nine years old. The oldest went back to February 1998, more than two years before Al moved to Ashland. As they shuffled through the files, Clair and Samara recognized the names of some neighbors, friends, and more.

"Hey, here's your name, Mom."

"And I've found Duane's," called out Patrice.

"Now, this is interesting," Samara remarked. "This one is labeled 'Patillo.' "

"The guy who questioned me on Christmas Eve?" asked Patrice.

Samara read the top form. "It says 'First Name: Paul.' Yup, it's him. Now, all we have to do is figure out what's in these files that's worthy of blackmail and murder. Let's each take one of these three and see if anything jumps out."

Clair shrank back when her daughter tried to hand her one.

"What's wrong?" Samara asked.

"You said, 'see if anything jumps out.' Well, I can't stop my reaction. Of course, I know what you meant."

"Yeah, look for anything odd," Samara said. "Sorry, I should know better."

Twenty minutes later, they closed their respective files. "Anything, Aunt Patrice?" Samara asked.

"I'm afraid I have no idea what I'm looking at, other than a bunch of legal mumbo-jumbo on refinancing forms signed by Duane S. Chanesky."

"Mom, how about yours?"

"These are from my home equity loan in 2006. They've got my signatures, even the smears from the lousy pen they gave me to sign with. I don't see anything odd."

"Patillo's is another home equity loan," Samara said, "but nothing looks out of the ordinary. Now what?"

"Say, why don't you have your nice young man take a look?" Patrice suggested. "He's an accountant. Ryan, uh, what's his last name?"

"Bennett." Samara groaned. "We could put these back and let the police figure it out."

"I thought you didn't trust the police, especially the one whose file you're holding," said Patrice.

"Do both," Clair said. "Show these three to Ryan *and* give them all to the police."

"How do I explain where I got them?"

"Tell the truth. Always tell the truth, Samara. Lies are

wrong. They only make things more complicated."

****

Sam wasn't sure who to face first, Ryan or the police. It was a toss-up, but she decided on the lesser of evils. It would have to be Monday evening when she could corner Ryan at home. He was on duty today.

Monday evening, she drove all the way into Richmond to pick up some Thai-hot takeout from the restaurant he liked. Food would make a good door-opener…and a bribe. She set the bag on the floorboard by the heat vent, but by the time she arrived at his doorstep, it wasn't even lukewarm. At least it still smelled enticing, along with the rest of her car.

"What are you doing here?" Ryan held his door half-open, one hand on the doorframe, one on the doorknob.

The odor of bacon and onions leaked out of his apartment.

Sam raised the take-out bag and faked cheerful. "I brought dinner."

"Too late."

"That's okay. You can put it in the fridge for tomorrow. It's Thai-hot. You won't even have to reheat it to feel the burn."

He sniffed the bag. "Get in here so I can close the door."

He took the proffered bag to the kitchen and returned. "Now tell me why you're really here. I sure hope it's not to bail you out of the trouble you keep brewing."

"Can we at least sit down for a bit?" She leaned on a chair back, taking the weight off her left foot—playing the sympathy card.

"Yeah, sure."

Sam chose the sofa; he sat in a chair opposite.

"It would be easier if you came over here. I have something to show you."

Ryan grudgingly complied. She dug into her oversized shoulder bag, retrieved three files, and handed him one.

"Don't tell me where or how you found these." He thumbed through the first few pages. "Looks like typical loan paperwork. What is it you want me to see?"

"I'm hoping that if you dig into it, you'll find something that I don't know to look for. Some underhanded dealing, anything illegal or unethical, you know—a smoking gun. Put that accounting hat on."

He gazed out the window and heaved a sigh. "If I do this, what are you going to do with the files after I'm done?"

"Turn them over to the police, along with the rest of the files."

He scowled. "How many are we talking about?"

"I didn't count, but it's two heavy cartons' worth."

"You shouldn't hang onto this stuff any longer than necessary. I'll study these tonight and return them to you tomorrow *if* you promise to turn the whole shebang in immediately."

"Thanks. You're a sweetheart." She grabbed Ryan and planted a big smacker on his lips, then popped up to go.

"Wait." He snagged her hand and pulled her back onto the sofa. "If you're going to do something, do it right." He wrapped his arms around Sam's waist and kissed her long and hard. When he came up for air, he said, "Okay, you can go now."

Sam wasn't sure if her legs would support her when she stood.

****

The next day, Ryan entered the bookshop just as Sam had taken the first bite of her sandwich.

She stashed it back in the baggie and mumbled, "Mariah, can you cover the floor for the next few minutes?"

"No prob. Go."

Sam showed Ryan to the stockroom, where Mom cleaned up after her lunch and pulled two chairs up to the desk.

"Good to see you again, Mrs. Hobson," Ryan said, extending a hand.

Mom gave a brief nod in reply. "Please call me Clair, at least until I change my last name back to McNeer."

News to Sam, but it made perfect sense. "I can't stand it, Ryan. Tell me, did you find anything?"

"When I prepare tax returns, many of my clients show me closing statements, thinking they can deduct their closing costs for buying or refinancing a home. I have to give them the bad news that, for the most part, they can't."

"Please get to the point."

"On my first look at these three loans, the only thing I spotted was that the appraisal fees looked about a hundred dollars higher than most of the ones I've seen around here, so I gave the appraisals a closer look. And there it was." He paused and held one up.

"You're enjoying torturing me, aren't you?"

"I spent the whole morning at the courthouse working on this." He leaned back in his chair. "Patience, Grasshopper."

First Mariah, then Patillo, now Ryan. Why did everyone expect her to be patient?

Mom's brow furrowed. "My daughter is Samara, not Grasshopper."

"He's quoting from an old TV show, Mom. Get on with it, Ryan."

"These appraisals from 2006 are way higher than they should have been. Real estate values have fallen a lot since then, but not this much. So I looked up property transfers of similar homes from that time period and confirmed it. Bottom line: the appraiser inflated the valuations. And all three of these were done by the same appraiser."

"So the appraiser would be the guilty one. How could that implicate anyone at the bank?"

"I'm getting to that. In 2006, banks thrived in the hot real estate market. They were more than glad to issue mortgages to any warm body wanting a house. The major limiting factor on a mortgage loan or a home equity loan was the appraisal. They couldn't issue a loan for more than the house was worth. More loans equal more underwriting and processing fees, so they encouraged refi's and home equity loans, in addition to writing original mortgages for home purchasers. Here's where Al came in."

Mom sat up stiffly straight at the mention of Al.

"From what you've told me, he pushed the idea of putting home equity to use by refinancing, upping the mortgage amount, and taking cash out. Any time that's done, the purpose of that money is supposed to be to improve the property, like for additions or remodeling, or maybe to consolidate loans or pay for college. Those sorts of things were written into the paperwork for these loans."

"Al never told me about any remodeling," Mom said.

"All he did was insist my equity could generate more money in that hot investment of his. At closing, so many forms were shoved at me to sign that I didn't read any of them. He lied to me. How could he get away with that?"

"Nobody from the bank checks afterward," Ryan said. "Even if they did, the bank has no right to enforce how the money is used. In Duane's case and yours, Clair, Al steered the money into Madoff's fund. If Al didn't already know about the high appraisal racket the bank had been running, he couldn't have missed it when he saw the appraisal for your loan."

Mom stared at her desktop and squared up her papers, but Sam could visualize an army of her brain cells decoding Ryan's message and fitting it with the other intelligence they'd gathered.

"Everyone was one big happy family as long as home values kept inflating, but then the bubble burst. Those houses are now worth a heck of a lot less, often less than what the homeowners owe. Values of the houses have fallen below the 'water line' of the loan amounts, hence the term 'underwater mortgages.' When—"

"Been there, done that. Lordy, will you ever get to the point?" Sam rolled her eyes.

"If you quit interrupting, Sam, I'll get there faster." He paused for a big breath. "With the economy tanking, lots of those homes ended up in foreclosure. When a foreclosed home is sold, it often can't bring in enough to pay off the mortgage or a home equity loan. Whoever owns the loan ends up taking the loss. Whatever outfit bought a batch of bad loans might sic their lawyers on the original lender. A subpoena for the bank's loan files could expose the entire racket."

"Wouldn't digital copies of the paperwork be enough

to prove wrongdoing?" Sam asked.

"Yes, but you know how lawyers love to wave fistfuls of physical evidence in front of a judge or jury. Besides, there's always the chance that someone at the bank monkeyed with the paperwork when they digitized it. The bank would be up the creek if the two didn't match."

"Now I see where you're going." Sam continued sketching the scenario. "It would be most convenient for the bank if all the original paperwork disappeared. I'll bet Mardigan weeded out the loan files with inflated appraisals and gave them to Al to destroy. But Al kept some as insurance, a bargaining chip in case he ever needed one. Somehow Mardigan became suspicious that the files still existed, so he searched everywhere Al could have put them—Al's place, Mom's apartment, the bookshop, even burning Duane's attic after overhearing him tell Al to clear out his stuff. But Mardigan made a big mistake when he fired Al. He pushed Al—broke and unemployed—into cashing in his chip."

Sam wanted to pace the floor like a prosecuting attorney doing a summation in front of the jury, but considering her impaired foot, she settled for perching her butt on Mom's desk.

"And that, lady and gentleman," she continued, "brings us to the night of December 20. Al went to Someplace Else to collect the blackmail from Mardigan. He got his money, but Mardigan had no intention of letting him keep it. He spiked Al's drink, and when Al ran out, leaving 'a fresh Franklin' from his new wad, Mardigan followed him. When Al became woozy, he pulled off the street into the nearest driveway, at the church. All Mardigan had to do was load him into his car, drive into Richmond, and pitch him off Huguenot Bridge. Either the fall or the river finished the job. For a crowning touch, Mardigan tossed the empty packet from the drug into Duane's trash."

"Sam, you've collected all the pieces of the puzzle," said Ryan, "but you have no way to prove that's how they fit."

The three of them silently pondered the situation. The bells on the shop's front door sounded a distant jingle.

"What about the crooked appraiser?" asked Clair.

"I'll bet if we looked in the rest of the folders, we'd find his name on all of them," said Sam. "He had a good deal going with Mardigan. The appraiser earned a bonus fee, maybe even a kickback, too, and Mardigan booked lots of high-dollar business. If he knew his actions played a part in a murder, the appraiser might negotiate a lesser plea in exchange for testifying against Mardigan."

Ryan shook his head. "Sorry. There's one tiny problem. Our shady appraiser is no longer licensed in Virginia. The clerk in the records office knew him well. In early 2007, the guy retired to God's Waiting Room—Florida—then permanently retired via a heart attack on the golf course."

"Funny thing how I didn't see a single file dated after January of 2007," Sam said. "Must be hard to find a corrupt appraiser these days. You know I hate to do it, but I don't see any other choice. I'll have to give the files to the police and let them handle it. Unless either of you can think of a better course."

Clair turned back to her work. In Mom-speak, that meant no.

Ryan closed the file he'd been holding and handed it to Sam. "I'm relieved to see you've finally come to your senses."

****

"Mom, this time, I need your moral support. Will you go with me to turn the boxes in?"

Samara had set an appointment with Patillo for one o'clock that afternoon.

"Good. You're telling me what you need. I was wondering how you planned to lug both of those boxes by yourself. I don't like that place, but yes, I'll go."

It felt reassuring that her daughter, independent and headstrong as she was, still needed her. That's the way it should be.

"Let's talk through what we're going to tell Detective Patillo. I don't want to risk putting something the wrong way," Samara said.

"No need. We simply answer his questions, telling him the straight, unembellished truth. And we stick to the questions, not volunteering any extra information."

"I don't know," Samara said. "Not planning leaves me in a cold sweat."

"Plan, if you want, but the plain truth has always worked for me. You'll see."

By five minutes past one, Clair and Samara were seated next to each other in Patillo's office. They'd set the boxes beside his desk.

"Okay, you've got my curiosity up. What's in these, Mrs. Hobson?" Patillo asked. His chair squeaked as he leaned back and rested templed fingers on his chest.

Samara said, "These are—"

Clair cleared her throat. This time it was she who put a firm, cautioning hand on her daughter's. "These are loan files that have been missing from Ashland Community Bank."

Patillo sat up. He opened each box and peered at the contents. "Stay here. I'll be right back."

He left his office, his hard-soled shoes clacking down the hall. Had he noticed the tab marking his file in there? In five minutes, he returned, carrying a sheet of paper which he laid face down on his desk.

"Mrs. Hobson, where did these files come from?"

"I told you; Ashland Community Bank."

"No, where did *you* get these?"

"From Al's storage unit."

"And how did the boxes get into the storage unit?"

"Al put them there."

"Where were they before he put them into storage?"

"He stored them in my house."

"Did you see them in your house?"

"Yes." Clair enjoyed his clear, direct questions. He didn't ask complicated ones, like lots of people.

"Where did you see them?"

"They were stacked in my foyer the day of my house fire." Pointing, she said, "That one was on the bottom, and that one was on top."

"Mrs. Hobson, I'm placing you under arrest for accessory after the fact and the possession of stolen property."

Clair froze, dumbfounded.

Samara jumped to her feet. "You can't do that. We're returning these. We didn't steal them. What's more—"

"Shall I arrest you, too, Ms. McNeer? Mr. Mardigan reported these files stolen." He flipped the sheet of paper and slapped it, faceup on his desk. "Here's a copy of the police report from Ashland, dated Monday, December 29. You can see for yourself. The property was in her house, and she admitted she knew it."

Patillo read Clair her rights. When he asked if she understood, she mumbled, "Yes." What more was there to say?

As a uniformed officer led Clair away in handcuffs, she turned toward her daughter and cast a pleading look.

The tears welling in Clair's eyes matched Samara's.

Chapter 22

With the gauntlet of procedures Mom had to endure, and the scrambling Sam did to arrange for her release, plus the flurry of phone calls to Mariah, Patrice, and Ryan, it was after 10 p.m. before she'd driven her mom back to the apartment.

"Mom, I'd be glad to spend the night here on your sofa. Just say the word. You've been through a terrible ordeal."

Mom's gaze never left the floor. "Go home." She trudged up the stairs to her loft. A moment later, the bedsheets rustled, then nothing.

Sam went home and followed suit, too wiped out to even vent over the phone to anyone. She flopped on her bed, fully clothed, staring at the ceiling as if a way out of this debacle might magically appear. So much for her mom's "tell the truth" approach. So much for Ryan's "turn it over to the police" idea. By three a.m., exhaustion trumped anxiety.

The next day, much as she wanted to do otherwise, Sam couldn't bring herself to turn Amy down when she asked her to accompany her on a visit with Duane again. With the memory of their last depressing visit with him, plus Mom's arrest the previous day, it required every ounce of her resolve to re-enter that jail.

Duane slouched in his chair, barely making eye contact. Amy gave him an upbeat report on their boys' latest successes in school, but that brought tears to his eyes, followed by an uncomfortable silence.

He blinked the tears back then looked Sam's way. "Two weeks since you've come by, Sam. Getting tired of visiting a lost cause?"

"I've not given up on you yet," she said, "but I'll be tempted to if you don't show some appreciation for what I've been through for you."

He listened impassively to the story of her mom's arrest.

"What did you expect? Mardigan and Patillo are tight. It's no wonder Patillo would hammer your mother over the stolen boxes. It'd make his friend happy. Not only did Mardigan get his property back, but an immediate arrest tied it up with a neat bow."

"What brought those two together? I wouldn't expect a bank president and a detective to run in the same social circles."

"Maybe not. But around the poker table, everybody's money is the same color."

"Patillo and Mardigan were in your poker group?"

"Hell, no. I don't have that kind of money to throw around. That's the high-stakes game. Al asked me to join in once, but Amy would have killed me."

"You've got that right," said Amy. "You shouldn't have been in the other one, either. It's not like we have money to burn."

Duane shrugged, but he wouldn't look at her.

Sam asked, "You're saying that Al, Mardigan, and Patillo all played in a high stakes game?"

"Yeah. I think that's part of why Patillo wants to nail me against the wall."

"Why? To divert any suspicion from Mardigan and

himself?"

"That and more. Al told me Patillo was a sore loser and the other poker players gave him lots of opportunities to show it. Al said one night Patillo even accused him of cheating. Mardigan played peacemaker and settled them both down. Of course, by the end of the night, Mardigan held most of the chips. With as much as Patillo lost, I imagine he still owes Mardigan a shitload."

When they left the jail, Sam's thoughts were spinning. She'd never contemplated a personal link between Mardigan and Patillo, but that would account for his quick arrest of her mom. She drove straight to Ryan's. She needed a sounding board.

As soon as he saw Sam in his doorway, Ryan pulled her into his arms, pressing her head against his shoulder. "You've had me pacing the floor. Why didn't you call to let me know what happened after your mom was arrested?"

"She's been charged and released, but I didn't get home until eleven. I was in no mood to talk with anyone. And I'm mad at you for insisting that I turn over those boxes."

He loosened his embrace, looking her in the eye, confused. "Then why are you here?"

She stepped back and motioned toward two chairs in his dining room. "I need you to listen, that's all. Don't tell me what to do; just listen."

Sam unloaded the entire tale of the previous day, then added today's conversation with Duane. Next, she raged about Patillo, trying to comprehend why on earth he seemed to have it in for her mom. When Ryan started to interrupt, she shut him down. He persisted.

"Don't be such an ass. I've got something to show

you, for a change. Wait a minute. I need to get something from my office."

He returned and spread out a handful of papers in front of Sam. One glance, and she gasped.

"I thought you gave me all the papers back. You'll get us in more trouble. Why'd you keep these?"

"I didn't keep any originals. These are copies I made to take to the courthouse for research. I wasn't going to walk in there with a pile of stolen folders. Good thing I hadn't recycled these yet."

"What good can they do? The police have the originals."

"They'll never see what I saw. You've just given me the explanation for something that didn't make sense. Patillo took out a sixty-thousand-dollar home equity loan, supposedly to build an addition onto his house. Before going to the courthouse on Tuesday, I drove past his place to see if any work was done. The place is a dump—a decrepit bungalow—with no addition. Nothing even worth building onto."

"He probably invested the money with Madoff, like Mom and Duane."

"More likely, he used it at the poker table. I wouldn't think a detective's salary would go far in a high-stakes game. And from the looks of his house, he's been on a losing streak. If he lost it to Mardigan, who knows? Maybe he lost more than he could pay back, and Mardigan's got his neck in a noose." He sent a smile Sam's way, but it faded. "Hey, why the dejected look? I may have given you another piece of the puzzle."

"All these 'what ifs' don't amount to a hill of beans unless we can prove what happened. As long as Patillo is running the investigation into Al's murder, he'll sidetrack anything that works in Duane's favor."

"Focus on what you can do. Get your mom off the hook. Patillo's case against her is so wobbly; it'll topple with the first light breeze of truth."

****

For the third day in a row, Sam found herself in the company of police. She'd been summoned for questioning regarding the theft of the loan documents. At least she'd get the chance to tell her side of the story. Yet as she drove into Richmond, she wished she was headed to the jail to visit depressed Duane; anything would be better than facing Patillo again. When she entered the station, the desk officer sent her to see a detective named Dominic Dimitri. Puzzling, but she was relieved.

"Good morning, Ms. McNeer. I'm Nick Dimitri. May I call you Samara? I hate the Ms. and Mr. thing. Call me Nick, if you don't mind."

"And I prefer Sam."

Was this Patillo's counterpart—the good cop? He was everything Patillo wasn't—short, round-bellied…and broadly smiling. With his wide-set eyes, turned-up nose, and chubby cheeks, he reminded her of a particular teddy bear who loved pots of honey.

"Sam it is, then. I'll be handling your mother's case, so—"

"Pardon me for interrupting, but why isn't Detective Patillo doing it? He was the one who arrested her."

"He handles the major felony cases. I get the small stuff. All I need from you today is a statement of what you know about these boxes. It shouldn't take long."

He was wrong; it took an hour. In addition to recording their conversation, Detective Nick furiously scribbled notes.

Sam related the whole box saga, including the day of the fire, the suspicious break-ins, Mardigan's mention that her mom's file was missing, finding the key, the call about the storage unit in Charlottesville, discovering the boxes, finding Mom's file in it, and turning the boxes in to the police. She kept a laser focus on the boxes, ignoring Al's murder and carefully sidestepping any mention of her mistrust of Patillo. The last thing Sam needed was a defensive cop protecting one of his kind.

Mardigan's financial shenanigans did not benefit from the same discretion. If she could draw attention to his underhanded dealings, then use the boxes to tie Al into the picture, he couldn't help but come to the same conclusions she had. By the time she ran out of ammo, Nick had offered to take a shot at her target.

"Sam, I truly commend you. You've followed that trail more doggedly than a K-9. I'm going to open a case to investigate the appraisal misdoings. That's not my bailiwick, so I'll be passing it to Detective Lawson." He gathered his notes into a neat stack.

"What about my mother's case?"

"Sorry about that; you got me so sidetracked. After I corroborate the details you've provided, of course, I'll see about getting the charge against your mother dropped. I'll be back in touch soon. It's been a pleasure."

"The pleasure has been mine." Sam grinned so wide her cheeks hurt.

Nick wasn't a good cop. He was a great cop.

She could have skipped out of the police station but kept a lid on her soaring hopes until she sat in her car.

With the car door closed and no people nearby in the lot, she threw her head back and yelled, "Yes!" She snatched the phone from her pocket and punched Ryan's number.

"Hi, Ryan. It's my turn to ask you for a last-minute date. Would you like to go out to dinner to celebrate my exceptionally good, spectacularly awesome day?"

"I didn't think you played the lottery. With an offer like that, how could I refuse? What time?"

"I'll pick you up at six. Dress casual."

"You're not going to tell me anything more than that?"

"Not a word until this evening. Bye."

Her bare fingers tingled from the cold. She started the engine, blasted the heater, hustled back to the bookshop, and greeted Mariah with a bear hug.

"Mariah, I wanted you to be the first to know, uh, make that second, that I've had an exceptionally good, spectacularly awesome day. And it's not over yet."

"Who beat me out for first, Ryan?"

"Yes, but—"

"Don't 'yes, but' me. Our Friday movie nights have ceased, and we haven't had an ISC Convention for what seems like a decade. What gives?" Mariah raised one eyebrow. "Is it a proposal already? Or perhaps a proposition? Ooh, don't tell me."

"I won't right now, but how about a convention later tonight, say, about nine or so?"

"You're on."

****

When Sam drove into the packed lot of the Smokey Pig, Ryan said, "Ah, an Ashland tradition. Good choice, whatever we're celebrating."

Over a messy but satisfying rack of barbecued ribs, she told him all about the meeting with Nick Dimitri.

"I have to hand it to you, Sam. You did a great job of

laying out enough to warrant investigation, giving him 'the facts, ma'am, just the facts,' without accusing Mardigan of murder. Police like to solve their own cases; they're funny that way."

"Mom was right. The truth isn't always the easiest way to go, but it's the best. It felt so awesome to have a detective listen with an open mind for a change. And you were right. Clearing Mom first has started the ball rolling on clearing Duane and nailing Mardigan."

"I have another great idea for you. Why don't we continue this celebration back at my place? I'll even provide a movie and popcorn."

"I can come in for a while, but only for the popcorn. No time for the movie. I promised Mariah I'd stop by to give her the news."

****

It started with the popcorn, which, of course, demands comfortable seating on a sofa and a video running for the background atmosphere. They hadn't even gotten past the opening scenes of *The Da Vinci Code* when Ryan hit the pause button.

"All right, it's time. Way past time, don't you think?" He draped his arm softly over her shoulder.

She recognized that hungry look in his eyes, and it had nothing to do with popcorn. *Play it slow. Maybe I'm mistaken. Maybe I'm not ready.* "Time for what?"

"You know I've had a crush on you ever since high school." He played with her wayward curl, wrapping it around his index finger.

"You sure had a funny way of showing it then. Battle of wits, teasing…" Did she ever tell him to stop, go away?

"Yeah, well, what did I know? I was just a stupid kid.

Now I've learned more effective ways to go after what I want. How about you? All you wanted back then was to one-up me in everything—grades, debate club, even the friggin' science fair. What is it you want now? Could it be this?" He ever so slowly stroked her cheek and kissed the tip of her nose. The tingling didn't stop when he drew back.

"Ah, not…"

"Maybe this?"

Now a full-on kiss sent a tremor of heat through her. He was right. Way past time and time to let go of the past.

"Mmm, maybe. Try again." *Let's see what happens when he tries harder.*

"Or this…" A hand slipped to her thigh while his lips worked their way down her neck, to the top of her breast.

"Getting closer." She had been ignoring what not only her heart but also her body had been trying to tell her since she first saw Ryan in that hospital bed. Her gaze drifted to his staircase.

His followed.

"Great minds work alike."

****

At eleven-thirty, Sam opened Mariah's door, calling, "ISC Convention."

"In the kitchen," Mariah said. "Why are you so late? Your hot chocolate is now iced chocolate."

"Ryan talked me into watching *The Da Vinci Code* after dinner." Did Mariah hear the slight sigh at the end of that sentence? "But enough about the night. You'll never believe the morning I had."

After hearing the story, Mariah said, "Sounds wonderful, but I want to caution you not to get your hopes too high. With all the wild turns you've been through since the fire, I wouldn't be surprised if a few more cropped up. If you're building a bridge from two boxes of files to bringing a murderer to justice, there's still a long way to go."

"I realize that, but at long last, it's heading in the right direction. Don't be such a wet blanket."

"You don't have any stops to make on the way home, do you?"

"Of course not. Not at this hour."

"Okay. Just thought that if you did, you'd want to rebutton your blouse properly, first."

****

Mid-afternoon on Monday, Mariah answered the phone at the counter and waved Sam over, covering the mouthpiece. She whispered, "It's Nick Dimitri for you. That's quick work."

"Hello, Detective. Sam speaking. You have good news already?"

"Not exactly. We'll probably be dropping the theft charge shortly, but there's a problem. We don't know how this happened, especially after all you went through to get those boxes, but, uh…they're missing."

"You're kidding."

"I don't kid about stuff like this. They were sent to the evidence room, tagged as possibly related to the Hobson murder due to his involvement, and checked in properly, but they couldn't be found when Detective Lawson went to retrieve them to start on the case. I'm hoping they were merely stored on the wrong shelf. Unless they turn up, there are no files to investigate. The only good news is that it makes the case against your mother look bad on our part."

"I might be able to help get the investigation back on

track. Let me check into it. I'll get back to you. And I want to thank you again for what you're trying to do." Sam hung up.

"What was all that about? Please don't tell me I jinxed you."

"Maybe not. The boxes disappeared from the evidence room. If Patillo is wrapped up in this, that move could give him away. Ryan had better have saved those copies he made."

Inside of two hours, Sam handed copies of the copies to Detective Nick.

****

Wednesday evening, Clair called her daughter on the antique wall phone. Before Clair could speak, Samara asked, "Mom, are you okay?"

"I'd be better if you'd remember to charge your cell phone or turn on the ringer or whatever. Can you come over to see this letter from the life insurance company? I don't like what they're doing."

"I'll be there in a flash."

Two minutes later, Clair met Samara at the apartment door, waving the letter. "Look at this. I thought you said things were going better with the police."

"Hold on. Let me in the door first."

Samara stepped in but didn't bother taking off her coat. It didn't take her long to skim the one-page letter.

"What the insurance company is telling you is that they won't pay the claim until it's determined that you played no part in his murder. Looks like you'll have to wait until Al's murderer is convicted. I can't believe that idiot Patillo. How can he say you're a 'person of interest' when he has a suspect locked up? Maybe I can talk with Detective Nick and see if he can twist Patillo's arm."

"That would be stupid. He'd get a lot further if he convinced Patillo to change my status."

Samara shifted her feet, then sighed. "Looks like this calls for another visit to the station. I'll do whatever I can. In the meantime, don't worry about the insurance. They'll pay. It's just a question of when."

Samara didn't ask, and Clair didn't volunteer to go with her to the police station.

****

The next afternoon, when Sam popped her head in Dimitri's door, he said, "You're getting to be a regular around here, Sam. What can I do for you?"

"It seems there may have been an oversight in the investigation of Al Hobson's murder. My mother was questioned and never charged with anything, but her status hasn't been cleared. She's still listed as a 'person of interest.' Could you get this corrected?"

"I'd love to, but it's not my case. Detective Patillo would have to sign off on that. Do you want me to see if he's free now?"

"I was hoping to avoid him. We've not been on the friendliest of terms."

"I understand where you're coming from. He can be gruff, but he closes more cases than many of the others. I'll ask him to treat you nice." In his brief phone call to Patillo, he did just that.

When Sam entered Patillo's office, she forced herself to shake his hand. He grasped hers reluctantly, then dropped it.

"You've sure stirred up a hornet's nest with Mardigan. He's ticked that you're sticking your nose into private bank business. There'd better be a strong case there—he said you're going to find yourself in court for slander. Why are you here?"

So much for treating me nicely.

She told him the same thing she told Nick, but Patillo was dead set on keeping Mom on the hook.

"Your mother's affect is off. She smiles at the wrong time. And her answers are abrupt and short. That's how people avoid giving themselves away."

"It's also a trademark of the behavior of someone with Asperger's Syndrome, a high-functioning form of autism. Are you familiar with it?"

"You're saying she's autistic? Can you prove it?"

"She's not been diagnosed, but I've read the definitive book about it. She has all the traits."

"So you've read a book. That makes you an expert, right?"

This was destined for a dead end.

"Would you believe it if she got a professional diagnosis?"

"I might reconsider it. Other than that, wait until Chanesky is convicted. When the case is closed, her status will automatically be cleared. Now, I have work to do."

He opened a folder and picked up his pen.

Chapter 23

Before heading home to a quiet evening, Sam stopped at her mom's apartment.

"Why do I have to pay a doctor good money to tell me what I already know for certain? I'm different; that's all there is to it."

"Do you want to get that insurance check, Mom?"

"Of course I do. Then maybe I'll consider getting a diagnosis."

"Are you okay with waiting a year to get the money? Because the diagnosis is the only way you'll see it sooner."

"I've been poor before. It's not like I'm starving. I can stand more months of having no money in the bank."

"I was just trying to help."

"I'll ask for your help when I need it."

Sam gave up and went home. Time to lose herself in a fictional world, where every problem worked itself out within a few hours of reading. The moonless night set the perfect mood. Snug in her overstuffed chair, tucked under an afghan, she opened *Maisie Dobbs*, a mystery featuring a young British woman who becomes a psychologist and investigator in early twentieth-century England.

In the middle of chapter three, Sam's doorbell rang. She checked her cell phone—dead again. Ryan had probably tried to phone. If she didn't get more reliable about recharging the darn thing or trade it in on one that had a longer-lasting battery, she'd have to get the landline reinstalled.

"Coming," she called.

She looked in the foyer mirror and tucked that wayward curl back. On second thought, she dangled it over her forehead. Then she opened the door. *What's Elena doing here?*

"Hope I'm not disturbing you. I tried your cell, but it immediately rolled to voicemail. I need your help on a little matter."

If Elena needed help, why hadn't she simply gone by the bookshop during the day?

"No problem. Come in. It's cold out there."

When she stepped inside, Sam caught a whiff of alcohol on her breath.

Elena locked the door. "You can never be too careful."

"Hey, this is Ashland, but you're right. Thanks."

Sam's senses sharpened. Something in Elena's demeanor—something more than alcohol—was off. Maybe it was the way Elena looked at her and then scrutinized her living room as if assessing a situation.

"When you stopped by with the death certificate a couple of weeks ago, you said you'd be leaving shortly. Nothing's fallen through with your new teaching job, has it?"

"No, it's just taken me longer than expected to wrap up a few details. Actually, that's why I'm here. My landlord is giving me a hard time getting my security deposit back. I need that money. I thought you might know a lawyer or someone with pull who could help me change his mind."

"I'm not sure if he deals with that sort of thing, but I

was impressed by Marcus DeVaughn, the fellow who's defending Duane."

Elena shuddered at the mention of Duane.

"Sorry, I wasn't thinking. Maybe I could dig up the name of the guy who helped us retitle our house and the bookshop's building after Dad died."

"That sounds more like it."

"I meant to ask you the other day; how'd you manage to get hired to teach in the middle of a semester?"

"Long story. I don't want to keep you from whatever you were doing."

"Oh, I was only reading. How about I make us some decaf, and we can chat a bit."

"I'd appreciate that." Elena's mouth wore a smile, but her eyes, not so much. A mismatch, almost like one of Mom's expressions.

As Sam walked through the dining room toward the kitchen, she glanced out the window to the street. No car was parked in front of her house.

"Say, how'd you get here, Elena?"

"A friend was coming this way, and she dropped me off. My car's in for repairs."

"Well then, will you need a ride home?"

"Oh, I can walk. It's a nice night. I could use the exercise."

Sam took another look outside. The only nice part about the freezing night was the pretty coat of frost sparkling in the wash of the streetlight. Across the street and down one lot, a small cloud of exhaust from an idling car almost spoiled the scene. Although the vehicle's front was obscured in a dark spot and its lights were off, its black rear end had the trademark squared-off look of a certain SUV.

No one on Sam's street drove one of those. But Mardigan did. A black one, too.

When she glanced back at Elena, that odd smile was still plastered on. She seemed to relish seeing Sam's shock as comprehension slapped her in the face: Mardigan sitting beside Elena at Al's funeral, comforting her with a big hug. She'd probably even lured Al into the engagement for the sole purpose of learning where he'd hidden the incriminating boxes.

"You know, you ruined everything," Elena said. "If you'd just returned the files to the bank, as he told you to do, well…"

Sam eyed her dead cell phone on the coffee table. As best she could with her booted foot, she lunged for the phone, flipped it open, and pushed a few buttons.

"Get out now. I'm calling the police." Sam tried to make her bluff sound firm and strong, but her insides were jelly.

Elena snatched the phone out of her hand and looked at its black screen. "With this?"

Sam backed away. Elena dropped the cell to the floor, stomped it with her boot, and then sauntered toward Sam.

Sam lurched into the kitchen and upended the kitchen table against the doorframe. As Sam reached her back door, Elena casually slid the table aside, laughing.

"Did I ever tell you I run marathons?"

Even without an injured foot, Sam could never outrun a marathoner. Or Mardigan, who must be lurking out there. Change of plans. Sam lifted the earpiece off the antique phone's hook, turned the crank, and waited. At the sound of the ringing bells, Elena burst into derisive laughter.

Sam leaned close to the mouthpiece. "9-1-1! Send the police! Elena's here. She's in cahoots with Mardigan."

Still laughing, Elena ripped the earpiece out of her hand and yanked its frayed cord from the wooden cabinet.

"The police will be here any minute, so you'd better leave while you can, Elena," Sam said loudly, hoping the intact mouthpiece still caught every word.

"Another fake. What a joke! Where'd you get that old prop? From a movie set? Oh, we're leaving all right, leaving for good, thanks to you, but not until we teach you a little lesson about the price of meddling in someone else's affairs."

She grabbed Sam with both hands and slammed her against the wall. Sam slumped to the floor, her head spinning. Pain shot through her shoulder; she couldn't move her left arm. In addition to being a runner, the woman must lift weights.

"How about a little farewell toast?" Elena leaned back on the counter, folded her arms, and studied Sam. "Got any whiskey around here? I sure would like a nip."

Sam wanted to piece together some witty comeback, but the thoughts ricocheting through her aching head refused to cooperate.

Elena chuckled, opening cabinet doors. "Oh, don't trouble yourself. I'll find it."

A siren sounded in the distance. Shortly afterward, a second one joined it in an offbeat chorus. Through wavy vision, Sam watched Elena cock an ear, then hurriedly open one kitchen drawer after another. *That's stupid.* Even if Sam had whiskey, which she didn't, she'd never stash it in a drawer.

When Elena came to the cutlery drawer, she paused to study its contents, then held up a serrated six-inch knife. "I'll have to make this quicker than we'd wanted, but that's the way it goes. After what you've seen, we can't risk—"

A key grated in a lock, and the back door burst open. Mom surveyed the scene: Sam crumpled on the floor, clinging to one arm; Elena on the other side of the kitchen, a knife clenched in her raised fist; the upended table near the doorway. She leveled a pistol in Elena's direction and pulled the trigger.

The bang blasted Sam's eardrums. Elena collapsed, screaming in rage. The knife clattered to the floor, out of her reach. She pressed hands to her bloody thigh and moaned.

"Are you okay, Samara? What did she do to your arm? Are you hurt anywhere else? What do you need?" Mom lowered her gun and moved toward Sam.

Elena took advantage of Mom's distraction to inch closer to the knife.

"Keep your gun aimed at her. If she creeps any closer to that knife, shoot her again."

Her mother swung Elena's way and raised the gun. She stood in that pose, still and silent as a tree on a windless day.

"Bitch."

Sam couldn't tell if Elena hurled that at Mom or her, but she didn't care as long as Elena complied. The last thing she wanted was to hear another gunshot.

Pounding rattled the front door. "Police! Open the door."

"She locked it, Mom. But don't walk near that woman. Call out the back door and tell them to come around."

As soon as she poked her head out the door, a deep

voice shouted, "Put your weapon down. Now."

Mom eased the gun onto the back stoop.

"Now turn around and put your hands behind your head."

Again she obeyed, her arms now trembling. Three officers appeared in the doorway.

"That woman shot me, officers," Elena said through gritted teeth. "She's crazy. She came in the back door and, without saying a word, she shot me."

"Is this true, ma'am?" one officer asked Mom.

"Yes."

There was that mistimed smile again. The officer removed handcuffs from his belt.

Sam interrupted his move toward Mom. "Ask her *why* she shot her, please."

"Yes, ma'am, I was getting to that. Why did you?"

"Because she was attacking my daughter with that knife." She tipped her head toward where the knife lay against the baseboard by the sink.

Another officer pulled on a pair of latex gloves, picked up the knife, and studied it. "There doesn't appear to be any blood on this."

"That's right," said Mom. "I shot her before she could use it."

"I'm bleeding to death over here," Elena whined. The proof puddled around her. "Are you going to talk all night, or are you going to call an ambulance?"

"One's on the way."

"Make that two. I think she broke my shoulder," Sam said.

Another officer radioed in the call. The third officer bagged Mom's gun.

"Is that your gun, ma'am?" the lead officer asked

Mom.

"Yes."

"Until we sort this out, I need to take you into custody. Please put your hands behind your back."

She obeyed but started rocking.

The officer had trouble hitting a moving target. "Hold still, ma'am."

She froze. He slipped bags over her hands, then cuffed her.

"This is so wrong," Sam cried. "My mother saved my life, and you're treating her like a criminal."

"We're just taking her in for questioning. Standard procedure in any shooting. She'll be released if no charges are filed." He stepped aside to let the paramedics in and then led Mom out by the elbow.

As the paramedic team tended to Elena, Sam warned, "Be cautious around that woman. She's dangerous."

"She's not in any condition to cause trouble now. She's lost consciousness."

They rushed the stretcher out the door. At the spot where Elena had fallen, a bright red pool covered the light blue vinyl. The bullet might have hit an artery. Sam prayed she wouldn't die. She wanted to see Elena suffer in jail for the rest of her life. But more than anything, she couldn't stand to see her mom accused of murdering a murderer.

When the second paramedic team wheeled Sam away, the antique phone, now looking forlorn without its earpiece, reminded her of when she was a child. She'd use that very phone to call Mom from her playhouse. *Hey, it's started raining. Could you bring me an umbrella? Please?* This time, it had taken much more than an umbrella to rescue her.

On the way down her drive, Ryan rushed to her side.

"Are you all right? The guys at the station phoned me when they realized it was your address on the dispatch."

He laid a hand on hers but withdrew it when Sam groaned. She broke down, not as much from the pain as from the deep concern in his eyes.

"I think my shoulder's broken. Elena tried to kill me, but Mom shot her." Her sobs made any more words impossible.

"I'll follow you to the hospital. You'll be okay."

The ambulance doors banged shut.

****

Sitting back against pillows in a treatment room at Memorial Hospital, her arm cradled in a sling, she looked down at her charming hospital gown, then up at Ryan. She hoped her appearance wouldn't banish all visions of more romance from his head. X-rays showed a slight fracture of Sam's collar bone, plus she had a mild concussion from her head smacking the wall.

"Don't worry," he said. "They say that gown is the latest style. It even matches your face—white."

"I guess I won't be wearing any more of my favorite turtlenecks this winter." She gazed at the shreds of the turquoise shirt they'd cut off her. "And as if the broken bone isn't enough, my head is killing me."

He chuckled. "Welcome to the concussion club. Sorry for laughing, but you and headaches seem to go together."

"If you're trying to cheer me up, you're doing a lousy job. You can do one thing to help, though. Please check on Elena's status."

He phoned Memorial's information desk. "Elena isn't listed as a patient there. They must have taken her to the

283

Level 1 Trauma Center at VCU Medical Center." He tried their number next. "She's there, but no word on her condition yet."

"Could you make one more call? Check with the police about my mom."

At that moment, a uniformed officer stepped through the doorway. "I might be able to help with that. Your mother is still being questioned regarding the shooting, and I'm here to ask some questions, too, if you're up to it."

"Absolutely. Elena tried to kill me. If Mom hadn't stopped her, I'd be dead. And Mardigan's also involved. I think he killed Al Hobson."

"Wait. Are you talking about Squire Mardigan, the man who's wanted for loan fraud?"

"Yeah. That fraud led to Al's murder."

"He was there tonight? Wish we'd known. We figured he was long gone."

"What do you mean?"

"When we went to pick him up for questioning this afternoon, he was nowhere to be found. Not at the bank. Not at home. Mrs. Mardigan was furious when she found his closet cleared out and all his suitcases gone. You wouldn't happen to have any idea where he'd go, would you?"

"No," Sam said. "I don't know much about him, other than the old joke that our noble Squire hailed from a West Virginia farm."

"If he's headed back there, we could be in luck. A jackknifed fourteen-wheeler caused a big pileup on I-64 near Afton Mountain. If he was caught in the accident or the miles-long backup, we'll get him. Excuse me a minute."

The officer stepped into the hall to radio in a brief report. Ryan used the break to readjust Sam's pillows and lower the head of the bed a bit.

"You never know, you know," the officer said as he came back. "Now, where were we? Oh yeah, why did Elena attack you?"

Sam told her whole story, blow by blow.

"Say, how soon will they release my mother?"

"These things take time."

As Sam pictured her mom in a small interview room, rocking in a chair, tears filled her eyes.

"I can see you're in pain. That's enough for now. Take care of that shoulder."

After a two-hour observation, Ryan drove Sam home, only to find crime scene tape sealing her door. "Should have guessed this. You can spend the night at my place."

"A sweet offer, but I'd rather associate your place with more pleasant times." Her cheeks flushed. "Please take me to Mariah's house. I'll tell you the way."

"It's two a.m. Do you really want to disturb her at this hour?"

"Trust me; she'd be more disturbed if I didn't. That's the way it is with best friends."

At Mariah's house, Sam was surprised to see lights on inside. Ryan knocked at the door, but Sam merely turned the handle. Mariah was among the Ashland residents who rarely locked up.

"Thank God you're here! Come in and sit down, both of you." Mariah fussed over Sam, getting her comfortable on the sofa, then ran into the kitchen to put on a pot of coffee. "Don't worry, it's decaf," she called out.

While the coffee brewed, she said, "Clair told me what happened. My God, that crazy woman almost killed you."

"Sure did. Hey, how'd you end up talking with my mom?"

"She called me from the police station an hour ago and asked me to take her home. Don't worry; she's shaken, but she's stronger than you think."

"Thank goodness! With a second arrest in only a week, I thought it could push her over the edge."

"Why didn't you answer your phone? I called a few minutes ago, and it rolled to voice mail."

With coffee in hand, Sam repeated the sordid story. At the end, she added, "The funny part about all this is that I didn't know Mom even owned a gun, let alone knew how to shoot one. The sight of her with that handgun nearly made me pass out."

"Kind of like my first sight of you in pain on that stretcher." Ryan slipped on his coat. "Well, Sam, it looks like you're in capable hands. If there's anything you need—absolutely anything—give me a call."

"How do you suggest I do that?"

He paused. "Oh, yeah. Slight problem."

"Got it covered," said Mariah. "Unlike Sam, I still have a landline. Until further notice, she's staying here where I can keep an eye on her. Come by any time; we can double-team her." She wrote down her home and cell numbers and handed the slip to Ryan.

****

The smell of baking biscuits lured Sam into the kitchen. She found Mariah seated at the table, reading the morning paper.

"How do you make those smell so irresistible? Ooh, my head and shoulder hurt." She reached for Mariah's cordless phone with her good arm.

"If you're calling your mom, don't bother. I already did. She's on her way. Ditto for Ryan."

Sam parked the phone back in its cradle.

Mariah added, "You might want to exchange those pajamas for a shirt and sweatpants. Pick anything out of my closet. I'll handle the buttons for you. Lately, somebody's been having a hard time hitting the right buttonholes, even without an arm in a sling." She flashed a sly grin.

"Oh, this is gonna look great. The shirt will be too baggy in the bust, and your pants will look like capris on me. So I don't embarrass myself in the shop, you'll have to retrieve some clothes from my house."

"No need. You're not going anywhere. I rose early, went to the bookshop to post a 'Sorry – We're Closed Today' sign on the door, then came back to cook breakfast."

"But I—"

"Forget it. You're in no shape to work, and I'm taking care of you. End of story."

Ryan and Mom arrived minutes apart. Conversation buzzed about the previous night's events, but Ryan cut in.

"I have an update you'll all want to hear. On the way over, I phoned a friend of mine at the police station. Elena is expected to make a full recovery in the secure ward of the hospital. She'll be charged with assault with a deadly weapon. Clair, I'm pretty sure they're not going to file any charges against you."

Mom and Mariah heaved sighs of relief, but Sam *humph*ed.

"Mom, that's absolutely as it should be. Anything less would be a travesty. But what about Elena? Even though Mardigan is in the wind, he'll find a way to throw

287

his money at a bigwig lawyer, and she'll get off with a light sentence. That's not good enough. She's still getting away with Al's murder. So is Mardigan."

"At least it's not your murder, Sam. Let's eat before everything gets cold," said Mariah.

"Long as you don't mind me speaking with my mouth full. There's more I need to talk through."

As the four of them tucked into warm biscuits, bacon, and eggs, Sam brought up the topic of Mardigan's and Elena's relationship.

"Before last night, a link between those two never occurred to me. Elena's whole engagement to Al must have been a sham to get her close enough to Al to learn where he'd hidden the loan files. Did any of you see that coming?"

"Not exactly, but didn't you ever question why Elena kept trying to build a friendship with *you*, Samara?" Clair asked.

"Not before last night." Sam suddenly found her slice of bacon to be of exceptional interest.

"First, she invited you to sit with her at Hanover Café, divulging all kinds of personal stuff, blatantly going against the wishes of both her fiancé and his lawyer. When you love someone, you're not supposed to do that. I would never have treated Preston like that."

"True, but I thought she was just upset about the arson charge, jumping to Al's defense."

Mom ignored Sam and moved on. "Next, she offered to get the death certificate I needed for the life insurance claim. How did she even know about the policy? Or that I was the beneficiary? Al might have mentioned it, but, as guarded as he always was about his finances, I doubt it. Seems to me Reliant Financial Services wouldn't tell anyone but the beneficiary. Of course, Mardigan knew all about it. He's the one who told us."

"Why didn't you bring this up when Elena first mentioned the policy?"

"I wasn't in on that conversation. She phoned you at home, not me. Besides, like you, I wanted to get the insurance claim going. How she learned about it didn't seem important. When you told me she'd asked us to her house, I focused on the chance to get my clock back."

Sam pushed the scrambled eggs around on her plate. "I'll bet the only reason she invited us was to find out if you had any of Al's files in your storage unit. Ironic. I gave her the perfect opening for her question when I asked the same one in reverse: did she have his files somewhere in her place? You know, I can see her being frustrated that she couldn't find the missing boxes for Mardigan. And angry when I persisted in uncovering his financial mischief. But I would think it would take more than that to drive her to attack me physically. Or 'teach me a lesson,' as she put it."

"Bad people do bad things. She's a bad person, that's all." Mom said.

"Enough about Elena," said Mariah. "Back to your original question, Sam. How could those two carry on a long-term affair—which appears to be the case—and not one of us heard the first whisper of a rumor? So un-Ashland."

Ryan shrugged. "They were slick enough to commit a murder and set up Duane to take the fall. Keeping an affair hidden must have been no sweat for them."

Sam thought back. "Son of a bitch. They say the best way to hide something is in plain sight. Before leaving Al's funeral, Mardigan gave Elena a big hug. And his wife was right beside him. Now, why would a man hug the fiancée of a disgraced employee he'd fired? I was so sure that Mardigan had acted alone, yet it would have been much easier for two people to hoist Al over Huguenot Bridge's high railing. I learned last night that woman is strong."

"And violent," Mom added. "Women aren't supposed to be. Men are usually the violent ones. Plus, Mardigan has a wife and children. Bankers are supposed to be trustworthy, but he broke the most important promise, his marriage vow. Why would anyone do that?"

"Can't help you with that one, Mom." Sam finished the last crumb on her plate. "But I've got a question for you. Why didn't you ever tell me you had a gun?"

"Preston made me promise not to. *I* don't break my promises. He said if you knew it was there, you might get curious and try to play with it."

"How old was I when he said this?"

"Four."

Sam groaned. Ryan kept a straight face but rolled his eyes, which then crinkled in silent laughter. Mariah tried to suppress a laugh, too, yet when she turned her back to rinse the dishes, her shuddering shoulders gave her away. Good thing Mom had never tuned in to body language.

Mom had stuck to a promise decades after a reasonable expiration date. Yet Sam felt ashamed about how they all, including her, had laughed at her and her iron-clad sense of honor. How many other times in Mom's life had she been ridiculed for being true to her values, revered values many folks compromise whenever it's convenient?

The woman never lied, always followed through on everything she said she'd do, always told it like she saw it, but was ostracized for being different from the vast majority who could never be so unfailingly honorable.

Stifling the threat of tears, Sam asked, "When did you get the gun?"

"Preston bought it for me in 1974, shortly after we were married. He took me to a shooting range and taught me to use it. I always keep it clean and close by, but out of sight, just like he told me."

"Where?"

"I don't tell anybody that," she said, taking the last biscuit.

Iron-clad.

"I'm curious, Mom. Why did you shoot Elena in the leg?"

"I didn't mean to. I was aiming at her gut."

The others grinned, but Sam was left to wonder why her safety-conscious dad would ever give a gun to a woman with point-blank aim no better than that. Only one answer came to mind; Dad must have been desperately afraid of something.

After Mom and Ryan left, Mariah talked Sam into going back to bed. With the combination of a filling meal and good pain meds, she drifted back to sleep. The next thing she knew, Mariah was quietly saying, "Sam, I brought you some lunch. Let me help you sit up."

"What time is it?"

"One-thirty." Mariah rearranged the pillows and set a tray on the bed. "Detective Dimitri phoned and left a message. He said you'd never believe it, but…"

"Oh, no. Not again."

"Let me finish. He said some Fridays the thirteenth were lucky. Those boxes with the loan files showed up this morning in the evidence room as if they'd never left.

He knew that news would cheer you up."

"Not much good without a guy to prosecute."

"That's the best part. They caught him."

"All right!"

"He escaped the mega-backup on I-64, only to slide into a second pileup near Staunton. As soon as police ran his plate, he was a goner. And forgive me, but Detective Dimitri told me to put it this way: He's now on ice in our local jail."

"Cop humor; gotta love it." Sam sighed. "Loan fraud might send Mardigan away for a few years, but I'm hoping for more. There must be a way to get him for Al's murder."

`

Chapter 24

That night, Mariah asked Ryan to come for dinner. She'd also invited Sam's mom, but Clair claimed she wanted a quiet night in her own place. After the three of them finished a feast of roast beef, fresh asparagus, and homemade mashed potatoes, Mariah set a pie in the center of the table and cut three big slices.

"If I'd known you'd baked that for dessert, I would have saved room for two pieces," Sam said. "Ryan, have you ever tasted brown sugar pie?"

"Can't say that I've ever heard of it. What else is in it, aside from brown sugar?"

"Not much. Think of it as a pecan pie without the nuts."

After the first bite, Ryan requested the recipe.

"You cook?" Sam asked. "Most guys I've known, even my dad, couldn't fix anything they couldn't heat-and-eat using a microwave."

"I eat well; therefore, I cook. I look at it as building something in a workshop, except I get to consume the finished product."

A man who's not afraid to tackle the domestic arts can be very sexy. "What's your favorite dish?" she asked.

"Enough about cooking, already," Mariah broke in. "I thought you wanted to discuss the trail of those wandering file boxes, Sam."

"Yeah, I did." *Spoilsport.* Another minute and Sam

might have wangled an invitation for a home-cooked dinner, a movie... She sighed. "Let's start at the beginning. Patillo had to have a hand in making them disappear. Would there be any way for him to get them out of the evidence room without a paper trail?"

"Doubtful," said Ryan. "Police are sticklers for rigid procedures and proper paperwork. More likely, the boxes were simply stashed in the wrong place."

"That's what Detective Dimitri suggested, but if that happened, how did they magically reappear today?" asked Mariah.

"Ryan, I think you're right," Sam said. "The boxes couldn't have left the evidence room, but I'd bet dollars to a policeman's donuts that Patillo still engineered the disappearing act. Let's say Patillo owed a bundle in gambling debts to Mardigan. When Mom and I delivered the boxes to Patillo, he phoned Mardigan to let him know. Maybe Mardigan asked him to make the files disappear, offering to cut him some slack on his debts, but instead of destroying them as Mardigan wanted, Patillo could easily have gone in the evidence room and buried them in some obscure corner. Patillo, like Al, wanted a bargaining chip in his back pocket."

"Wait." Mariah frowned and shook her head. "That corner couldn't have been very well hidden. It only took a few days for them to be found."

Ryan picked up the dangling thread. "No, I doubt they were found by accident. Sam, once you delivered my copies of the three loan files, there'd be enough solid evidence to convict Mardigan of fraud. If Mardigan were headed for jail time, he'd have trouble collecting a gambling debt. For Patillo, the risk of his complicity with Mardigan coming to light was suddenly much more dangerous than the risk of double-crossing an incarcerated man. All Patillo would need to do is put the boxes back where they belonged."

Mariah shook her head again. "All very plausible, but not an ounce of that story you've woven is provable. Some things may never come to light." She looked Sam's way.

Sam's train of thought screeched to a halt. She'd been so entangled in coming to grips with a tragic past and a messed-up present, she'd not looked very far ahead. The few glimpses of the future she'd envisioned showed Duane rotting in jail for a crime he didn't commit and Mardigan and Elena getting away with murder. She readjusted her arm sling to no avail. Time for another pain pill. "Maybe it's like Mom said. The answer will be in the last place I look. The trouble is, I don't even know what I'm looking for."

"They must have dropped a hint somewhere," said Mariah. "Review everything you watched Mardigan and Elena do or say."

That's exactly what Sam planned to do over the next few days.

****

Ryan popped in at lunchtime Saturday, bringing Sam his remedy for shoulder pain: a quart of double dark chocolate ice cream and goofy Get Well and Valentine's Day cards. On Monday, in spite of still feeling lousy, Sam told everyone she'd be fine and sent Mariah and Mom to work.

By Tuesday, she was going stir crazy, so Ryan offered to take her cell phone shopping after a client meeting he'd scheduled for two o'clock. The morning hours seemed interminable, and the afternoon followed

295

suit. She'd been sifting through her memory, reconstructing every encounter with Mardigan or Elena, reliving that terrifying moment when Elena gripped the knife, leaving no doubt they both wanted her dead.

That could be it. If only...

Sam grabbed Mariah's phone and called the shop.

"When you cleaned up my kitchen, did you find any loose trash, anything you didn't recognize?"

"Hello to you, too. No, I only scrubbed the bloodstains."

"Are you sure you didn't see anything on the floor below a cabinet or something?"

"No. All I saw there were stray crumbs and a colony of breeding dust bunnies. What's this about?"

"I have a theory." The doorbell rang. "Gotta go. Ryan's here. Thanks. Call you later." She hung up and hobbled to the door.

"Ready to go shopping?"

"I'm almost set." She dashed as best she could into the kitchen and snatched a zip-top plastic bag from Mariah's pantry. Back in the living room, Ryan helped her put her good arm in one sleeve of her coat, draped the rest over her bum shoulder, and then gently drew her close for a kiss. When he stepped away, her eyes remained closed, face upturned, savoring the moment.

"More later when you heal up a bit. Cell phone shopping, remember?" They headed out the door.

When he put his car in drive, Sam said, "I need to drop by my house first. This is really important." She could hardly sit still.

"Another experiment?"

"Not exactly. I need to test a theory."

"Have you thought of the proverbial 'last place to

look?'"

"Maybe."

"Do you know what you're looking for?"

"Fly poop in the pepper. Maybe. Sort of. But I don't know exactly what it will look like."

"Are you going to tell me what it is, or are we going to continue playing twenty questions?" His tone conveyed equal parts of amusement and annoyance.

"Neither. We're almost there. Oh, don't pull in the drive. Park at the curb, in front of my neighbor's house."

Ryan was doing a great job of following orders. The Army must have trained him well.

Step by step, Sam made her way along the edge of the street, probing clumps of leaves and debris in the gutter with the toe of her booted foot. Her unfastened coat flapped in the cold breeze, but she didn't care.

"This might go quicker if you tell me what you're searching for," Ryan said, his brow knotted.

In her best Groucho Marx voice, she said, "Congratulations! You said the secret woid—quicker." She talked as she moved along. "When Elena had me cornered in my kitchen, she casually asked where I had some whiskey, but her whole demeanor changed when she heard the approaching sirens. Hurriedly she began searching my kitchen drawers, saying she needed to make this *quicker* than they'd wanted. By *this*, I'm sure she meant killing me. She'd planned to drug me with a spiked drink, and Mardigan was waiting outside to help finish the job. Shades of Al's murder. Same method, new victim."

They'd arrived at her driveway. She focused on the side where an overgrown forsythia hedge threatened to take over.

297

"Got it," said Ryan triumphantly.

"You found it already? Where?"

"No, I just *got* what you're leading to. With police on the way, what Elena brought with her would be useless. And incriminating."

"Then she pretended to pass out, so they wouldn't talk to her on the way out. As they wheeled her down the driveway, she ditched her weapon, if you can call it that." Halfway up her drive, Sam spotted a shiny glint against the dull, dry leaves and barren forsythia branches. "Maybe…"

She quickened her awkward pace. The glint came from a clear snack-size baggie that looked empty. When she bent down closer, she could see a smidgen of light powder in the bottom. Turning the bigger baggie she had brought inside-out, Sam used it like a glove to pick up the smaller one, then reversed her bag again and zipped it closed, the same process she'd used for picking up puppy poop without touching it.

"I hope this teeny bit is enough to turn the tide."

"I'm calling the police right now," said Ryan, taking out his cell. "That needs to go straight to a lab. Great piece of deduction, Sherlock. We need to pray there are fingerprints on that, and the powder inside is the same drug used on Al."

Sam's elation nosedived when it hit her how close she'd come. She could visualize herself, woozy from a drug, powerless to prevent Elena and Mardigan from tossing her off Huguenot Bridge.

****

Clair sat at her kitchen nook, following each step Preston had listed. She knew them by heart but always had the instruction sheet on the table, so she could enjoy seeing his neat writing while she worked. After the last step, she sat back.

Thank you, Preston. Your foresight saved our daughter.

She retrieved the blue plastic box of cleaning cloths from under the sink. After removing the top three-quarters of the cloths, she put the folded instruction sheet and cleaning kit inside and covered them with one cloth. Then she carefully nestled the gun on the next layer and replaced the rest of the cloths.

She gave thanks for one more thing: Elena or Mardigan, whichever one searched her apartment, hadn't done any more than lift the lid.

Chapter 25

Amazing how the linchpin in a murder case can be exposed by one careless word: quicker. Two days later, Marcus DeVaughn, Duane's lawyer, phoned Sam with an update. Good thing she was now reachable by the number she'd given him, thanks to Ryan taking her phone shopping.

"I've got great news on Duane's case. He asked me to share this with you since you've been such a huge help. Testing on that baggie showed it matched the brand and size recovered after Hobson's murder. The powders inside both bags had identical chemical compositions: Rohypnol, known on the street as 'roofie.' Even the inactive ingredients matched, so they're sure the drugs came from the same source."

"What about fingerprints?" Though she wasn't into superstitions, Sam crossed the fingers of both hands anyway, fumbling to hold onto the phone.

"The evidence you found had not only prints matching Elena's but traces of her blood, as well. A partial print had been found on the inner lip of the baggie from Duane's trash. It didn't match Duane's prints when they tested it right after the murder. This week they tried it against Elena's. No luck there, either."

"Is the drug evidence alone enough for a case against Elena for Al's murder?"

"Actually, there's more. When they caught up with

Mardigan, they impounded his vehicle. After hearing your suspicion that Elena and Mardigan had conspired together, police techs gave his car the full treatment. In addition to recovering several of Elena's hairs from the front passenger seat, they found traces of Hobson's blood on the back seat, plus Elena's suitcases next to Mardigan's in the cargo area. For a bonus, the partial on the baggie from Hobson's murder turned out to be a close match to Mardigan's right thumb."

"Is Elena still in the hospital?"

"No. She's recovered enough from the gunshot wound to be transferred to Richmond City Jail. Duane will be released as early as tomorrow, as soon as the papers can be processed."

"Yes! Is it safe to assume my mom will no longer be considered a person of interest in Al's murder?"

"No word on that, but I would think it likely."

Sam knew better than to count on that happening. But even if the justice train arrived slowly, at least it was approaching the station.

When Sam phoned Mariah and told her what had happened, Mariah's yelp of joy probably carried throughout the entire bookshop. "This calls for a major celebration. While you share the news with your mom and Ryan, I'll make a reservation for four tomorrow night at the Smokey Pig. My treat."

"Thanks, but I'm going to pick up the check. I owe you big time for all the help you've been."

"My idea, my money. No argument."

Why do Mariah and I always have to get into a tug-of-war over who pays? "I'll give in for now, but remember, next one's mine." Sam crossed her fingers again, one hand behind her back. *Unless I can grab tomorrow's check first*. "What time will you pick me up?"

"Not me. Your mom can ride with me straight from the shop. I'll have Ryan pick you up at six-fifteen. Customer's coming up. See you later."

Unless Sam missed her guess, Mariah had just sacrificed their upcoming Friday Night Flicks to give Ryan ample opportunity to step in.

****

As Sam knew she would, Mariah requested the booth in the back corner. Mom claimed her customary place facing the wall, and Mariah slipped in beside her. That left Sam and Ryan side-by-side, facing them. Not a bad place to be, but his proximity made it harder for Sam to concentrate on the conversation.

When their drinks came, Mariah tapped the side of her iced tea glass with her fork. "I propose a toast to Duane and Mardigan trading places. Now they're both where they belong, thanks to Sam."

They clinked their glasses, or in Ryan's case, his beer mug.

Sam added, "And here's to Mom saving my life!"

Her mother looked up to touch everyone's glass, then dropped her gaze to the table. The corners of her mouth twitched up in a tiny smile. She even blushed.

Mom set her glass down and fiddled with her napkin. "I'm proud of you, Samara. You paid attention and put all the clues together."

The praise caught Sam by surprise. Her words wrapped her in a hug as well as any arms could have.

"When you reconnected Preston's antique phones, I never imagined they'd help me look after you. But please, be careful about who you let in your front door."

"You can count on it."

Mom is, first and foremost, a mom. And now I owe my life to her—not once, as we all do, but twice.

Ryan raised his mug again. "And here's to a fitting use for Mardigan's first name, as police *squired* him to jail."

They all laughed, even Mom.

Sam said, "What a contrast to thinking of him inviting Mom and me into his immaculate office. I doubt he'll be telling all his new inmate buddies to call him Squire. What do you bet he'll go by either Mardigan or his middle name—Tom, I think?"

"He may find his buds dub him with a new title, not one of his choosing," said Ryan, grinning.

"Mom, since the police should be taking your name off the person-of-interest list, that life insurance money could be coming soon. Will you use it to save your house and move back in? The repairs should be done in a few months."

"Definitely not. I need to stay close to you. You need me."

True. Their gazes met for a rare moment. Whether Mom would ever put it into words or not, Sam read that she needed her daughter, too.

"I can rent the house out and use the income, along with some of the insurance money, to get caught up on the loan, just like we originally planned. Besides, I don't want to move again, and I've already ordered the seeds for refurbishing Zena's gardens. She doesn't know as much about gardening as I do. I will save most of the insurance money and put some toward appointments with a psychologist to make it official that I have Asperger's Syndrome. Then people like Mr. Patillo and Mr. Truitt will know why I don't act the same as everyone else.

303

They made big mistakes when they misjudged me."

They weren't the only ones. Sam had overestimated her mom's challenges and undervalued her strengths. It was high time for her to begin understanding this complex woman.

After they'd eaten and plates had been cleared, the waiter set the check at the end of the table. Mariah nonchalantly picked it up, beaming a knowing smile Sam's way. She knew her too well. Mariah had made sure Sam was trapped on the inside seat of the booth, the arm she'd need for a check-grab trussed up in a sling.

"I'll be good to go as soon as I get my receipt," said Mariah.

The waiter took her credit card and returned with the slip and a black plastic pen with a white cap.

Mom said, "Last time I saw that color combo on a pen was at Al's funeral. It's like the fancy pen Michael Hobson used to sign the check he gave Elena. You kept staring at that pen of his, Samara."

Sam tied a short chain of knots in a straw wrapper, then dropped it into a half-full glass of water and watched the paper swell and try to straighten. "You know, one thing still doesn't add up. When Elena raised the knife, she said, 'After what you've seen, we can't risk…' That's when you burst in, Mom, cutting Elena off mid-sentence. I'd locked my attention on the knife, not Elena's words. But what risk was she talking about? The only compromising things I'd seen were Mardigan's bad loan files and his car sitting out front. Their game was up on the bank business, and I'd seen that they were working together, but that's not reason enough for them to want me dead, especially when they were on their way out of town."

Ryan said, "I see what you mean. The risk for them increased if they hung around to do you in." He gave Sam's uninjured shoulder a glad-you're-still-alive squeeze.

"Right. The only higher stakes would be if I unknowingly witnessed something damning about Al's murder. But what? Nothing from our visit to Elena's house jumps out. Nothing when she brought the death certificate to the shop. That only leaves seeing her at the funeral. All I saw was Hobson's father writing a check and giving it to Elena. After Elena left, he told me he was paying for the gravesite and the marker."

"Makes sense. Not knowing the town, he probably had Elena take care of that."

Sam nodded. "But there might be more to it. He also said he came to Ashland for one reason, and one reason only: he didn't trust anyone else to make the funeral arrangements. He had to take care of them face-to-face, so 'the great Hobson name' would be treated with proper respect. He had zilch in the way of respect for Al. He despised his adopted son, who'd dodged the draft, and then his only natural son lost his life in Vietnam. With as much as Michael Hobson cared about protecting his precious name, perhaps he'd tracked Al's doings through the years and knew about the two prior scam marriages."

"Fat chance news of a third would have been welcome," Ryan added.

"Right. He didn't want to see 'the great Hobson name' dragged through the dirt again. Particularly when he was being vetted to become a justice on the Connecticut Supreme Court. Then Al's arrest for arson pushed him clean over the edge. How would it look if a son he'd raised were to be convicted of a felony? I bet the cold S.O.B. paid to have Al killed. Hence, the check to Elena at the funeral. And when I ogled the pen, Elena feared my expression meant I'd seen a suspiciously large dollar amount on the check and would eventually realize it was a payoff."

Their waiter came by with a pitcher of water, but Ryan politely waved him away. "Little did your Aunt Patrice know how prophetic her words were. Al's third marriage sure wouldn't become the charm. But I see two problems with your theory. First, only someone with the intelligence of a graham cracker would pay for murder via personal check. Instead, he'd pass the money in some untraceable way, like through an offshore account." He caught Sam beginning to scowl and changed his tone. "You could be on the right track, though. Did you see anything else change hands between Elena and Michael?"

"I did," Clair said. She'd been silent so long, the others startled when she popped in. "Before Elena left the funeral, she picked up a slip of paper from the ground and tucked it into her coat pocket. Didn't you notice that, Samara?"

"Yes. I assumed the paper had fallen out of her purse or pocket, but I didn't see it drop."

"I saw it. Mr. Hobson dropped it when he pulled the checkbook out of his inner coat pocket. He could have been passing her a bank account number or the location of a satchel of cash. If Elena thought you'd seen the paper flutter to the grass, she'd be afraid you'd wonder what she was doing, sneakily taking a slip of paper from Al's father."

"You could have the answer," Sam said. "Kind of like getting caught passing a note in school, but a lot more sinister."

Ryan said, "Good job, Clair. You've come up with a plausible solution to problem number one, but we might have more trouble with my second issue. How did Michael Hobson ever connect up with Mardigan or Elena?"

"Hmm, I haven't worked that part out yet," Sam said. She picked up another straw wrapper and tied a few more knots.

"I can't imagine how those two would ever cross paths with Al's dad. It doesn't look like he'd ever been to Ashland, except for the funeral," Mariah said. She stood and slipped on her coat. "Well, this has been great fun, but I'm bushed after the long day. You coming with me, Clair?"

Mom gathered her coat and purse and motioned for Sam to do the same. "Come on, Samara."

Without missing a beat, Mariah said, "If Ryan gives Sam a ride back, and I take you, it gives me the chance to spend a little time at your place. You've told me about your upcoming spring gardening, but I'm having trouble visualizing the layout you've planned. It would be so much clearer if you'd walk with me around Zena's yard. Do you have time this evening?"

"Sure. It would be easier in daylight, but I can use my flashlight like a pointer. I'll have to show you my bedroom, too. I've set up a sort of greenhouse there, and seedlings have already started sprouting. Even in winter, the skylights and the windows flood the room with light. For my tomatoes, this year, I'm trying a new cultivar called…"

As the two went out the door, Mariah looked back and winked.

Sam and Ryan had the table to themselves. Ryan

made no move to leave.

"Mariah's a real pro," he said, grinning and shaking his head.

"She sure knows how to get Mom's cooperation. Mariah doesn't care about growing vegetables, just using them in recipes."

"Thank her for me when you see her. But she played you, too. Masterfully, I might add. You're one of those check-snatchers, aren't you? I saw that *gotcha* look she shot you."

"Guilty as charged."

Ryan shifted on the booth's padded seat, so he could fully face Sam. One forearm rested on the table, and the other draped along the seatback, his fingertips grazing the back of her neck. She'd have turned, too, but didn't want to risk moving out of range of that tingly touch. It tended to banish all thoughts but one from her mind. Yet she forced herself to put feelings for Ryan on a back burner while she turned the heat under the *perhaps* pot up to high. As she followed a chain of *what-ifs* through her head, she absentmindedly tied knots in a third straw wrapper.

"What's up now?" Ryan asked. "Don't tell me I did something wrong again."

"No. I was just thinking…"

"Oh, we're in trouble now. I see those wheels turning." He smiled, but his eyes told Sam he took her seriously.

"I'm trying to get them to turn, but I don't see how Mr. Hobson would ever have linked up with Mardigan and Elena. He didn't know them from Adam."

"Want an idea to get you rolling?"

"Sure."

"I can think of one possibility," Ryan said. "Let's say Elena or Mardigan contacted Al's rich dad, looking for hush money to keep quiet about Al's marriage racket and the arson charge, suggesting they might otherwise go to the Connecticut news media and ruin his family's reputation. Michael Hobson agreed to pay, but only if they eliminated the source of the problem: Al."

"No, I can't see that happening. Why would Elena and Mardigan take such a huge risk as committing murder? I think they simply would have held out for the bundle of money."

"Your turn. An open invitation to one-up me." He grinned at Sam.

A challenge.

"How about we look at your idea the other way around? If Al's dad had a P.I. keeping tabs on the wayward son, the P.I. might have caught on to the illicit affair between Mardigan and Elena. Michael Hobson could have threatened to expose them if they didn't kill Al, then he added a financial bonus to sweeten the pot. What do you think?"

"What if we combine the two? One party—it doesn't matter which one—tries to blackmail the other. Instead of dishing out the money, the second party flips the tables and says, 'How about we talk of what's in your dirty laundry basket?' They end up in a blackmailers' standoff."

Sam added, "Which is resolved by getting Al out of the way. Hobson pays Mardigan and Elena to do the dirty work. *Voila*! Mardigan no longer has to worry about the boxes of files Al had hidden, and Michael Hobson gets rid of the threat to his fricking name. They're each complicit in the crime, eliminating any future attempts at blackmail."

"Sam, you and I make quite a stellar team." Ryan squeezed her hand.

Sam gave him a discreet peck on the cheek. He met her peck and raised her one on the lips.

"Great minds not only think alike, they think even better together. However, we've created a hell of a tangle of *what-ifs*."

"Yeah. How can we prove any of it?" Sam dunked her latest string of knots into a water glass.

"We don't. We share all this with the police and let them work it out."

****

A week later, ultra-early on Sunday morning, breakfast in bed...his bed. Phoenix was curled up next to Sam, asleep. When Ryan delivered a tray, Phoenix perked up, only to get shooed off the bed before he could steal the bacon.

French toast stuffed with cream cheese and blueberries, bacon, and a bottle of real maple syrup, accessorized with a big mug of coffee, a folded page of the newspaper, and a kiss that almost led to her meal getting cold. Then he set up a folding chair beside the bed and sat facing her, poker-faced.

"Sorry I have to leave in a bit for my shift at the station, but I want to call your attention to this article first." He held the paper up so she could read while eating.

No mistaking which article he meant: *Bank President Pleads Not Guilty of Hobson's Murder.*

"Mardigan must have a lot of faith in his lawyer's skills. There's oodles of hard evidence against the man. He's going down in flames. And directly *to* the flames, if you know what I mean."

"Too bad, by the time his case is ready for trial, he'll probably finagle a plea deal to avoid the death penalty."

Sam scanned down the column. "Damn, this says Elena's already taken that route. According to some unnamed source, a deal will save her from the first-degree murder charge. Not good."

"Now read below the fold." He flipped the paper over.

"Well," Sam said, "who would have guessed? 'In exchange for testimony against a co-defendant, the prosecutor agreed to reduce the charge against Elena Fairchild to accessory before the fact.' That must be for supplying the drug used on Al, identical to the one almost used on me. She probably bought the roofie through a campus connection. She sure turned on Mardigan in a New York minute, though. She must not love him very much."

"Don't jump to conclusions. Keep reading."

She skimmed another couple of sentences. "At least she's still on the hook for trying to murder me."

"And…"

"All right! 'In yet another twist, the victim's father, Michael Hobson of New Haven, Connecticut, will be charged with conspiracy to commit murder and extradited to Virginia.' She ratted on Al's dad, not Mardigan! And she must have provided the proof we'd never have been able to find. I wish I'd seen her face when the detectives popped the connection to him on her. Let's see Hobson buy his fancy ass out of this one." Sam grabbed hold of Ryan's hand and raised it in triumph. "We did it! What a team!"

"Told you to leave it to the police, and for once, you

311

listened." Ryan pasted on a self-satisfied, told-you-so smile.

The meeting with Patillo five days earlier, sharing their conspiracy theory, had been anything but pleasant, yet for once, he'd listened, too. Maybe having Ryan sitting beside Sam had made Patillo take her more seriously.

"I heard you all those other times; I just chose not to take your advice."

His smile faded, replaced with scrunched brows. "If you'd taken it, you might have spared yourself a lot of pain and trouble, and me a bunch of worries. You always were the stubborn one."

"I prefer the term *strong-willed.*"

He tilted his head, stared directly into her eyes. "How about *obstinate*?"

"No, *persistent.*"

"Me, too."

With that, he set her half-empty tray on the floor, gently helped her to her feet, held her snug in his arms, and kissed her until her legs went limp. Then he set her unceremoniously on the edge of his bed and took a seat in the folding chair.

Cupping her chin with his hand, Ryan leaned in a foot from her face. "Sam, I think this is the beginning of a beautiful friendship."

Dad had replayed that classic line from *Casablanca* a zillion times.

"Love the sentiment, but this time you're the one who has Bogart's movies scrambled. In that scene, he was talking to Louie, not Sam. Sam Spade was in *The Maltese Falcon.*"

"I wasn't quoting from *Casablanca*. Jumping to

conclusions again, I see." He rounded up a dangling curl and tucked it behind her ear. "No more towels or bolt cutters, though, okay?"

"Deal."

****

Samara had fixed one of Clair's favorite dinners: crispy salmon cakes, rice pilaf, and fresh broccoli. When Clair started clearing the table, Samara stopped her.

"The dishes can wait, Mom. There's something important I need to tell you."

"What? Is this more news about the murder case?"

"No. It's about us."

Samara's tone was so serious. An old tension gripped her chest. *What could I have done wrong this time?*

Clair placed their plates in the sink but didn't rinse them. She braced herself against the countertop.

"I love you, Mom. And I need you. You saved my life, but it's even more than that. I need you in my life. You're so good at seeing what almost everyone—including me—misses. That's a rare and valuable talent. Our different abilities complement each other's."

A still minute passed. Clair's discomfort slowly melted into a deep warmth.

"Thank you for clearing me of suspicion in Al's murder. Without you helping me through these last awful months, there's no telling where I'd be. I need you, too... I love you, Samara."

She couldn't fathom why her daughter burst into tears.

Acknowledgments

Many thanks to those with autism who have shared their frustrations, unique talents, and triumphs with me. You've shown me the many colors of the spectrum and demonstrated the value of each individual. I created Clair as yet another unique person, not to be any one of you, but to be someone you might identify with at times. It's okay to be different. We all have differences that set us apart from others.

I owe a huge debt to the talented writers in my critique group who have patiently guided me through years of edits. Vivian Makosky (writing as Vivian Lawry), Susan Marusco (writing as Susan Ahern), Raab Reibach, Becky Kelly, Bronwyn Hughes, and Greg Smith have each contributed valuable insights that have greatly improved this book.

Here's a big shout-out to the fantastic folks at The Wild Rose Press, especially my editor Claudia Fallon, who saw the potential in my manuscript and helped me hone it to the best it can be. I am honored to become a new bloom in The Wild Rose Press garden.

And the deepest appreciation goes to my husband, Danny. He not only tolerated the untold hours I spent closeted in my office (his library), but he believed in me despite my years of rejections. That's true love, the love of my life.

A word about the author...

After earning her B.A. in Psychology from Duke University, Judy Witt began her professional life working with computers. Now she is deep into playing with words. She's an active member of James River Writers, Virginia Writers Club, and Poetry Society of Virginia. Her fiction, nonfiction, and poetry have won over twenty awards and appeared in *Hippocampus Magazine, Atlanta Review, The Quotable, RhymeZone*, and more.

When not at her desk, you might see her power walking through her neighborhood in Richmond, Virginia, or enjoying time with her family. Though only youngsters, her grandchildren are teaching her how far one can go armed with little more than a fierce determination to learn.

For more about Judy, visit her website:
www.judywittbooks.com

If you enjoyed this story, leaving a review at your favorite book retailer or reader website would be much appreciated. Thank you!